AWAKENING VEILED IDENTITY

FAE OF KYROSIA: BOOK ONE

 Formatted with Vellum

CONTENTS

CONTENT WARNING

READER DISCRETION IS ADVISED. THIS IS A LIST
OF POSSIBLE TRIGGER WARNINGS:

- Abortion
- Adoption
- Anxiety
- Child Abandonment
- Childloss
- Cursive (Joke)
- Death
- Domestic Violence
- Emotional Abuse
- Postpartum Death
- Sex
- Sexism
- Suicide

- Swearing/Slurs
- Toxic Relationship
- War

If you or someone you know is struggling with mental health and need assistance, please dial 988 which is the Suicide Prevention Lifeline.

I care deeply about mental health, but I am not a mental health specialist. Please prioritize your well-being; no book is worth risking exposure to your triggers.

BOOK INSIGHT

Awakening Veiled Identity is the first book in the Fae of Kyrosia Series.

Kyrosia is pronounced Kai-ro-sha.

Zylenia is pronounced Zy-len-e-ah.

This series, set in the present day, revolves around a rising generation of fae preparing for the Awakening Ceremony to *gain* their powers.

We meet the main characters as they are entering their final year of high school, a period that's crucial to the events that will unfold. As the series progresses we'll see them graduate from KAE and transition into adulthood.

Please note that although this story takes place during modern times, this is entirely a work of fiction. Unfortunately, this fictional world functions under a patriarchy.

Given the level of profanity and the nature of the sexual relationships depicted, I've chosen not to market this series as young adult. None of the sexual acts depicted are between minors.

My intention for this series is to invite non-fantasy readers into the fantasy world—a world where the focus is on the plot and characters, before magic begins to intertwine with the story. I want to show other readers that fantasy doesn't have to be strictly about world building, filled with thousands of unpronounceable names.

Fantasy is meant to be fun, immersing yourself into a world beyond our greatest imagination. I hope that this series makes you second guess everything you've assumed about fantasy, and it encourages you to pick up another book in the genre. Maybe you found a love for something you thought you'd hate. If so, then I've done my job and I've done it well.

Enjoy my fellow reader—

Welcome to Kyrosia.

FRIENDS' FAMILY TREE

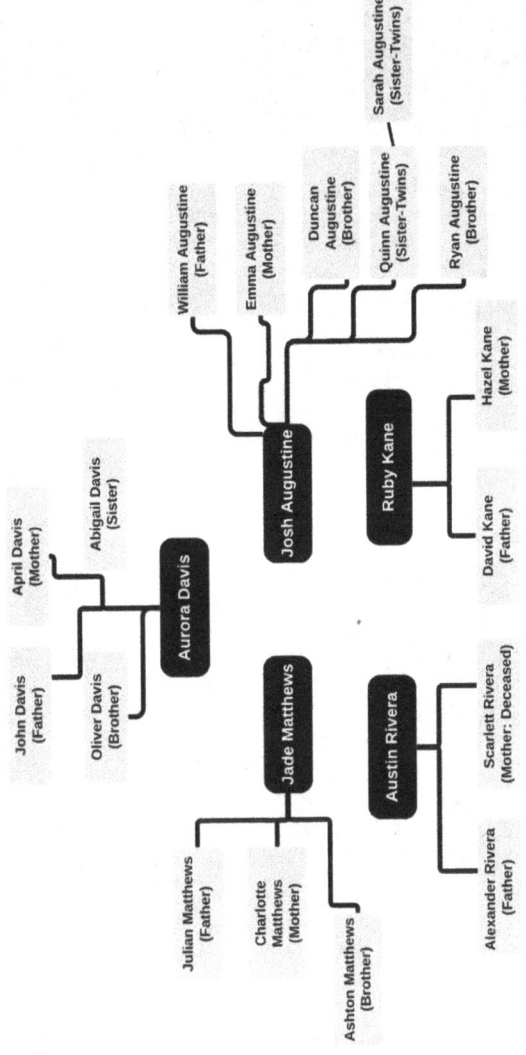

John Davis (Father)
April Davis (Mother)
Oliver Davis (Brother)
Abigail Davis (Sister)
Aurora Davis

William Augustine (Father)
Emma Augustine (Mother)
Duncan Augustine (Brother)
Quinn Augustine (Sister-Twins)
Sarah Augustine (Sister-Twins)
Ryan Augustine (Brother)
Josh Augustine

David Kane (Father)
Hazel Kane (Mother)
Ruby Kane

Julian Matthews (Father)
Charlotte Matthews (Mother)
Ashton Matthews (Brother)
Jade Matthews

Alexander Rivera (Father)
Scarlett Rivera (Mother: Deceased)
Austin Rivera

CURRENT FOUNDERS' FAMILY TREE

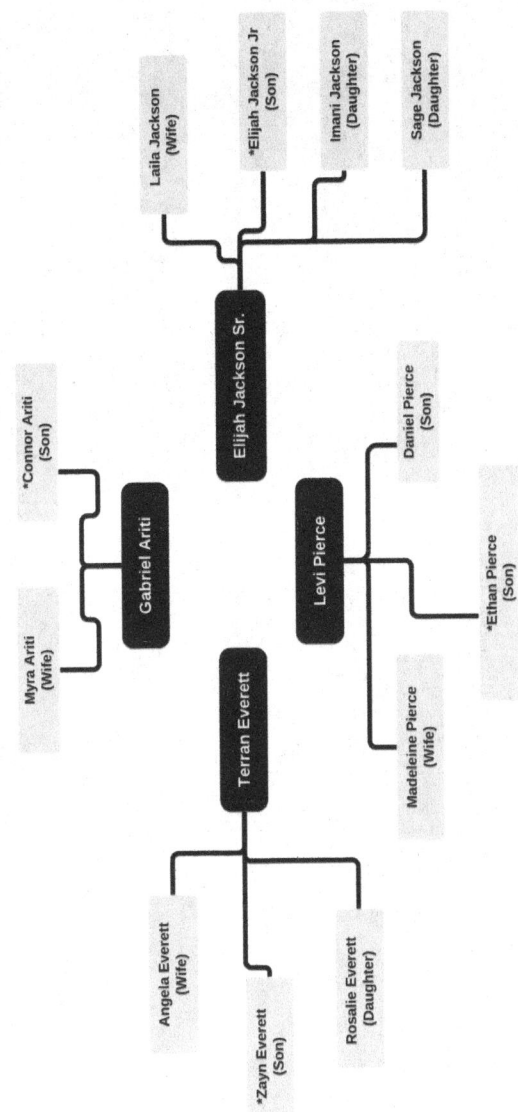

DEDICATION

For some, the journey to discover who we are begins at birth. For others, it is the result of losing ourselves along the way. How we begin the journey doesn't matter, it's that we embark on it in the first place.

To those who make their partners feel less than, shall you forever rot in hell. There is someone out there for everyone. Unfortunately, time and distance can be a bitch.

PROLOGUE

This story began many generations ago when there was a war between species. This war was the cause of the ultimate divide within the world.

Upon completion, four fae Generals decided to flee Zylenia. They took as many of their kind with them as they could. These men did not believe in a war within the species. They believed the only way to save their kind from extinction was to leave, to hide where no one could find them.

The generals packed as much as they could carry on horseback and left in the blanket of night with a plan to cover enough ground until they found somewhere to start over. These men, their families, and everyone together built Kyrosia—the beautiful city carved in the mountains.

Still to this day no one has found Kyrosia.

Zylenia had kept meticulous archives on all of the

species. Unfortunately, those chronicles were not brought with the generals.

This meant all of the fae who fled with the generals were unlisted. Even with the use of magic, it took decades to build Kyrosia.

Very few felt the importance of continuing to relay tales of what was once beyond the mountains. Especially as time went on and stories became folklore and memories were nonexistent. Because when those stories didn't match the narrative the founders wanted to portray, people had no choice but to stop telling them.

The people of Kyrosia originally worked together in community. There was no hierarchy despite the generals leading the movement. Over time, the founders' kin became power hungry. *As they do.*

They didn't all agree that their city should be balanced. They felt a sense of entitlement to what should be theirs. This began to plant seeds in the younger generations' minds on how they should run the city and hoard the power for themselves.

The first misstep of many was creating the Founders Council. This cabinet, or executive committee, was made up of the four founding families. All men, as they'd have it —no women were allowed to make executive decisions. They decided rather quickly that they needed to remain in complete control.

A few decades later, the Founders Council passed a law that every member of a founding family would partake in an arranged marriage. All marriages were arranged by the elders. This was to ensure that no one could disrupt the balance by marrying someone who would discredit or embarrass those in power. If a male of a founding family's wife was to die, then the man was to remarry a woman of the elders' choosing, yet again.

The daughters of the founding family members were to remain pure until they got married. A founding member could not marry a woman who was not pure.

If one was arranged with someone they could stomach, all was well. If one was not so lucky, however, one would Praise Lina to get through the day.

Lina Stormrider was the Queen of Zylenia, where the people of Kyrosia originated from. The peacekeeper of their continent. Over time her husband plotted to overthrow her. One day, he murdered her and claimed it to have been one of the Wolves. This initiated the series of events he had in place for the fae to be killed.

He was an Elve who was always envious of his wife's abilities. Despite her attempts to make life fair by creating elixirs and spells that diminished the fairies' powers. The women who fled after her assassination included members of her court and so, her story was passed on to women over time. It is one of the only remaining stories shared through generations.

No one would dare to mention her name where a man might hear.

Women and men became strictly prohibited from

discussing the queen. Again, the Founders do not want women to rule, to have power or voice. They want them to be seen as a body of flesh with a womb. A womb that is to bring heirs to rule and women for marriage.

Therefore, they do not want tales told of women in power. They do not want ideas placed in young women's minds of the possibility of a future outside of the Founders' control.

The most influential way the Founders Council could figure out how to play God was the use of magic. They searched for any way to keep power in check by everyone outside of their hierarchy. Such control started with the arranged marriages, ensuring power lines didn't cross to create children with higher abilities.

Until one day, they decided it just wasn't enough.

The Founders Council hexed the city so that one year, on May 31st, everyone who was under eighteen years of age was powerless. All the next generation were born with rounded ears and no magical abilities. Those who were eighteen could only get their powers back by performing a ceremonial ritual.

This created the annual Awakening Ceremony which is still performed on May 31st. If one's eighteenth birthday is to fall after May 31st, they would perform the ceremony the following year.

Immediately upon completion of the rite during the ceremony, the fae earn their ears and powers.

Unfortunately, some fae do not develop any magical

gifts. No one knows why or how. Those fae are considered the "Lessers" and are provided job details immediately by the Founders instead of moving on to the Academy.

The magical abilities one develops are based on several factors. The most influential being genetics. Magic is carried through generations. Sometimes certain powers will skip centuries before they reappear in another.

The Founders' have interfered with the law of magic by taking away a fae's magic at birth. Thus, interfering with balance. Certain specializations are given to a fae depending on what the world needs at that time. By removing how things are supposed to be, magic finds loopholes—ways to give the world what it needs when it is ready.

The Founders may think that they are in control, but magic always finds a way to regain balance.

All fae who have powers have elemental magic which consists of the four essential elements: earth, wind, fire and water.

Even though all fae have elemental magic, it is not equal across the board. Some fae are only able to push something across the table with a gust of wind, while others may be able to manipulate air currents to create a storm or a tornado in minutes.

Magic takes precision, focus, strength, agility, intelligence, and pure intentions. Traits not everyone possesses.

The main thing the ceremony determines is each individual person's specialization. At the completion of each ceremony, each person's specialization is documented.

Part of the reason the hex was placed on the city was so the Founders could start to record each fae and what magic they possess. They developed The Registry of Powers, which is available to the public of Kyrosia, but it only dates back so far. So, centuries went by with no record of anything past the birth of a fae.

Those who gain powers attend Kyrosia Academy of Enchantment upon completion of High School. High school focuses on the core curriculum such as: Math, Science, English and History. KAE's primary goal is to develop and cultivate their abilities. The academy's classes are dictated on an assessment of one's individual specialization, and potential job placement.

Job placements are usually determined by how an individual's specialization can meet the needs and expectations of a position. No one (with powers) is assigned a job placement until the completion of KAE.

KAE is a beautiful academy with modern architecture and tall buildings. It is located on the far side of the city, surrounded by woods on every side.

When school is in session, one is required to live on site. One side of the campus is primarily housing, while the other side holds the classrooms and training areas.

As generations evolve, there are those who begin to question the founders and their ethics. Things can only continue in one direction for so long, before people start to ask the questions that should have been asked all along.

Things need to change, rather it is done peacefully, or with no regard for those who resist.

CHAPTER 1
WHO AM 1
AURORA DAVIS

When I found out I was adopted, I was too naive to really consider what that meant.

Not realizing where or who you come from can affect your entire life. It just always felt like there were missing pieces to the puzzle, questions I didn't have answers to.

Why was I so different?

As much as I love my family, I always knew something was off. The older I got, I realized we had more differences than similarities. Eventually the questions grew, and I would pester my family for information on why we were so different.

Finally, one day, they sat me down and explained that I was adopted. I remember how upsetting it was when I first found out. I was so emotional. My life had always been stable, predictable, even. And now everything was different. I felt disconnected from those around me despite how much I loved them.

I couldn't talk to them about how I felt because they wouldn't understand. So, I was alone in my feelings.

At the time, my brother, Oliver was 10 and my sister, Abigail was only 4. After a few days, they sat them both down and explained it to them as they did me. Of course, Abigail barely understood, so it didn't make a difference to her.

Oliver on the other hand, didn't take it well. We grew apart for a while. I'd like to say I knew what was going through his mind, but I still have no idea. At first, he was quiet, then when he did speak to me, it was only long enough to spout hateful things.

I constantly tried to remind myself that he was entitled to how he felt, he was my brother, and his life had been flipped upside down just as mine had. That didn't mean it hurt any less. Deep down I knew it would either cause a permanent divide between us, or we would eventually be okay.

After some time, things went back to normal. I'm not sure if my parents spoke to him, or if he just needed time. I didn't really care; I was just happy that things returned to normal between us.

I never wanted to ask who my biological parents were. I could understand if they were too young, or they died, but what if they simply didn't want me? Once I entered that maze, I knew I wouldn't be able to get back out; constantly searching for more answers.

So, I took the easy way out by avoiding the subject all together. If I didn't know anything, then I could continue to live in my bubble of denial.

Until these last few months.

I suddenly found myself questioning everything.

I've tried to hide it from my friends and family. But, as time goes on I can feel myself changing, dimming. I know they feel it too. Everyone seems to walk on eggshells around me. As if they don't want to say the wrong thing. It's all just been exhausting.

I have no idea what to expect with the Awakening Ceremony approaching. My life has always been the same, steady. Now, I feel as if one foot is on the gas and one is on the brake. I live in my mind. When I pass people on the street, catch their eye, I wonder if they might be my blood family.

When I think about it, it all just sounds so cliché. Poor me, the girl who was adopted by an amazing family; while other people sit at home, hating who gave birth to them. I'm grateful, I really am. But that doesn't change the fact that not knowing who I am has been affecting me more than I would like it to.

I just want to go back to the way things were before I gave a shit about who my birth family was. Despite how much I am dreading the ceremony, I know it will be the only way to put everything behind me. So, now I just need to get through this school year because whether I like it or not, it's happening.

CHAPTER 2
BACK-TO-SCHOOL PARTY
AURORA DAVIS

S itting on my bed, I watch Jade get ready. She's propped up at my makeup vanity, curling her shoulder length blonde hair, feet barely flat on the floor.

Jade is like a sister to me. I can't imagine being so close to anyone else, despite us being polar opposites.

I am the dark to her light.

You would never know the weight she carries from looking at her. She hides it behind a dramatic, bouncy personality. She doesn't let anyone in, not even me, her best friend. She's forever keeping everyone at arm's length.

I get it though. I know what it feels like to not want to be a burden. I don't always want to discuss everything, myself. While I respect talking things out, sometimes it's easier to shoulder the weight of hardship than to drag others down with you. So, I try not to push her, just be there for her when she needs me.

As I wait for her to finish, I scroll through my phone and find my feed full of everyone's "summer dumps." I find myself less than amused when all I see are pictures of hot dog legs and keg stands. I throw my phone back on the bed beside me in a huff of irritation.

Summer has been a grateful distraction from the upcoming year, but I can't relate to those I go to school with.

It just seems like everyone around me is fine with the way things are. They're enjoying their lives, going to parties, dating, et cetera. No one seems to care that our entire life is mapped out for us. We don't get a single say on what we get to do, or how we get to live.

We're just robots programmed by the Founders. The only thing that matters is what we can give back to *them*.

My internal rant stops when my mom pokes her head in my room. "Hey honey, I just wanted to let you know I'm home. Hey, Jade. When are you girls leaving?"

Jade answers her before I have a chance to respond.

"Hi, Mrs. Davis! We should be headed out soon, we have to go pick up Ruby and Josh."

"Okay, well you girls please drive safe. If you need me to pick you up I will." *That's the last thing I will be doing.*

"Thanks, Mom, I'll let you know before we head out."

My mom is gorgeous. She normally keeps her cherry red hair in a slicked back ponytail and freckles litter her face. Her eyes are bright blue like my sister's; Abigail is her little twin.

Oliver, however, gets all his looks and height from our dad. They both have an olive complexion, lighter than me, but not enough for people to think too much into it.

Crap, I just remembered Oliver can attend the back-to-school party tonight. It's always held on the Friday night two weeks before school starts.

Oliver and Ashton—Jade's little brother—are both 15. Since they're entering their sophomore year they're allowed to go.

"Jade, please tell me the reason Oliver isn't coming home for dinner has nothing to do with Ashton and him going to the party?" I ask.

She shrugs her shoulders. "I hope not. Ashton didn't say anything to me about it. Not that he probably would, but I don't know for sure."

"Great, I can't wait." My response reeks of sarcasm.

Jade hops up. "Okay, I'm ready. Are you good?"

Walking over to my bedroom door, I close it so I can look in the full length mirror hanging there. My dark purple t-shirt body suit is tucked into my favorite pair of black jeans with rips on the knees, paired with my combat boots. I slip into my closet to grab a black cardigan, and check the mirror one more time. Once I have my sweater on, I pull my hair out and let it fall over my shoulders.

I began dyeing my hair before freshman year because I wanted red hair like my mom's. It doesn't look exactly like hers, but in the light, it's there.

Despite my mom's best efforts when I was younger, my

hair was often a frizzy mess. Before this summer, I put it in a bun every day because I had no idea how to style it myself. So, recently I started watching videos to learn how to style my hair and honestly, I have gotten pretty good at it.

When I realize I've been daydreaming, I quickly snap out of it. I look over at Jade who is eyeing me in annoyance. "Sorry, yeah, I'm ready. Let's go."

"Are you sure? Mirror, mirror on the wall—"

"Oh, shut up. Come on." I pull her out of my bedroom with me.

Jade sends a text to Ruby and Josh in our group chat letting them know that we are headed that way. Our group chat consists of Jade, Ruby, Josh, Austin and me.

I'm obviously closest with Jade. But I find myself confiding in Austin the most in an attempt to avoid burdening her with my shit. Not that she ever asked me to, I just don't know how I'm supposed to bitch and moan about my life with someone who clearly has things worse than I do.

It feels selfish and inconsequential.

Ruby and Josh are together and always in their couple bubble. The last year or so they have been hanging out a lot more, just them.

As we reach the bottom of the steps, I holler to my mom that we're leaving and grab my keys by the door on the way out.

If there's one thing about Jade, it's that she always has

to have control of the music. She immediately reaches for my charger when we get in the car.

We live a couple of streets away from each other, she doesn't have a car, so I drive us everywhere.

Even though Josh has a car, too, we want to take one vehicle so we can drink.

I check my back seat when we get to Josh's and realize the boys left all their school crap back there. I huff and throw the car into park to throw it all into the trunk.

Jade goes to the door to get them and by the time I'm done cleaning up their mess, everyone is loading into the car.

Josh looks at me in the mirror and asks, "I thought Austin was supposed to meet you guys at your house?"

"He was going to but, change of plans. He texted us that he had to help his dad with something first. Do you guys even bother to read the chat?" I mess with both of them.

Ruby giggles and Josh gives her a look, a look I'm not sure I want an explanation behind. Her beautiful doe eyes light up under his stare, framed by long lashes. She is beautiful, but in a shy, almost hesitant way. Standing at an inch taller than me—a detail she loves to point out.

Her outfits are quirky but stylish. She is heading into the woods wearing a linen maxi skirt and a knitted sweater.

She has her long brown waves braided back tonight. I look back in the mirror as Josh pulls the braid to her front, toying with the end of it.

Josh adores her, he'd shout his love from the rooftops just for the sheer joy of it. He is your average guy, tall, brown short hair, brown eyes, but his personality is larger than life.

Ruby's shy if you aren't friends with her, and Josh is the opposite. They have been dating since we've been in high school. They actually met at our first back-to-school party.

Her dad left when she was little, so her mom works constantly. As a result, Ruby spends a lot of time at Josh's house.

His life is picture perfect, white picket fence, a no-hidden-secrets family. He has 4 younger siblings so I'm sure they don't even notice her there most of the time.

His parents told us we can all stay at his house tonight.

Lancer Woods is full of cars by the time we arrive. It is more than just a hangout spot in the woods, it's beautiful. There are cabanas, fire pits, restrooms, grilles, the whole nine yards. People usually reserve the area for events just like this.

I text Austin to let him know we're waiting by my car for him.

The rich kids normally provide most of the alcohol, but almost everyone brings their own, as well. Obviously, most of the kids here aren't of legal age to drink, you must be 18, but that doesn't stop us.

Once Austin gets here, he opens up the bed of his truck and there are two coolers. Josh greets him with a slap on the shoulder. "Fresh cut my guy?" He points to Austin's, definitely shorter, dirty blonde hair. He has a hard part that pushes most of his hair to one side.

Jade interjects, "So much for having something to do with your dad, liar."

He laughs, shaking his head at her as the boys grab the coolers out and we make our way into the woods.

I enjoy Lancer Woods, truly I just enjoy nature. In the darkness, the streetlights cast a serene glow upon the trees. Their lush silhouettes painting the area with soft shadows. Their presence is a gentle reminder of the strength within nature.

The air hums with life as the trees sway in a soft breeze, leaves rustling together to form nature's delicate music.

The sweet smell of woods and pine drifts into the air in the forest's embrace.

While we walk to one of the cabanas to set down the coolers, I look around to see if I can spy Oliver or Ashton. Thankfully, I don't see either of them yet. Her brother parties a little too hard when given the opportunity and mine does whatever he wants to. So, neither one is going to attempt to listen to us if we tried.

After the guys set the coolers down, Ruby and Josh sit on one of the benches talking. I look around to see where Jade went when Austin comes up and gives me a hug.

"Hey Ro, you're quiet everything okay?"

"Hey, I'm glad you made it. Yeah, I'm fine."

"Try that again."

Austin and I have been close for years and he can read me like a book.

"I'm fine really, I was looking to see where Jade went. She just flew off."

Austin points into the distance. "There she is."

I click my tongue, she didn't even last 5 minutes hanging out with us. She stands in the middle of a group of people.

"Are you ready for your birthday?" Austin asks.

"Well, that's a loaded question." I sink down onto one of the coolers. "I just can't seem to shut my mind off. I try, and sometimes it works for a little bit, but then boom. Everything rushes back."

At this point Austin and I are the only ones left, everyone else has joined in the festivities.

Austin reaches into the cooler beside me and grabs two cans of beer as I talk. He pops the tab on one releasing a low *hisssss* and hands it to me before opening his own. "About the ceremony again?"

"It's not just about that." Staring down at the can, I swirl it around in my hand, searching for the right words.

The malty aroma hits my nose before I raise it to my lips. I wouldn't say I enjoy the smell, but it is preferable to the harsh scent and effects of liquor.

I finally take a sip, and the amber liquid goes down smooth. I am immediately thankful Austin didn't buy cheap piss water beer.

Breaking my silence Austin says, "Hey, it's me you're talking to, you know I won't tell anyone." He's clearly trying to negotiate with me to open up to him.

"Ugh, I know it's just that I have no idea who my father or mother are. I'm not talking about April or John, but my biological parents. How am I supposed to know if I am winning the genetic lottery, or if I have nothing—zilch? I could either be an exponential disappointment or have these great expectations I'm supposed to live up to. Or worse. I don't think I can stomach 'worse.'"

"I guess I didn't really think about that. If I am being real with you, most people have no idea you're even adopted. I think sometimes I forget you are, too."

"I know and honestly, it's fine. I just want May to hurry up so we can get the ceremony over with."

Austin nods delicately in agreement.

Jade runs up to us, thankfully breaking the awkward silence. "Why are you guys sitting over here alone, come to the fire with us!"

I look at Austin and gesture to our beers. "Bottoms up?"

Austin laughs and starts chugging what's left of his drink, crushing the can in his palm before shooting it into the nearby trashcan like a basketball.

We grab several more and make our way to our group. Once we catch up with Ruby and Josh, we all sit around the fire, laughing and drinking.

I relish the heat of the fire. It calms me. There is something unpredictable about an open flame. Each burst of heat is like a living, breathing thing. I can't imagine anything more vibrant and beautiful. It's hard not to get lost in it. To watch each flame dance and sing. As it moves you can hear each crackle and the larger it gets, it roars. It calls to you, like a sweet serenade.

I have to physically tear my eyes from the fire to look at everyone around me. They are having fun and their smiles are bright.

I glance around to see who all is here. In my direct line of sight are the Founders' kids, minus one, huddled with a group of people. They aren't even in power yet and they act like they run the world. Everyone bends to their will and searches for attention on their behalf. It's truly pathetic. Searching for validation from literal teenagers is quite troubling to begin with.

The four Founders' sons, those who are next in line for succession, are Ethan Pierce, Elijah Jackson, Zayn Everett, and Connor Ariti.

Connor is much younger, though; he doesn't enter high school until we leave. He'll be a freshman next year. I honestly don't know much about him.

Daniel is Ethan's younger brother, he may not be first in line, but he is best friends with Elijah and Zayn. The 3 of them are all in my grade. Rumor is, despite him being second born, their father doesn't believe he could ever rule. He apparently doesn't think he is 'leadership material.'

I watch them, my eyes gravitating towards Zayn. He may have the looks of a god, but he has the personality of a blood sucking mosquito. I swear every inch of his body was hand sculpted.

He has a black leather jacket on, matching his black curly hair, which is faded on the sides. It's always pushed back except for the one curl that hangs over his forehead.

Every time I'm near him, he looks at me with what feels like disdain, even though we have never spoken. I thought I was imagining it until one day, Jade noticed and asked me if we knew each other, which we don't.

Maybe he hates me on principle? Maybe it's how I look? I have no idea. I drag my eyes from him to the fire.

After a while I glance in his direction again, only to find Zayn's gray eyes boring directly into mine. As soon as our attention is on one another, he leans into Daniel's ear, whispering something before he stomps away.

What the fuck was that?

I sit at the fire for a while, my frustration building. I mean, his hateful looks are one thing, but that was just weird. Even if he was to catch me staring at him, his reaction would have been unwarranted.

Restless, I decide to go to the bathroom so I can rinse my face and cool down.

After I use the bathroom and wash my hands, I fill my palms like a bowl with cold water and tuck my face down into them. I repeat this action a few times, letting the water cool down my cheeks. I'm hot as hell from the fire or the drinking, or both.

I roughly grab a paper towel from the dispenser, drying my hands and face before opening the bathroom door. Just as I step from the threshold, I'm knocked on my ass.

Right as I gather my bearings and move to sit up, I hear a deep voice. "What the fuck are you doing?"

Startled from just falling onto the ground and primed from Zayn's reaction to my eye contact, I don't even look up before I start going off.

"Are you joking? I was coming out of the bathroom. The men's is on the other side, who the fuck walks directly in front of the—" I finally look up. *Shit, shit, shit.* It's him. Of all fucking people to possibly run into.

He doesn't attempt to help me up or look sorry. He pinches the bridge of his nose waiting for me to finish. *I obviously decide I won't be doing that.*

When it's clear I'm not going to, he turns to walk away. Finally, I come to my feet. As I start to brush off my clothes, I see him pause. He turns back towards me.

He steps forward. Reaching his hand up to my face, he tilts my chin up with his index finger. As soon as his skin touches mine, a shiver runs down my spine, causing my entire body to cascade in goosebumps.

Zayn stares into my eyes as if he's searching for something. I notice the way he towers over my 5'6" height, he has got to be over a foot taller than me.

"Hmm you have your father's eyes," he tells me, voice dark. Which is ominous as fuck.

He quickly walks away before I can even ask how the hell he knows my dad. I try to find him, scouring the woods, but come up empty handed. It's as if he's disappeared.

When I make my way back to the cabana, Austin reaches into the cooler for another beer.

"Grab me one please?" I ask before he closes it.

When he turns to hand it to me, I must look disheveled because he immediately asks, "Are you alright? You look like you are going to be sick."

Am I? I ask myself before responding to him. "Yeah I'm good, just had to splash some water on my face." He doesn't look like he buys the line, but he hands me the beer anyway.

When we get back to the fire, we find Oliver and Ashton talking to Josh. I look over to Jade who simply rolls her eyes.

Our brothers finally announce they're leaving and I'm hoping we won't be staying too much longer either. I've already had way too much to drink.

Not long after, Jade disappears and texts us that she's going to spend some time with her mystery man. I assumed she was going to bring him back to meet us, but I guess not. Ruby and Josh are too busy making out to pay attention to anyone else. So, that just leaves Austin and I. *Again.*

We sit and chat for a while, but I can't help my eyes from wandering around.

"Hey, are you looking for Jade? I'm pretty sure she left at this point."

It takes me a minute to realize what he's saying and I find myself needing to come up with something to say back.

"She wouldn't just leave without at least texting me. I'm going to shoot her a message just to make sure she's okay."

Eventually, she makes her way back to us. Since Ruby doesn't like to drink, we planned for her to drive my car. Austin will just pick up his truck tomorrow.

By the time we get to Josh's house, it's a little after one in the morning. We make our way to the upstairs living room and begin setting up our blankets as Josh goes to grab pillows. It doesn't take any of us long before we are all out cold.

The next thing I know, I'm being woken up by Josh's siblings running around like lunatics. I kept my eyes closed for a few minutes before opening them to chaos.

When I do finally open them, I notice it's just me and Jade left upstairs.

I kick her butt. "Jade, get up."

She rolls over and grunts. "I am up."

"Girl, what the hell happened to you, you didn't even look this bad last night?"

"Gee, thanks," she says.

I laugh at her expense. "You know what I mean."

"It's a long story. Better told at a time when my head doesn't throb and my back isn't aching from this shitty floor blanket." She scrubs her eyes as she inches herself up.

"Come on, let's go get some food. I'm starving." I roll my eyes at her dramatics.

CHAPTER 3

THE LAKE

AURORA DAVIS

W e spend a lot of time at the lake during summer. For starters it's free, and secondly, it's fucking hot outside. This is our last Saturday before school starts, and it is absolutely packed today. Everyone clearly has the same idea and most of them are in the water.

This is the only body of water in the area that isn't covered in shade by the trees. The sun beats down on the lake, warming it to perfection this time of year.

Ruby, Jade, and I sit at the edge of the water on our towels. Austin, Josh, Oliver, and Ashton are tossing a football back and forth behind us in the distance.

I live for days like this. All of us hanging out together; enjoying the peace.

I lay back on my towel and let the sun cover my skin. I try to drown out the sounds of those around us, to focus in on the movement of the water, but I can't. The voices and laughter is a frustrating reminder of everything I'm trying to escape. The breeze isn't too strong today, but enough that it whips my hair around. I close my eyes and between the sun and the breeze, a wave of calm washes over me and my eyes grow heavy. I doze off, but not for long before I'm jolted awake.

I jump up, flicking the water from my body. The girls aren't at their towels anymore, but I can hear Jade shouting profanities at someone. I look around searching for them before I finally see them; she's shouting at Elijah and Daniel, who are very—*shirtless*.

I find myself looking to see if Zayn is with them against my better judgment while I hurry to join them. Ruby has her arms crossed at her chest in a defensive position as Jade flings her arms out, gesturing wildly as she yells.

"Can you not fuck around anywhere else? You just soaked all of our stuff!" She screeches at Daniel.

He is quite a bit shorter than both Elijah and Zayn. His hair is long at the top with blonde highlights. I notice he has random tattoos everywhere.

"Aww, did I get you all wet?" he asks sarcastically, dripping with euphemism. He shoots her a wink with his blue eyes.

Her head turns to the side in a teasing way. "Don't be so confident, I'm sure it takes you more than that to get a girl wet. You're such a child."

He steps closer, tension filling the air. "Wanna bet, J?"

I almost feel like I walked into an intimate moment, the bickering feels a little deeper than getting splashed with some water, if you ask me.

Elijah stands behind Daniel watching the interaction with a huge grin on his face, showing his gorgeous, perfect white teeth. A stark contrast to his dark brown skin. I knew he was tall, but standing this close to him, he must be even taller than Zayn. It isn't his height that shocks me, it's his eye color.

Eyes that pierce your soul, best described as azure, blue. I'm pretty sure he uses them to siren all of the women he pulls. He is the absolute ladies' man.

My attention is pulled away from their conversation when I hear Zayn call out from the distance.

"Everything good over there?" he shouts. My eyes gravitate towards him. He just pulled his shirt down over his chest and I'm locked in on the exposed skin between his shirt and board shorts. The fabric drifts down his torso in slow motion and my eyes linger on the sharp lines of the V leading into his shorts. They are soaking wet; he must have just gotten out of the water.

I look up when I feel his eyes on me. He definitely caught me staring this time, and for a moment I forget to breathe. Not only was I staring but I was *very obviously* staring at his "shorts".

Just when I'm about to avert my eyes, I can't. I'm completely trapped in his gaze, watching as he inches toward us. He carries himself with such confidence, each step is as if he owns the ground beneath him. I have always found the way they carry themselves to be obnoxious... well until now. Now, it's addicting, he's impossible not to watch.

Instead of him walking up to his friends like I expect, he stops directly in front of me. Unlike at the party, his facial features don't hold the hateful look he normally sports. I feel suddenly naked as his eyes track my black two-piece bikini.

I shift on my feet, straightening my back. "Yes?" I ask, trying to exude confidence.

His eyes flick to my chest and back up to my face. When he doesn't answer me I ask again. "Are you going to say something, or are you just going to stare at me?" I feign annoyance.

"I don't have anything I need to say at the moment. I was just enjoying the view," he says as his eyes continue to devour my body. Before I can react, he immediately walks away, dismissing me entirely, leaving me standing there speechless and flustered. He clearly has a habit of doing that.

"Come on, girls, let's go, this is pointless." Ruby says, trying to pull our arms away from them.

She pulls us back towards where our towels lay. I grab my beach bag, ready to shove my things into it, but as soon as I do I drop it back down. I all but growl as I feel the weight of the sand and water in it. I look back towards the group and find the guys watching us, laughing.

32

I scowl at them as I tip my bag upside down and empty it onto the towel, wiping off each item before throwing them back in. We angrily pack everything up and walk to meet the guys who are still playing football, all completely oblivious to what just happened.

Ruby immediately greets Josh, hugging him tightly.

"What's wrong? Are you guys ready to go or something?" he asks.

I huff, "Or something..." under my breath.

"No, it's fine. People just have no respect. Some kids thought it would be funny to soak our stuff." She points behind her, motioning to our soaking wet towels that we threw over the bench.

The rest of their conversation becomes shushed as they talk between each other.

"I'm going to walk around for a bit. I'll be back," I announce before turning back to my bag.

"Do you want me to come with you?" Austin asks from a few feet away.

"No. I just want to be alone." It's not that I don't enjoy the company of others, I just need to think sometimes or my brain becomes jumbled. Things were so peaceful, until they weren't and now I just need to relax. I grab my hat and throw my hair into a ponytail, feeding it through the back. It would be great if my shirt wasn't all wet, so I could put it on over my bathing suit.

I head back down to the shoreline. The sand at the base of the lake is coarse from all of the sediment that washes up, but it doesn't bother my feet. I like to feel the water and if you go too deep it's hard to trek through, so I stay where it meets my ankles. I can barely see the black polish on my toes, even with how shallow it is here.

I look up at all of the people around me, the way they laugh at each other, throwing each other in the water, or simply lounging around. Do you ever wonder what is going on in someone else's brain? Ever imagine exactly what they are thinking? I've always prayed that I would never have access to reading someone else's mind. I can't imagine seeing someone's darkest, most private moments, listening to their insecurities. The world is depressing enough.

Not to mention, I sure as hell don't want anyone to see what's going on in my brain at any given moment. My brain is always on overdrive, thinking of any and every possible scenario. Someone would hop in and immediately beg to leave.

I hear footsteps approaching me and turn to see Zayn. It's clear he unnerves me, but I don't have the energy to argue with him.

"What is it now, Zayn?" I sigh in defeat.

"Not in the mood to quarrel?"

"I'm walking around for the peace and quiet. So no, not really."

"I like quiet, mind if I walk with you?" he counters.

I stop and fully face him. "If I say no, will you still come?"

"Yes," he fires off with a smile.

I don't respond, instead I turn away and continue to walk. Several minutes go by and he doesn't make a sound. I try to ignore my curiosity, but it gets the better of me and I look over my shoulder at him. He's simply gazing into the distance, but why does he feel both tense and relaxed at the same time?

I'm antsy when I finally ask, "Why would you even want to walk with me?" I try not to make the question sound as pathetic as it really is.

"What is that supposed to mean?" he rebuttals in question, now focused on me.

"Well, you're you and I'm me."

"Obviously," he interjects my statement.

"As I was saying." I roll my eyes. "We don't exactly run in the same circles."

"And? I don't give a fuck about that stuff. I am my own person. Elijah and Daniel are my best friends, not simply out of obligation. I don't have a 'circle' other than them."

"Oh." Is all I respond, feeling stumped.

"Say or ask whatever it is you're thinking," he half demands.

"I just don't get why you are walking with me in—well, silence—instead of hanging out with your friends."

"Well, you're better looking than them." he says behind his smirk.

I scoff and roll my eyes. *Good one.*

He laughs loudly and authentically and the sound takes me by surprise.

"You don't think very highly of yourself, do you?" He sighs before continuing, "That was a rhetorical question, don't answer. You intrigue me, Aurora, that isn't something that happens easily."

"I guess I'll take the compliment."

"Good girl," he says with a wink.

Obviously, he's joking, but my body doesn't think it's very funny. Instantly, my palms are sweaty and my stomach tightens.

Zayn surprises me. I wonder which half of him is the real one. Is he really the person everyone makes him out to be, or is he deeper than that? Deeper than all this shallow bullshit and hierarchies.

We continue walking until I see Austin jogging down to the shoreline.

Without thinking, I immediately turn to Zayn, wanting to create distance between us. "I think we're leaving, maybe I'll see you at school."

He tucks his hands in his pockets, eyeing Austin coming our way. "Yeah, maybe."

I jog in Austin's direction until I reach him. He follows alongside me but keeps glancing back at Zayn as we walk together back to our group. I distract him by reaching up to tussle his hair.

When I stop to grab my things, I take a chance to look back. Zayn is still in the same spot, watching me. I hold up my hand in a soft wave.

He nods his head and walks away.

I leave the lake thinking about how relaxing it was to just walk with him. Not to feel obligated to create conversation or put on a show for someone.

It's not often these days I feel that level of contentment, I enjoyed it while it lasted.

CHAPTER 4
COMMENCE SENIOR YEAR
AURORA DAVIS

I am rudely woken up by my alarm blaring in my ear. I reach over blindly to shut it off. I snuggle my blanket up into my neck and close my eyes. I have another alarm set; it will be fine to sleep a little while longer.

I always used to look forward to the first day of school. This year just isn't the same. The last few weeks flew by between babysitting Abigail and preparing to go back to school. Weeks seemed to have turned into days.

Ugh, I really need to get out of bed. I stretch my arms and legs and throw off my covers. I grab my towel from my closet door before heading to the bathroom.

I slip off my sleep shorts and tank top before stepping into the shower, I immerse myself in the hot water. I let the water soothe my aching muscles, like a makeshift heating pad.

My body has been tense since the lake. My mind

continuously wandering back to the interaction with Zayn; how unexpected it was and how curious I am to know more about the man beyond the disguise.

After, I lean forward above the sink and wipe the fog from the mirror. I style my hair before going back to my room to get dressed. As soon as I am in my room, I hear the bathroom door shut. Clearly Oliver's awake now.

Dressed, I sit down at my vanity to put some makeup on.

I'm texting back and forth with Jade and realize it's time for me to leave soon. I grab my book bag and head downstairs.

My mom is standing in the kitchen while Abigail eats. "Hey mom, good morning," I greet her with a side hug and reach in the fridge for the orange juice. I pour it into a travel mug to take to school with me when Mom asks, "Good morning, honey, do you want something to eat?"

I hear Oliver running down the stairs, so I put the orange juice back in the fridge. "No thanks, I'll eat with Jade when we get to school." Oliver runs into the kitchen with his book bag slung over one shoulder. He grabs a pancake from Abigail's plate and starts eating it.

"There is an entire plate of pancakes on the counter, get away from mine!" she shrills. He laughs as I shake my head.

We head to the car to pick up Jade and Ashton. I beep the horn upon arrival so they know we're here.

Jade immediately eyes Oliver in the front seat and

motions for him to move into the back. When he doesn't immediately, Ashton says, "Just do it bro, she is on a rampage this morning."

Reluctantly, Oliver pushes the passenger side door open, moving into the backseat.

Jade gets in and huffs, throwing her bag onto the floor.

"What happened between us texting and whatever this is?" I ask, motioning around her in a circle.

She dramatically twists in her seat. "Well, you see, someone here thought it was a bright idea to throw all my laundry onto the top of the dryer. My SOPPING WET laundry. In translation, all of my new clothes for school are wet. They smell like moldy gym socks. So, now I have to rewash them and pray the smell comes out, or burn them. Now, I'm left wearing the same shit people have seen a hundred times."

"Big whoop." Ashton says from behind me.

She shoots daggers at her brother, his matching green eyes narrowing into hers in challenge. She huffs and spins around, crossing her arms.

I chuckle and look back at the boys, they're holding in a laugh like their lives depend on it. I try so hard not to, but end up bursting into laughter, unable to control it any longer. Which, of course, makes the boys follow suit. By the time we get to school, I'm wiping the tears from my eyes trying not to smudge my makeup. Jade has a permanent scowl.

We eat breakfast in the cafeteria and start comparing

our schedules. The only period we have together is fourth. Of course, she ends up in classes with Ruby, Josh and Austin. I don't have them in any of my classes this semester. We clean up our trays and then make our way to first period.

The day drags on, so when the bell finally rings at the end of third period, I'm so excited.

We have fourth with Mr. Harrison for Science. I truly do not understand how they allow him to be a teacher. I'm surprised any of the girls even pass his class. It must be hard to find time to do their schoolwork between all the time they spend drooling over him. He's hot, but not worth the headache that would follow acting on it.

I step into the classroom and see two seats beside each other, immediately making a beeline for them. I throw my bag on the seat next to me for Jade. She comes in all giddy with a huge grin on her face. To hide herself from Mr. Harrisons view, she turns to the side and fans herself.

"Oh my god," she mouths silently. My smile is wide by the time she sets my bag on the floor between us and takes a seat.

She starts to tell me about her classes and as soon as she starts to mention her second period, Zayn and Daniel walk in. I try to look down and ignore them, but Jade notices. She squints at me as if she is missing something.

She is, but I'm not about to tell her that with him approaching us. Zayn kicks my bag out of his way as he

42

walks in the aisle between our rows. He takes a seat behind me and Daniel sits behind Jade.

To say I'm annoyed would be an understatement. He could have easily walked in the row to the left of our desks, but instead decided to walk through the middle and kick my fucking bag. I reach down and push it completely under my desk. At least now it won't be victim to any other abuse.

I'm shocked to see them. I've never had any classes with the founders before and now that we have run into each other, *twice*, here he is. This is going to be a long semester.

He leans into my left side. "This is going to be fun, what a nice surprise," he murmurs against my ear.

The tone of his voice is tormenting, causing me to instantly sag in my chair. Where is the guy I met yesterday?

We're halfway through class when I spy Jade flirting with Daniel. I grab my phone out of my back pocket to text her. As soon as I press send, her phone goes off.

FUCK, why doesn't she have her phone on silent? She shoots daggers at me as if I'm supposed to know her phone's on loud in the middle of school.

Mr. Harrison turns to the class. "You can tell me whose phone that was, or I can go get a list of everyone's phone numbers and call every one until I find out." Jade raises her hand and says it was hers and he makes a motion for her to bring it to the front. As she walks back to her desk, he starts to read my text.

Out loud.

To the entire class.

> What happened to the, "We don't waste
> our time on Founders?"

Half of the class chuckles while the other half seems too nervous to react. When Mr. Harrison stops reading, I breathe a sigh of relief. I think he knew the second message was best kept to himself.

"Jade you can get this at the end of my class. Aurora, if I see you with your phone out today, or ever again, it'll be given to the office," our teacher states.

My skin is on fire. I lean forward and put my head down on my desk for the remainder of class.

Later, when class finally ends, I practically feel Zayn's presence behind me as we leave. I try to scurry out of the classroom as quickly as possible. The last thing I need is to try to explain my text.

Jade heads up to Mr. Harrison's desk to grab her phone. As I get into the hallway, she comes up behind me, grabbing me by the arm to swing me around. "What the hell was that?" she hisses.

"Me?! Who doesn't turn their phone on silent?" I snap.

"I thought I did! That was so embarrassing," she says.

We were headed to the exit when I notice my

phone's missing. I swear it was in my back pocket. Pulling my book bag around, I dig through it to see if maybe I threw it in there. When I don't find it, I tell Jade I'll be right back and hand her my car keys to meet me outside.

Ugh, this is so fucking annoying.

I scan the ground as I retrace my steps back to the classroom incase maybe I dropped it. I get all the way back just to find the lights are already off and the door is locked. My parents are going to be pissed. I throw my head back in defeat and realize I'll have no choice but to check the office tomorrow in hopes that someone turned it in. I can hide it until then.

Jade, Oliver, and Ashton are already sitting in the car by the time I make it back. I get in and pause when I see my phone in the cup holder. Weird.

"What the hell, I just looked everywhere for this?"

"It was sitting on the hood when we got to the car," Oliver answers. "I'm guessing someone knew it was yours and left it here instead of bringing it to the office."

That's sketchy as fuck. How would they have known it was my phone when my lock screen is a picture of me and my friends? My case is plain black, so they just *knew* it was mine out of the 4 other people in our group?

During the entire drive to drop them off, I can't stop thinking about who had my phone. I kick off my shoes as soon as I get home and lay down on my bed I get a message.

Unknown: You know you should be more aware of your surroundings, Aurora.

Me: Who is this?!

Unknown: The person who politely returned your phone to you.

Me: Someone doesn't "politely" return a phone and then mysteriously text from an unknown number and not say who they are. Now, who is this?

Unknown: Feisty, I like it. I won't be doing that yet, but I will be enjoying the idea of you trying (and failing) to figure it out.

CHAPTER 5
THE BIG 18
AURORA DAVIS

Today is my birthday. After school, my parents are celebrating by having my friends join us for dinner. I'm excited because my parents don't have people over very often; they are more reserved. That and they are normally exhausted from work.

The only two who have free roam without asking are Ashton and Jade. My parents treat them like family.

We're all sitting in the cafeteria discussing the plan for Saturday.

Since Austin's dad travels to the other side of the city for business a few times a month, staying in the city when he does, they've decided to throw me a party at his house while he's away. He's aware Austin is throwing a get together, but what he doesn't know is that they have basically invited the entire school.

I jump into the conversation. "Guys, we really don't need to do some big thing," I remind them.

"Umm, of course we do, it's your 18th birthday. *And,* before you roll your eyes at me, this *is* exciting. You and I are the only two remaining to turn 18 this year. I, for one, want to enjoy every free moment we have left. You will love it. Trust us," Jade lectures me.

"I promise we aren't going crazy, but we will be celebrating you." Austin leans in and knocks my shoulder.

"But there will be beer pong right?" Josh asks. "That's the only reason I'm coming."

"Josh, shut up," Jade and Ruby say together and we all burst into laughter. Josh either says the most inappropriate things or makes everyone laugh at the perfect time.

The bell rings and we go to dump our trays. Austin comes up beside me.

"Hey, what can I bring to dinner?"

"Oh, you know my mom said you guys didn't have to bring anything tonight," I tell him.

"I know, but I love your mom, and she's going out of her way to cook for all of us. It's the least I can do. What if I make her those orange blossoms she likes?"

I can't say no to that, my mom is obsessed with them and eats almost the whole basket when he brings them. "Honestly, I think she would love that, but if you don't have time, it's fine."

He winks. "I'll make time." Austin walks me to third period. Class drags on and before the teacher dismisses us, he assigns a bunch of homework. I guess I don't get out of homework because it's my birthday.

Once in fourth, Mr. Harrison takes attendance. Unfortunately for me, when he gets to my name he wishes me a *Happy Birthday* in front of the class. I can feel my face flush in embarrassment. I've been avoiding drawing any attention to myself in this class, hoping if I fade into the shadows, Zayn and Daniel will forget I exist.

I feel Zayn inch up to my left from behind. "Happy Birthday Aurora," he whispers, keeping his voice low.

"Thanks," I choke out.

Shortly after, Mr. Harrison begins to discuss a class project we will be working on over the next two weeks. We are to create a renewable energy source. It will be worth 40% of our grade. He informs us we will be working on it every day in class, but if we need more time than that to meet the expected deadlines, we are to meet up outside of school.

He split us into groups of four. When I hear my name and the names of my group partners, I think I'm being punked. Sure enough, he was one hundred percent serious.

It is me, Jade, Zayn, and Daniel.

Once all groups are assigned, we divvy up into our sections with instructions that tomorrow, each group will take turns presenting their plan for the project with the class.

We aren't even a half hour into the project, and we can't agree on anything. We have been going back and forth, trying to decide what to create for it. Jade suggests demonstrating solar panels powering something and explaining how it works.

Zayn immediately shoots that down. "That is too easy, I for one, need to ace this. We won't do that by doing the bare minimum."

"What about a wind turbine?" I suggest. The guys look at each other, clearly trying to communicate with their eyes instead of just opening their mouths. I continue to explain my option. "If we create a wind turbine, we can explain how important it is to harness wind energy to produce electricity. We have wind turbines in our city. Thus, showing the importance in why we chose it."

Zayn doesn't respond, but Jade and Daniel both agree it's a good choice.

The 10 minute warning goes off, marking the end of class is approaching. Since we already have our project chosen, we have to draw it up and map the design. And because tomorrow everyone will be discussing their project, we can begin to materialize the plans on Friday. The bell rings, and the class disperses.

Jade comes home with me, so that way I don't have to drive back to her house to pick her up before dinner. Leaving her in my room, I head to the shower.

When I step out of the bathroom, the smell of food wafts upstairs from the kitchen. Instantly, my stomach growls. I decide to run downstairs knowing I need a snack or something to hold me over until dinner.

As soon as my bare feet hit the cold tile downstairs, I see Austin is already here. Backing up a step, I quickly glance down at my towel, checking to make sure it's wrapped tight around my chest. When I know it's secure, I look back into the kitchen, hoping no one has noticed me so I can escape upstairs.

As soon as I do, my stare meets Austin's. *So much for no one noticing me.* He looks up at me, before his eyes drift to my towel. Almost unconsciously they start to roam the length of my body.

Of course, my mom has her complete focus on the food in front of her. I feel grateful for her distraction.

I inch forward causing his attention to be pulled from my body. His face flushes and his adams apple bobs in his throat. A rush of heat flows through me. I've never been attracted to Austin, but his reaction to seeing me stand here in a towel is affecting me. Shaking the thoughts away, I continue to walk towards the kitchen. I try to hide most of my body behind the bar while I white knuckle my towel.

"Hey, I didn't realize you would be here so early, I wouldn't have taken so long to shower," I greet my friend.

He looks back down at the cutting board in front of him, burying his head in his current task. "It's fine, I just wanted to come early to help your mom prepare dinner."

"Thank you again for that, Austin, you are so sweet."
She responds to him as she reaches over into a basket.
Realizing by its contents, clearly he brought it. She makes a
show of smiling at us and shoving one in her mouth.

I decide to abandon the snack I was planning to grab,
and start to back away from the bar. Telling them both that
I'm going to go get dressed, and we will be down shortly.
My mom throws up her hand to wave me off.

I avoid looking at Austin before turning around. I run
upstairs heading straight for the bathroom. When I reach it,
I close the door quietly behind me. I take a deep breath,
leaning my head back against it and shake out my hands
that are stiff from holding the towel so tight.

Heat pools in my stomach and I try my best to ignore
the thoughts forming. Honestly, I don't think it's just Austin
that has me so worked up.

The way Zayn's eyes roamed my body felt different
than when Austin did. It was more than a physical reaction.
Not that he didn't provoke that, too. I haven't been able to
stop thinking about him and the lines on his body. *Ignoring
his hot and cold personality.*

Every time I see him, I flash back to the sight of him on
the beach. Closing my eyes, I place my hand on the inside
of my thigh. It glides up and underneath my towel, wanting
to relieve the pressure that's building. As soon as I'm
almost there, my phone vibrates, causing my arm to
instantly sag in pain.

When I finally grab my phone, there's a text from

Austin. I hesitate before unlocking the home screen to read it.

> Austin: Hey, I feel like I need to apologize. I should have said something before coming by. I hope I didn't make it awkward.

> Me: Of course you didn't, sorry I just would have gotten dressed before I came down. We are good. I'll be down in a few.

> Austin: It never takes you "a few" to get ready. LOL.

Okay great, he's joking, so maybe we can just enjoy dinner without that coming back up.

I return to my room to finish getting ready. No wonder Jade didn't come looking for me. I find her out cold in my bed. I can tell she hasn't been sleeping well lately.

I do my best to get ready as quietly as possible, waiting until the last minute to wake her up for dinner.

Downstairs, I sit down at the bar to talk to my mom while she finishes preparing dinner, Austin and Jade begin to set the table. Ruby and Josh should be here in about 15 minutes for dinner.

Oliver walks through the door with Ashton. As soon as Jade notices them, she yells to her brother, "I wasn't aware you were invited."

Ashton gives her a side smirk and leans on the bar

beside me. Shooting me a wink before he asks my mom, "Hey Mom and Ro, mind if I stay for dinner?"

"Ashton, they are already setting 10 places," she answers before directing her question to Jade. "Jade, did you not count how many plates you have?"

I can't help but laugh along with my mom. Jade and Ashton are basically extensions to our family at this point. Jade, knowing she lost, continues to set the plates at each seat. Ashton offers to start bringing food to the table.

The doorbell rings and I jump off my stool to answer the door. Josh and Ruby stand behind it, I step forward to hug them both. Austin comes up behind me causing my body to immediately stiffen.

Austin has never made me feel uneasy, he is normally the most caring and levelheaded of our group. But something feels possessive about the way he made his presence known from behind me. I may be thinking too much into it, but this is my house, I don't need help answering the door.

I usher everyone into the dining room, my dad and Abigail come in from playing outside.

Once everyone has settled into their seats, I glance around the table. They're each deep in their conversations. Bright smiles pouring out laughter that warms my heart with a sense of appreciation.

Gratitude blooms in my chest for my friends and family and a smile plays on my lips as I soak in the moment, not wanting it to pass.

Jade reaches over and grabs my hand in hers, settling it on my thigh, a silent acknowledgement of my happiness.

Friday afternoon, we separate into our groups. Yesterday, each group presented our plans in front of the class and Mr. Harrison was impressed with ours and how it correlated with the building of Kyrosia. I felt like we were off to a great start.

Daniel has started designing mockups for our design. Zayn keeps rebutting that certain aspects of the design will ruin efficiency and now it feels like we have gotten nowhere with the end of class creeping closer. The design has to be finalized so we can collect the materials we will need to build it.

Clearly frustrated, Daniel asks us if there is any way we can meet up this weekend to work on it.

"I can't tonight, I have an event with my dad. Can we meet tomorrow?" Zayn asks.

"We can't tomorrow," Jade declines, clearly avoiding having to elaborate.

Not that it works. Daniel picks up on her lack of explanation when he asks us why we can't. As if it is any of his business. I immediately become aggravated, having no interest in where this is going.

The moment it clicks for Daniel, he gives us a mischievous smile. "Oh, that's right, Birthday Girl. Sounds great, we'd love to come. I'll get with Zayn on the drawings, and we can bring them tomorrow. It shouldn't take long to discuss what we will need to get started on Monday. J, text me the address."

He makes a show of ripping the corner off one of the trash drawings and writing his number down before handing it to her. She crumples it and shoves it into her pocket. Meanwhile, Zayn is sitting in his chair listening to the conversation with a blank expression.

I want to ask him where his mind is at. I am entirely uncomfortable when I can't tell how another is feeling. Him sitting there, emotionless, eats at me.

It only makes me more curious about him.

Jade and Ruby insist on me picking something new out for my party. I don't think it's necessary but somehow, I find myself walking around the mall anyway. We have gone into a few stores, and I haven't spotted anything I like yet. I'm growing sick of trying things on and getting tired of being here.

I agree to try one more store before we leave. When we walk into Xilos, I look around skeptically. I would prefer a floor-length dress, so I look at the bottom of the racks. That way, I don't waste my time looking at any that are short.

That's when my eyes catch the sight of a dress layered with black lace.

I push the hangers apart to get a better look and the dress is beautiful. I really love it, but it feels like it may be a bit much for a house party.

Ruby comes around the corner and eyes me staring at it. As soon as she looks at it, she gasps. "Ro, this would look amazing on you!"

"Are you sure?" I ask.

She grabs my size off the rack and hands it to me. "I want to see it on you, go try it on." She shoos me away.

Once inside the dressing room, I hang the dress up on the hook. It has long sleeves with a plunging neckline and slits up both legs. Under the bodice begins a layer of black lace that travels all the way down to the floor. Stepping out of my boots and then my clothes, I slip the dress on.

I open the door to exit into the hall and as soon as I see Jade and Ruby's faces, I know this dress is the right choice.

I can't hide my excitement; I'm obsessed with it.

Ruby claps her hands together. "That dress is absolutely beautiful on you."

"Holy shit, you look incredible. Why must you hide this body away in jeans and turtlenecks every day?" Jade throws her hand on her hip.

"You are ridiculous," I reply. "I have never even owned a turtleneck. But, as much as I do love it. Is it worth it? This is my entire birthday allowance."

They both nod their heads, assuring me that it is.

Jade circles me, inspecting it further. She pushes one of the slits open to see if my boots are on, they aren't. *Yet.*

Her green eyes are wide as she begs me not to wear them, "Please tell me you will at least wear heals or sandals tonight?"

Ruby effectively shushes her. "Ignore her. I think it will look sexy with your boots, gladiator meets fuck-me-neckline."

We laugh at her comment. Ruby is so very sweet, but also not frigid in the slightest. She's vocal and I love that about her. They're still ogling me like an anomaly when I look in the mirror.

"Okay, stop staring I'm getting it," I announce as I walk into the dressing room.

Ruby is bouncing up and down and I hear Jade say, "This is going to be fun."

I freeze at her choice of words. That's exactly what Zayn said to me in class. Now, I'm thinking about running into him at my party. This was a lot less stressful before he was coming.

I stare at the dress in the mirror, nervously running my hands down it. I start to ask myself if he'll like it before immediately regretting how desperate that sounds. It doesn't matter if he likes it. I don't need his approval.

But do I want it?

I purchase it, and ouch, that hurt. We have a few hours to hang out and get ready before the party so we stop by Ruby's on the way back from the mall. Jade and I wait in the car while she runs in to get what she needs. She isn't in her house for 10 minutes before she comes out with a bag in her arms.

"Isn't that a lot just for the party?" I ask.

"I grabbed clothes to stay at Austin's with you guys, too," she answers.

Jade and I don't respond. Both of us know that is way more than needed for an overnight stay. Ruby has it hard enough without the third degree from us.

Back at my house, we each take turns showering and getting ready. Oliver is under strict instructions to take Abigail out of the house so we can get ready in peace.

Tonight, I go a little heavier on my makeup than I normally would. I style my curls, and once they're dry, I pull the top half of my hair into a top knot. I decide on my silver dangling crescent moon earrings for my first lobe holes.

It's not long before I go ahead and put my dress on and lace up my boots. We all finish getting ready at about the same time. Jade is wearing a royal blue long sleeve body con dress that has a turtleneck with short black heels. *Ironic, no?* Ruby is wearing a lavender baby doll dress and brown sandals.

Jade states it is a must that we take pictures before we leave, knowing I hate pictures, but I smile through them knowing this is my last birthday before the ceremony.

Once she is satisfied we head out the door.

Austin's house is much larger than any of ours. It has a

large circle driveway with a fountain in the middle, which is already lined with cars. We park and head inside. As soon as we open the doors, we're greeted with loud music. I can't help but smile. From the music playing, I can tell he chose one of my playlists. Austin never skimps on the details.

Jade leads the way towards a table set up with everything from water to alcohol. I stand there watching her make us drinks when I feel a hand reach for the small of my back, in hello. I turn to find Austin.

Josh came early to help Austin set up. He is standing at Austin's side and moves quickly to give me a hug and say happy birthday first. As soon as he releases me, he turns to Ruby, sweeping her off her feet and pressing his lips to hers. She returns the kiss with passion as if they haven't seen each other in days.

I envy to be loved like that.

To distract myself from my jealousy, my attention floats back to Austin. He sets his drink down on the table to reach up and wrap both arms around me. "Ro, you look absolutely beautiful. Happy birthday."

"Thank you, Austin, and thank you for the party it looks beautiful in here."

He lets go of me and reaches behind me to grab his drink. Maybe, just a little too close. "You're welcome, I hope you actually take the time to enjoy it."

As the drinks kept coming, time became a blur, and the house transformed into a pulsing sea of bodies.

Each room vibrating with music. I lost myself with every song that played, dancing freely amongst the crowd.

I am almost out; do you want another?" Jade shouts over the music, pointing to her drink.

"I'll get it, I need a break anyway," I yell back.

"Are you sure?" she asks.

I nod while laughing. I think I can handle getting drinks. I head out of the living room still swaying with the beat.

I go to reach for the tequila bottle without paying attention and my hand touches someone else's. I look up to see it is Zayn, I yank my hand back. I was so focused I didn't see him when I walked up, nor did I notice him arrive.

He starts to speak barely loud enough for me to hear. "It's your party, why are you over here making yourself a drink?"

I cast a quick glance around the room trying to look for Daniel since we need to discuss the project. When I don't respond to him he continues, "Relax, I'm not going to roofie your drink. You look like you're trying to send an SOS."

"I wasn't." I try to justify myself awkwardly. "My

friends are dancing. I don't need anyone to fetch me a drink."

"You don't seem like the type who needs much help for anything, Aurora." He looks puzzled. "That doesn't mean that people wouldn't want to help, if given the chance." He reaches for my cup and silently waits for me to hand it to him. Reluctantly, I do and he starts to make my drink for me. I sit there in silence as he works.

When he's done, he hands me my drink.

I stare into the contents of the cup. "I never told you what I was drinking."

He motions with his finger for me to try it. I lift the cup to my lips and the moment it touches my tongue, I know it's exactly how I would have made it.

He leans down to whisper in my ear, "I'm very observant. Which also means the longer I stand here with you, I question how your friends let you out of their sight for this long in that dress."

When I go to step back and put some distance between us he swiftly moves one arm around me, effectively halting my retreat. He pulls me in hard enough that my chest hits his torso, spilling some of my drink onto the floor. Sensation pulses through me when I notice the way his arm feels wrapped around me.

I lean my head back to look at him.

The alcohol I consumed must be thinking for me. I don't even realize what I'm saying as my mouth opens.

"What about my dress?" I ask quietly.

Before I have a chance to regret what I said, Zayn takes his left hand and tucks my hair behind my ear. His eyes scan my face, searching for something before grabbing the hair at the nape of my neck softly to pull my head back further.

I'm sweating with anticipation as his finger trails the plunging neckline of my dress.

"If you have the nerve to ask that, then I should have given you more credit." He pushes his lower body flush against mine. "But, as you can obviously feel, I think you look sexy as fuck. The second I got here I saw you dancing, your head was tipped back in euphoria. Those beautiful red curls wild and free. I saw the sweat dripping down your neck. I watched you, I wanted you Aurora."

I'm breathing heavy. My pulse is racing. This is all so new to me. These feelings, his words, the way he is touching me.

I reach my hand out to his chest to catch my footing. At the same time, I look up into his smoldering gray eyes. His hands reach for my hips, and he starts to walk me back into the hallway out of sight.

My back hits a wall and I let out a gasp. He wraps his hand around the underneath of my thigh to pull my leg up around his hip. I can feel his fingertips dig into the flesh there. He takes his left forearm and places it firmly against the wall behind my head.

I have one hand on his chest and the other dangling

somewhere. I have no idea what's happening. I'm too turned on to think straight.

"I am doing everything within me not to take advantage of you. I can see how erratic you're breathing. Even with this dress, I can feel the heat radiating off of you." He pushes his hair back with his left hand, the one curl falling immediately as it always does.

Without thinking I reach up and push the curl up into his hair. I run my nails through his scalp to the back of his head and he leans it back in ecstasy.

The way his head tips back only turns me on more. Seeing how affected he is by my touch, I lean forward. "So, take advantage of me," I murmur seductively.

Zayn wastes no time, he grabs my wrist and pins it to the wall behind me. It's like he becomes unhinged, when he slams his mouth against mine. His kiss is fast and hard. His tongue enters my mouth and dances with expertise, and I find myself trying to keep up with him, not entirely sure of what I'm doing. With heat, I push my core harder into him. His dick jolts to attention with pressure.

His hand drifts up my thigh farther into the dress's slit.

I tip my head back slamming into the wall behind me and close my eyes. My left hand leaves his chest and grabs his hand, stopping it. He instantly slides his palm back down my thigh in response. Putting distance between him and my pussy.

He needs to know we can't have sex.

I hesitate, I'm either going to make an absolute fool out

of myself or by some chance, he understands. He must notice because he stops kissing me. He looks down in question.

"I'm sorry, I shouldn't have let it get this far, I wasn't thinking," I say.

His eyes go from guilt to rage in an instant. "Were you promised?" he asks me. His hand on my thigh loosens and he lowers my leg to the ground.

I reach for his hand instinctively, needing to explain. "No, it-it's by choice. I was originally holding off for the ceremony."

His eyes soften and he grips my cheek with his hand. "Aurora, you can't—"

A throat clears behind us, and I know it's Jade without having to look. Zayn pulls back from me immediately.

My eyes don't leave Zayn's until Jade begins to speak. "I have been searching for you everywhere, I ran into Daniel, and he said he couldn't find you either." She motions to Zayn. She seems to notice the tension between us because she asks, "Now, am I walking away and pretending this didn't happen or are you coming back to the group?"

Zayn looks at me. "It's okay, we were done here anyway. Happy Birthday, Aurora."

I stand there for a second, watching him walk away as if nothing happened between us. The burn I feel from his disassociation leaves me feeling like I've been struck.

I have tried my best not to ever be put in a compromising position. My mom sat me down before high school and explained what it meant to be a woman, that those of our social standing are free to have sex. I didn't have to wait until marriage, but a lot of women in our city do so they can possibly be chosen.

She told me it was entirely up to me. It wasn't that I wanted to be a Founder's wife, or even that I thought it was possible. I just thought that I needed to leave my options open. Then, I got older. Became aware of how little power women hold, regardless of your hierarchy. Holding onto my virginity was no longer about keeping my possibilities open, but *a lack of desire*.

I just never found anyone I wanted to kiss, let alone fuck. Now, I'm 18 and completely untouched. I'm the only one of my friends who is pure.

We walk back into the living room, abandoning my drink, despite how bad I need one right now.

His kiss still tingles on my lips, the phantom ache reminding me of his absence. I reach up and rub them absentmindedly. I try my best to act as if nothing is wrong, but I can't stop trying to figure out what Zayn was going to say.

I can't, what…?

CHAPTER 6
CONVERSATIONS
AURORA DAVIS

When I realize I'm no longer enjoying myself, I tell my friends I'm heading to bed. Everyone is mostly gone anyway. I march upstairs for the room where Jade and I are staying.

Beside my bag on the bed lays a folder. In it, there are two drawings of possible designs and a list of supplies each design would need. A sticky note on top reads:

These are the two designs Daniel and I liked the most. Pick which one you ladies want to move forward with and have Jade text Daniel which one. HBD.

-Z.

I wonder if he put this here before or after we were

together? How did he even know which room we were staying in?

I go to stick the folder in my bag; planning to show it to Jade tomorrow when I notice my bag is open. Which is weird because I haven't been in here since we brought our stuff up earlier.

I snag my toiletry bag and head for the en suite bathroom to take off all this makeup, change into my pajamas, and throw my hair up in a bun.

When I come out, I find Jade sitting on her bed still all dressed up.

"So, are we going to talk about it?" she asks unbuckling her heels and tossing them to the side. My initial response is to act like nothing happened. But, I know her and she isn't going to let it go. I lay back onto the bed for a minute and then lift my head up.

"Jade, what the hell was I thinking?" I ask rhetorically.

"I need every single detail, from the beginning," she says.

"When I went to grab a drink, he was there at the table. I hadn't even noticed until his hand touched mine, completely stunning me. He made my drink for me and made a comment about how sexy my dress was. He actually told me he was watching us dance and his words were...descriptive. When I tried to back away, he pulled me into him and, Jade, I could *feel* how hard he was. Then, he started making out with me! I've never, ever felt like that. When he started to seem like he was going to go further, I had to stop him. Ugh, I'm an idiot, Jade."

"Excuse me for a second, I'm a little shell shocked. You stopped Zayn Everett from going farther with you? Okay, that doesn't even matter." She shakes her head. "What did you say? What did *he* say?"

"I told him that I shouldn't have let it get that far, I wasn't thinking and that I was sorry. I didn't say I was a virgin, but he inferred by asking if I was promised. He really thought I was stopping him from touching me because I was already set to marry someone else," I scoff. "I shot it down, but why would his mind jump to that? He went to tell me 'I can't—' something before you walked up. I have no idea what he's thinking. He was completely unreadable." I throw my arms up in the air staring back at Jade.

"Okay, with all that being said," Jade starts, "I didn't go looking for you. Daniel texted me and said I should probably go get you before you do something you regret. I didn't know what he was talking about because I instantly went looking for you without responding. I'm guessing he knew you were a virgin or at least assumed. He had to have seen you guys or something before he texted me."

"I think I'm even more confused than when we started this conversation. Why would he text you instead of just walking up to us if he wanted to stop it?"

"Ro, I think Zayn likes you. Think about it, he is always

looking at you. You guys have barely had any interaction besides class, and he sticks his tongue down your throat."

I huff. "He doesn't know me enough to like me. It was just an in-the-moment thing."

Jade puts her hand up to silence me. "Okay, stop. What I can't do is idly sit by while you act like you couldn't possibly be liked. People don't have to 'know each other' for there to be an attraction. You are drop dead gorgeous. Whoever gave you your gene pool certainly did at least one thing right. Now, you have Zayn falling at your feet and you are here questioning everything. Look in the fucking mirror, like you used to. Before you started overthinking your very existence."

She continues, "I know everything with Zayn has you rolling, but there is something you do need to decide. If it is Zayn you want to pursue great, hop on him. Literally, please. But, you need to open your eyes. Austin has been so in love with you and you are too blind to see it. I think at this point he might wait his whole life for you. If you don't want that, you need to tell him.

"It's worth mentioning, I've never seen you look at Austin with the raw passion I saw between you and Zayn tonight. So, I tell you this with love: figure out who it is you want and tell them. Then, do whatever the opposite of 'getting the fuck over yourself' is." She grabs her overnight bag and heads into the bathroom.

She's entirely right. I haven't been myself. What I should have realized by now is how Austin felt, or maybe I did but I subconsciously chose to ignore it to remain friends.

I don't feel the same heat under Austin's stare as I do Zayn, or the curiosity to dive into his mind. Maybe it's because we've been friends for so long, but the pull I have to Zayn feels unstoppable.

When Zayn looked at me tonight, it was like he couldn't decide if he wanted to devour or kill me. In the moment, I think I would have stayed for either, which feels a little dangerous. And the craziest part is, that feeling is addictive.

I hear the shower start to run, so I go down into the kitchen and grab a glass of water. Austin is shirtless cleaning up the mess and I glance around to see if Ruby and Josh are still up, but don't see them. They must have gone to bed.

Crickets fill the air. I start to pick up some cups on the counter and go over to the bag Austin is holding.

"You don't need to clean up after your own party. I'm only down here still because I want to sober up some before I go to bed," he says.

"I don't mind helping, Jade is in the shower." I shrug him off.

We work together cleaning up the remaining cups and

bottles and agree we will finish cleaning the counters and floors tomorrow. I go ahead and grab us both a cup of water. Right before we go to head upstairs, I stop him.

"Austin, can I ask you something?"

"Obviously," he mocks.

Here goes nothing. "I like you, I think that's obvious. But, you are also one of my best friends. I can't help but feel like I'm leading you on and that isn't my intention. I just can't handle the idea of us not being friends," I say, staring into my cup. "If we became more and it didn't work, I can't risk losing you as a friend. Maybe that's self-ish, but sometimes I feel like you are the only person I can talk to. I know I am really dumping it out there, but I just needed to be honest with you."

As I wait for him to respond to me, the pressure is weighing on my chest.

"Aurora," he leans against the wall. "I'm going to do my best to say this and act like I'm not entirely too drunk for this conversation. There is a reason I've never acted on anything. I want you as my friend. I'm not so sex craved that I am too blind to see how it could ruin us. I love you in more ways than one. But, I'm not stupid. Rumor spreads fast. Several people saw you and Zayn at the lake and tonight. I was shocked at first. But, I can't blame him for wanting you."

I'm stunned, we were just cleaning and everything was so normal. I had no idea he had any clue about what happened between Zayn and me.

"Austin." His name weighs heavy on my tongue. I feel guilty for not having this conversation sooner.

"Stop, it's fine. I will always be your friend, Ro. Now, I'm not saying if you didn't change your mind one day I wouldn't react, because I will. I'm just a man after all," he says with a wink, trying to lighten the mood. I smile and give him a one armed hug with our glasses in the other hand. We head up the stairs to retire to our rooms.

I creak the door open quietly, in case Jade is asleep and crash into the bed. Staring at the ceiling, I replay the events of tonight in my mind. If tonight was any indication on how my 18th year is going to be, I need to turn back time.

At least Zayn will be Monday's problem.

CHAPTER 7
ASSUMPTIONS
AURORA DAVIS

Sunday, we all worked together to finish cleaning Austin's house before we left. Everyone was normal and we joked around the entire time which was a relief. I talked to Jade in the morning about what was said between Austin and me and she was happy that I finally talked to him. We were friendly all day until we went home.

At breakfast, I showed her the project folder. We decided to go with option two, the design seemed to be more aesthetically pleasing with the least amount of mechanical engineering. I explicitly told Jade not to text Daniel which option, I would tell Zayn.

In second period, I go back and forth on what I'm going to say to Zayn when I see him. Maybe the easiest, and most petty, way to handle it is to write a note back to him. That way I won't forget what I want to say once I'm in front of him.

With my notebook and pen in front of me, I start to write:

Zayn,

While I understand we left things in a weird place, telling me to have Jade text Daniel with which design we wanted was a cop out. I'm sorry if I led you on by not stopping things sooner. That wasn't my intention. But, if you are so "observant" as you claim to be, then you should know my choices are mine. I am not chosen, it's not about that. I have no idea where life will take me. So, I have decided not to make reckless decisions to possibly impact that trajectory. I know that may not be what you are used to. I have no idea what you were about to say before Jade interrupted you, what can I not do? One minute it seems as if you don't hold anything back when you talk to me and in another, what you say is so vague. You are impossible to decipher.

Feel free to tell me to fuck off, or don't. Either way, I was able to say my piece.

If you want to write me back, you know how to find me. Or, we can do this with modern day technology.

-Aurora 8-293-282-8459

At first, I'm worried he's going to think I'm clingy. Then, I'm concerned about giving him my number. I don't think I've ever second guessed anything this much before. The bell rings before I can think about it any further. The paper rips from the spine of the notebook and I stick it inside the folder. When I get to fourth, I see him already sitting in his seat. I am normally one of the first here since it is so close to my last class.

I hand him the folder. "There is a note in the front for you."

He opens it and takes the sheet of paper from inside the pocket before I even turn around. I sit down and pray to Lina Mr. Harrison starts talking before Zayn has a chance to say something to me. Maybe, the note is a bit more ballsy than I intended.

Mr. Harrison walks in and immediately jumps into discussing the project. I mentally thank him. He calls on a person from each group to receive an update on the status of their developments. When it's our turn, he asks Daniel for our groups status. I immediately see Daniel look towards us in guidance. Jade turns in her chair and nods her head. He tells Mr. Harrison we have finalized our design and we are going to begin gathering materials. Some of the other groups have not finalized their plan yet, so those who still need to will be doing that today.

He breaks us up into our groups to begin working. Since we have already created the design, we'll just have to divvy up who is getting what from the list of materials.

I stand to turn my desk when I see Zayn's eyes are already watching me. A sweat breaks out over my skin. From the corner of my eye, I catch Daniel and Jade look between us and back and forth with each other.

"What is going on right now?" Jade asks. I shoot daggers at her for probing.

It takes Zayn a moment before he starts to speak, almost as if he is gathering his thoughts. He leans forward on his desk crossing his arms.

"Well, Aurora was so kind to leave me a note before class. I thought about sending her a good old modern day text, but then she would have my number," Zayn says, calm and cool.

Fuck. I instantly feel my face getting red with heat. Maybe this was not my best idea.

He continues. "Which would have made her realize I was the one who took her phone on the first day of school."

"Are you shitting me?" I question, becoming annoyed instead of embarrassed.

"Can I continue?" He raises his brow in question.

When I don't entertain answering him, he starts again. "I heard Jade's phone ding twice. So, either that's how she has her text tone set up, which seems unlikely, or Aurora sent two texts. I saw the way Mr. Harrison's face tensed after he read the first message. It was clear there was another message he didn't want to read out loud."

I look over at Jade anxiously, who is watching Zayn without blinking.

"Curiosity got the best of me, so I took your phone out of your back pocket on the way out of class. Sitting behind you makes it pretty easy to see your password," he says shamelessly. "I was aggravated that Daniel invited us to your birthday party, not because I didn't want to go, but because you have always piqued my interest, something I didn't want to explore. Running into you at the back to school party only made it worse. I avoid girls that are out of the Founder's circuit because of what it means for them to be associated with me. You have no idea what life has been like for some of the women involved with the Founders. I would never force someone into this life."

At least he's not blind to it like everyone else seems to be.

"So, when I thought you were chosen, I got angry. Someone I finally liked, even if it was essentially forbidden. The idea that you had already been arranged to be with someone else, made me crazy."

While I'm flattered, why should that matter to him? Hence the, 'forbidden' part.

"Honestly, it was stupid, but I thought you weren't a virgin from that text you sent to Jade. Yunno, the one that said, 'There's no point of fucking a Founder. Their daddy's choose who they get in the end.'"

Daniel whips his head in Jades direction. I furrow my brows at them, wondering what the hell that was about. I want to point out those weren't my words, but saying that seems futile; it doesn't make them any less true.

"It was rather—forward. My attempt to read between the lines was poor. I thought because you saw them flirting and you went straight to a joke about them fucking that could only mean one thing. Looking back, it was ridiculous." He shakes his head, clearly trying to rid himself of that notion. "Not that it mattered. I was never going to have sex with you."

Ouch that hurts. He must have seen the pained look on my face because he tries to redeem himself.

He holds his hands up in surrender. "Hold on, not because I don't want to, but because I promised myself that if a woman was forced to be pure to marry, then I would be, too. I know, shocker, since you seem to know me so well, but I haven't had sex yet either."

…what? I certainly wasn't expecting that.

"I found out young how sexist our fathers are. How outdated their practices are. That night, I was going to say that you can't let them control you. So, here I am having no idea what is best for you. I either encourage you to fuck someone, or you are available to be cherry picked. Either one being a shitty choice.

"I have no intention of telling you to fuck off. What I was going to do was sit on the sidelines until I could figure out how I wanted to handle all this. What I can't do is push you into the arms of someone else because you got the wrong idea. So, now I have no plans to sit back. Are you ready for that?"

"What does that even mean?" I question sheepishly.

Daniel snickers, clearly amused by my lack of under-standing. Which only causes me further embarrassment.

"What it means is that I don't do anything half speed. If you want me to leave you alone, I will. If you don't, then I hope you are prepared for what that entails," Zayn responds, his expression genuine, eyes never wavering from mine. He meant for his statement to be matter of fact, but it is really a question. I need to decide what it is that I want from him.

"How am I supposed to know what that entails? We don't even really know each other."

Zayn's smile spreads across his face. "It would mean you are mine, only mine, and I don't share."

I swallow the lump in my throat, with an audible gulp. I look around to see Daniel and Zayn are wearing matching smirks, and then I look over to Jade whose jaw is currently on the floor. I cannot believe he just said all of that in front of the two of them. I mean, I couldn't make this shit up if I wanted to, Jade never ever would have believed me.

Mr. Harrison begins to speak and instructs us to move our desks back. I haven't listened to anything he has said since, desperately trying to wrap my mind around every-thing Zayn just told me.

Do I want him? Is it worth it?

I'm still sitting there like a love struck fool when class is over.

Zayn's hand reaches for my shoulder. "Red, I wasn't joking. I get that you are processing, but you can't sit here all day. Get up, let's go." He grabs my book bag and motions for me to walk out of the classroom.

"Can Jade drive?" he asks.

"Why…?" I ask in return.

He rolls his eyes. "Because you drive her and the kids to school. I want to take you somewhere, but I can't do that if you have to take them home. Now, I'll ask again: can Jade drive?"

Should I be lying and saying no so that I have an excuse not to go? Will he see straight through that?

He stares a hole into the side of my face, so I answer honestly. "Yes, she has her license, just no car. I can have her bring the boy's home."

"Excellent," Zayn replies in satisfaction.

We head outside and everyone is waiting at my car, per usual. I walk over to Jade to ask if she can take the boys home. She agrees, so I hand her the keys and let her know that I can drive her home later when I'm back.

When I turn around, I see Oliver staring at Zayn with a death glare.

CHAPTER 8
VANILLA & JASMINE
ZAYN EVERETT

RETELLING OF EVENTS UP TO CURRENT DAY

I have become utterly fascinated with Aurora.

For so long, I have spent my time watching her from a distance to avoid getting too close, so she won't find out the truth. Keeping my distance was working well until I ran into her at the back to school party. All I've wanted to do since is find a reason to be around her again.

When I saw her sitting by the fire at the party with her friends, she looked different. It didn't take me long to pinpoint it. Her hair. She was wearing it down. Her red curls were glowing from the fire and I imagined that hair wrapped around my fingers, getting lost within the curls.

Before I ran into her, I was staring at myself in the bathroom mirror. *She should be off limits. Engaging with her could mess up everything for me.* I splashed my face with cold water and took a minute longer looking at the man staring back at me. Reminding myself that I am not my father, despite our resemblance. I need to be smart, strategic. *And I need to calm the hell down.*

I stepped out of the bathroom to head back to the fires when something rammed me in the chest. Still flustered and pissed off, I rushed out, "What the fuck are you doing?"

I looked down and realized it was her. *Yeah, real cool. Be an asshole. Women appreciate that.*

That's when she really surprised me. Hearing her yell at me made a smirk tug at the corners of my lips. I mentally smacked it away. *Remain passive.* In any other situation I would have offered to help her up, but if I did that, then she would have felt my hands sweating like a 14 year old fan girl. Instead, I waited for her to get her footing on her own. So, I placed my hands in my pockets to keep them to myself.

I went to leave, needing to get away from her but when I glanced back at her, I saw how the color of her eyes bounced off of the darkness.

My feet moved on their own accord until they stood right in front of her. Without thinking, my hand reached for her chin. When her eyes met mine, I focused on the honey golden color, the way they were so intricate, warm and yet, there was something else.

They were exquisite. It's normal for brown eyes to sometimes reflect brighter in the light, but they weren't like that, they were much greater. It was as if the gods tailor-made them by melting gold from our very sun to forge something new.

I wanted to stare into them, count each golden fleck, create a name for the color not yet discovered.

Lost in her presence and gaze, I almost said too much. Realizing my mistake, I quickly pulled away to leave. I needed to get far away fast before she asked questions she may not want the answers to, *answers that could get her killed.*

What is it about this girl that makes it so unbelievably challenging to just stay away from her?

After the back to school party, I told myself it was fine. I would just go back to keeping my distance from her. We never had a class together before, so I doubted that we would this year. That was, until I saw her in the hall heading straight into Mr. Harrison's classroom at the same time I was.

I took a deep breath, closing my eyes. A string of curses playing on a loop in my head. I waited for as long as I could before I needed to go in or I would be late. Just as I was entering the classroom, Daniel came running up to my side. Scanning the room, I noticed there were only two spots left, and they just so happened to be behind Aurora and Jade. I looked at Daniel and his eyes told me what I already knew.

Someone, somewhere, was laughing at me.

Her bag was in the middle of the row and I kicked it to the side frustrated. As soon as I did it, I regretted it. I was trying to stay away from her, not treat her like shit. I tried to make a joke, but the way her shoulders tensed, I didn't know if that was the right thing to do either. When I'm around her, I find myself overanalyzing every move I make.

Instead of listening as Mr. Harrison spoke. I watched Aurora look at Daniel and Jade with question. Clearly, bestie didn't tell her they were seeing each other. I decided to save that detail until it was convenient. Daniel owes me, anyway.

I was brought out of my trance when I heard a phone go off. At first, I didn't realize it was Jade's, but she was clearly trying to grab it and silence it quickly. That's when it beeped again. After some questioning, Mr. Harrison made her bring it to the front. He read her message out loud. But I caught how his face contorted, meaning there was more. I needed to know what else she said. Was it about us Founders, too? My interest was piqued, wondering what could follow up that first message. I made a plan to grab it from her pocket when we left class.

She was right in front of me, which made it easy. Once I had it and got out of the classroom, I walked in long strides to gain distance between us. I knew her password from glancing over her shoulder, so it was easy to unlock.

> I remember it was something like,
> "There's no point of fucking a Founder.
> Their daddies choose who they get in the
> end. Some outdated bullshit"?
> HAHAHAHA. Quit flirting.

I quickly read the message so I could return her phone to her car before someone realized it was me who took it. I was trying to decipher her message as I walked. She wasn't wrong. The Founders are generations of sexist men who have been horrible to women.

Before I left the phone on the hood of her car, I called myself from it, so I had her number. Then, I deleted my outbound call from her log.

I decided to mess with her later in the day. I'd be lying if I said I wasn't disappointed she left me on read after only a few short messages.

Her personality intrigues me; the time she yelled at me and then her texts. The feisty side of her is sexy as hell. It's an unforeseen advantage to this predicament I have found myself in.

The next day, Daniel invited us to her birthday party, much to my annoyance. He knew I had been trying to stay away from her. He just wants to be close to Jade. I also didn't love that it was at Austin's house. I'm pretty sure he has feelings for Aurora. Which shouldn't matter to me, but yet again, here we are.

We arrived at the party later than most. I saw her and her friends grab drinks a few times and watched her dancing from the hall.

All she had to do was look up at any point and she would have seen me watching. I leaned against the wall with my arms and ankles crossed.

Her eyes were closed as she swayed to the music, like she belonged to it. Her hair bounced as she danced and she had her arms stretched up behind her head where she lifted her hair from her neck. I watched the beads of sweat glisten down her exposed chest. The way her neckline drifted down her breasts almost to her naval had me feeling feral.

I watched as people stared at her, her head tipped back and eyes closed. The way she trusted everyone around her, clear by her posture and not needing to watch her surroundings.

All I wanted to do was run up to her and rip the dress off her and lick the sweat from her body. To lay her back onto the coffee table and feast, so everyone in there knew their eyes didn't belong on her.

Jealousy is a bitch, and she isn't mine to take. *Yet.* If I'm lucky.

She reached down pushing her dress out of her way, I watched as the slit of her dress exposed her long, dark leg as she danced. I found myself wondering what the silk of her skin felt like. That's when my eyes landed on her boots. I laughed to myself. She may be the only girl in our school who would choose to make such a bold statement.

Girls flock to us Founders' sons as if that will get them somewhere. Somewhere other than Elijah's bed, that is. Those same girls are money and power hungry carbon copies of their mothers. Nothing makes them remotely interesting, continuously boring me with their existence.

The girls who are worthy, *of anyone*, aren't out flaunting their bodies, they are forbidden. Like Aurora. She is *different*.

She doesn't seem to care at all about what the status quo is. I have never seen her force herself onto anyone. When I am around her, she is magnetic. She pulls my attention entirely in her direction. She is sexy, smart, and edgy yet it's not in your face. I find myself wanting to know everything about her, from her. It isn't enough anymore to find out information from afar.

Aurora stopped dancing, so I headed to the drink table, knowing she would eventually make her way there. I could smell her perfume as she approached; it was rich with nodes of vanilla and jasmine. I reached for the bottle just as our hands collided. When her warm hand covered mine, she flinched.

I instantly missed her touch when she pulled away. She was clearly nervous being alone with me. I tried to ease her nerves by making a joke, but again, that didn't work. I decided to change tactics.

I made her drink, and it was clear she was shocked. She questioned how I would know what she drank. Silly girl. I finally just told her to take a sip of it.

I'm not sure she even realized it, but when she was done drinking, she slowly glided her tongue across her lips. Which drew my attention to the deep red she had them painted. Just like her hair.

Loosening my leash, I whispered into her ear. "I pay attention to everything, Aurora. I am very observant. Which also means the longer I stand here with you, I question how your friends let you out of their sight for this long in that dress."

Her chest was heaving at my words. My dick stood at attention with the idea of her being turned on. The reaction my body has to her is different than anything I've felt in the past.

She began to step back away from me but I reached out and pulled her into my chest. I could practically feel her heart beating in sharp erratic bursts. She didn't even notice when I grabbed her drink from her hand to set on the table beside us after she spilled it.

Every ounce of my self control ditched my body when she asked, "What about my dress?" in the most sultry voice I had ever heard.

It wasn't even what she said, but how she said it. Teasing me, wanting more…it was clear.

I crashed my lower body into her, erasing all distance between us. It was obvious she was just as affected by our closeness as I was. All I could think about was grabbing her hair and yanking it back to devour her neck. But maybe that wouldn't be the best first moment for us.

Instead, I trailed my fingers down her chest. Her entire body was so warm even though the sweat had since dissipated. It felt like she was burning me from the inside out. Red, my own little ball of fire.

I knew I should have just walked away, but I didn't want to. Instead, I whisked her out of sight. I needed to taste her plump red lips, see them swollen from my touch.

I pressed her into the wall and lifted her thigh up to wrap around me. When I did, I could feel her pussy radiating with heat through her dress. I was hungry for her. I wanted to lift her and wrap her legs around my neck. But I knew better. She was drunk, or at least tipsy. I'm not an asshole; I wouldn't take advantage of her. Not to mention from how Daniel talks about Jade, I think she would slit my throat.

I tried to satiate my cravings for her by slamming my mouth against hers. desperately trying to tame my desire but not being able to fully restrain myself any longer. She started grinding against me and the friction of my jeans and boxers against my dick made me ache with every swipe. I wanted more, needed to feel her. My hand started to drift up her thigh slowly.

She suddenly stopped me.

Fuck, is she not single, did I just mess this all up? I thought to myself.

She looked up at me with heavy eyes. She started to apologize for taking it too far, but hesitated. There was something she wasn't saying. I tried to mentally fill in the blank.

And then it clicked. "Were you promised?"

Her eyes searched mine, trying to understand what I was asking. "No, it-it's by choice. I was originally holding off for the ceremony."

My body instantly sagged with relief. Of course, she's just a virgin. I was clearly wrong thinking otherwise.

"Aurora you can't—" I began when I was cut off by Jade. I wished Aurora a happy birthday in a sad excuse to walk away.

I recoiled at the fact I just asked this girl if she was promised, basically gesturing that the only way a woman can be a virgin is if someone already had his proverbial chastity belt locked on her. What a stupid thing to say. My mom would have slapped me in the face if she just heard me.

I found Daniel to get the folder from him and tell him to meet me in the car. I rushed upstairs searching four rooms before I found a room with double beds. There was two bags in the room, clearly belonging to women. I had no idea which was which, so I peaked in both to determine which one was Aurora's. After zipping it closed, I set the folder on the bed that had her belongings and Daniel and I left immediately after.

I spent the whole night and the following day thinking about my run in with her. I was trying to figure out what to say when I saw her on Monday. The only thing I did know was that, as much as it killed me, I couldn't let it happen again. It was a moment of weakness. I needed to learn how to control myself around her.

At least that's what I thought before I saw the look on her face when she informed me of her note.

As I read it, I could feel this passion in her, the need for control. She fights it tooth and nail to stay buried.

But I want it out. Let it free and see what happens. I realized I was the one who snapped her control. I'm not sure one would consider that a good thing, but it was at that moment I knew I didn't want to keep forcing her away.

CHAPTER 9
ABANDONED SPRING
AURORA DAVIS

After I gave my keys to Jade, we headed to his car where he opened the door for me, taking me by surprise.

His car is really nice, way nicer than mine. All of the windows are down and it feels amazing outside. He sits, leaning back with one arm out of the window and the other stretched to the steering wheel.

As we pick up speed my hair starts blowing every-where. I try to hold it back as best as I can. He looks over at me in the middle of a fist fight with my curls and I cringe at how awkward I am.

He turns down the music with the steering wheel buttons. "Do you want me to put the window up?"

"No, it's fine," I snap. "It feels good. My hair is just pissing me off. I didn't plan on being kidnapped, so I left my arsenal of beauty supplies in my own car." Okay, maybe that was unnecessary.

He swaps hands on the steering wheel and reaches in front of me, opening the glovebox. He grabs a clip from inside. I'm horrified and the expression on my face says it all. *Oh god, he's handing me another girl's hair clip. Could this be any more awkward?*

When I don't grab it right away, he laughs. Hard. "You should see your face right now, Red, it's my mom's," he chortles as he rolls up the window.

Be right back, I'm going to die of embarrassment now. And what is it with the nickname? I've only ever been Ro or Aurora.

"'Red,' I don't know if I like it or hate it. Doesn't feel too original, I'm sure every redhead gets called that."

He looks puzzled. "I don't call you that because your hair is red."

Wait, what? "Then why do you?"

"I call you Red because you have this fire in you. From what I've seen. You're mostly quiet or stick to yourself. It's rare you let that side of you out. When you do, it is almost as if you're stepping out of your skin. It's riveting. I would never have expected it. It's what I have enjoyed the most about you."

I try so hard *not* to show that side of me. I guess I haven't done the best job at it lately. I certainly have never heard someone say they like it before.

I stare out the windshield deep in thought. I watch as

the road around us snakes up through the mountains, the landscape surrounding us left entirely untainted by greed.

Zayn's car glides effortlessly through the winding roads. Each twist and turn executed with precision and grace. Unlike my car which is more like a white knuckle affair.

It takes me a second to realize I still never put my hair up, so I finally use the clip he gave me. It's much smaller than the ones I normally use for my hair, so I do the best I can.

I see him glance over at me from the corner of my eye as I finish. He brings his hand in from outside to hit the switch to roll my window back down. Then, he turns the music back up. All without me having to say anything.

He always anticipates the next thing. Like he knows what I want, without asking me.

I stare at him as he places his arm back out the window, hand open feeling the cool air wind through his fingers before tapping them on the outside of the door to the music. He doesn't seem to notice me watching, so I take a minute to appreciate his relaxed pose.

"How do you do that?" I ask with genuine curiosity.

"Do what, create nicknames? You see, I—"

My eyes roll to the ceiling. "Okay, smart ass, I meant notice everything without it being said."

He doesn't seem like he wants to answer me at first, avoiding the question by rubbing his face. "My mom. She made it clear to me that I needed to be observant. Always be able to read people and what they aren't saying. I can't turn it off even when I want to."

I sense that trying to read people becomes tiring. I consider asking why his mom thought it was a necessary trait for him to learn, but I suspect it may be too intrusive.

I opt to switch topics instead. "Are you close with your mom?"

That seems to have done the trick, because he smiles. "I am. My mom is amazing. I'd be lying if I said otherwise."

The love he has for her genuinely rings through in his voice. I can only imagine how happy it would make her to hear him speak about her like this. Does she know? Or, does he act all *'too cool'* around her?

I wonder what she's like. I've obviously seen his mom, Angela, at Founders' events, as well as his little sister, Rosie. His dad is much more ominous. You don't see or hear from him much. He isn't as forward-facing as the other Founders.

"That's amazing. I'm sure she appreciates you."

Our conversation dies down, and we return to silence. I have no idea where we're going, but we have already been driving for about 45 minutes. I grab my phone to text my mom and realize it's dead.

"Shit, my phone died, can I use your charger?"

"Yeah, here," he says, unplugging his phone to hand me the charger.

After several minutes, it turns back on. I already have multiple missed texts from Jade. She is desperate for details, apparently. She said she is going to wait at my house for me. Before locking my phone, I text my mom and let her know I will be home later.

When the car starts to slow down towards a parking lot, I look around. I have quite literally no idea where we are.

The lush deep green trees form a barrier, their overgrown branches intertwined like a wall, suggesting the area has been abandoned.

Zayn turns the ignition off after sliding into a space, and we both get out of the car.

Immediately, I revel in the scent of the air. It's fresh and earthy, damp. From the lack of rain we've had, I can tell there's water up ahead.

There is a sign, but it isn't legible beneath the layers of dirt and moss covering it. Just beyond it I finally see a narrow pathway between the trees, barely visible but wide enough to pass through.

Zayn goes in his trunk and grabs a bag, shoving things into it before closing the trunk behind him.

"Where are we?" I ask as we enter the clearing.

I gaze upward; awestruck by the dense canopy overhead. With each step the opening widens, revealing the artifice of this hidden path. It's clear magic was used to conceal and craft this perfectly formed tunnel.

The leaves rustle in abundance, a melodious song in the wind.

"We're almost there. I promise you'll love it. I don't get to come out here often enough. It's my favorite place. I thought after how things went down earlier, it would be nice to get away from the noise. Spend some time with you and talk," he explains.

As the pathway ends, my eyes widen in shock. We reach a beautiful, sparkling body of water surrounded by large rocks and trees. In the distance, I can hear an echoing rush of water. I walk faster around the bends of the spring, inching towards it with anticipation. Finally, I find the source of the rushing water.

The water plummets in a solid sheet over the cliff's edge. Cascading into the spring, leaving behind a refreshing mist. The waterfall is magnificent. I stare in appreciation. The sound of the water pounding off the rocks below, the smell of the cold water, the magic it holds, despite it being powerless and nature made.

My smile is wide as I spin around and see Zayn watching me in the distance. His eyes don't leave mine, staring into the depths of my mind. I focus my gaze on him only chancing a glance to the waterfall once before approaching him.

He throws his bag on the ground and leans down to reach inside. He pulls out a pair of bathing suit shorts only to walk away without saying anything. After a moment, he comes back with his jeans in his hand and the shorts on his hips.

Those strong arms reach behind his neck and pull his shirt over his head. *Fuck.* Why is it so much sexier when they reach behind their neck versus grabbing it at the hem?

I can't help myself taking note of every line and muscle. He has a large tattoo on his chest I never noticed before.

"Here, you can put this on," he instructs. "There is a spot around the corner where I just came from that you can change."

As I approach him, I try to get a better look at his tattoo, but he turns before I have the chance. Disappointed, I grab the shirt from him and go to change.

Replacing my clothes with his shirt, I fist it in my hand and bring it to my nose. His shirt, while clearly expensive, isn't bathed in cologne like other guys. Instead, his scent is subtle. A mix of laundry detergent and his body wash.

As I walk out to him, I am slightly self-conscious about the way his shirt is swallowing me whole. I become suddenly aware of how much larger he is than me. I mean, there's his height and the fact his body is an advertisement for lean muscle milk. Somehow, I manage to put one foot in front of the other.

I carefully wrap my undergarments in my folded clothes like an awkward gynecologist appointment.

When I come around the corner, I find him treading water near the rocks. "You can throw your clothes beside, or in, my bag. No one will touch them out here," he hollers.

I place my clothes beside his bag and go to take a seat in front of him where I dip my feet into the water. It's absolutely freezing at first.

"It's beautiful out here. How do you know about this place?"

"It's on the Founder's side of town," he explains. "No one really comes out this way unless you're a Founding family even though they don't sit around lounging. I was driving around one day to clear my head and heard water running. I pulled over and followed the sound and that's when I found this spring. Clearly, people came around in the past because there are signs. I just think it's been a while because I've never seen someone here."

"Why did you bring me here, Zayn?"

"Are you always so apprehensive? Or is it just because it's me?" he questions as he pushes the water around in circles with his arms.

"I thought you hated me. You always gave me dirty looks when our paths crossed," I try to explain the motive behind my apprehension.

Zayn shakes his head in frustration. "You don't understand. I could never, and have never, hated you, Red. My life is mapped out for me. I don't get a choice or a say. If I hated anything, it's what you represented: everything I am not supposed to have."

He discusses his future as if it's such a burden. I never thought any of the Founders were plagued by their responsibilities. I thought they craved the power they would one day have.

"Sorry, I didn't realize. I just assumed—"

"Haven't you learned anything from assuming?" he asks harshly before softening his tone. "Sorry, let's enjoy the water. Join me."

I take his extended hand, allowing him to pull me into the water. My body is still slowly adjusting to the cool temperature when Zayn dunks his entire body under the water.

When he emerges, he rakes his ink black hair back. I watch as it slowly drips down his neck.

"How the hell are you able to do that? The water is so cold. I'm trying not to clench my teeth," I ask.

That, and trying to cover my breasts because my nipples could cut glass right now.

Zayn laughs. "The quicker you submerge yourself, the quicker you warm up to it."

I curl my mouth up in disgust. Which only makes him laugh harder.

The next thing I know, he pounces on me, trying to dunk me under by my hips. The second I feel his hands wrap around my waist *I try* to fight him off. I sink completely under and when I come back up to gasp for air, he is so close to me.

My, *his*, shirt drifts up in the water while I try to push it back down.

"Thankfully, I can swim! You could have killed me!" I jokingly shouted at him.

Ignoring my dramatics, he reaches up with both hands and smooths my sopping wet hair behind my ears. "You are fine. I wouldn't let you drown."

His touch causes me to forget about the shirt riding up. He clearly takes notice because his eyes drift down. You can't see anything through the water, it isn't clear enough to expose me, but instinctively, I reach for the hem to pull it down.

But my hands don't make it there. He grabs them and places them on his chest, pulling me in even closer. I allow him to pull my chest in, but purposely push my lower half back, creating as much distance as I can.

When his eyes finally meet mine, they burn with desire.

I look to where my hands are pressed and realize I can see his chest tattoo clearly now. It's beautiful. My eyes trace over each delicate line.

It's of a lion with his teeth bared to a lioness. She seems scared. It is as if he is overpowering her. There are these geometric mountains with trees in the background and it reminds me of Kyrosia. An owl with gray eyes is stationed on a branch watching over them, while a beautiful sun sets behind them in oranges and purples. The tattoo starts at his collarbone and goes all the way down to his belly button. It's like a mural.

The detail is astounding. It looks like a picture rather than ink in his skin. I cannot stop looking at each hair-like line on the mane. My hand moves to trace the details of the lion's fur.

His eyes penetrate my soul. I have never seen a tattoo like this before. Whoever must have done it, it would have taken them forever.

Zayn doesn't pull away from my touch so I allow my hands to roam. Running my fingers along each line of his sculpted chest, to his arms, and up to his neck. His body is sculpted and toned, but he doesn't carry the excessive bulk that some gym rats have. His muscles are chiseled and lean. When I finally look up into his eyes again, they watch me with such intensity.

"What made you get this?" I run my hand along his chest again.

He closes his eyes for an extended blink. When he finally reopens them, gone is the desire they held, now replaced by reluctance. "It's just a tattoo," he says, his defenses up.

His change in demeaner makes a knot form in my stomach. I go to pull my hand away from his chest. But he wraps his large palm around my wrist to stop me.

"It's not that I don't want to tell you. It's just complicated."

"I get it, you don't owe me an explanation."

"Clearly, I do, because now it feels like something I am keeping from you," he continues in a strained tone. "It's symbolism for my family. My dad is bigger than the rest of us, he is the predator. My mom is always between us, trying to protect our innocence and peace. All the while, I watch over them, unable to interfere."

"What about your sister?" I search his chest for another animal I must have missed.

"No where near the fucking rest of us. Somewhere safe," he spits.

My hands wrap around his neck, pulling him into me.

"Thank you. You didn't need to tell me, but I appreciate that you did. You said you wanted to come out here to talk. What did you want to talk about?"

"Not about, just talk. Tell me something about you. Something I don't know."

What am I supposed to tell him? What you see is what you get. "I really don't know what there is to tell. There isn't anything about me that stands out. You've seen my brother around, I have a little sister, too. You know who my friends are. That's really it. What else do you want to know?"

"Why do you do that?" he asks, unyielding.

"Do what?" my brows crinkle in misunderstanding.

"Dull yourself down" Zayn stares firmly. "Try to sum yourself up into this box. As if nothing about you makes you stand out. None of us are one thing. Be real with me."

I feel my body heat up. I have no idea why it irritates me so badly. I don't try to fit into anyone's box. All I was saying is that there isn't anything about me that makes me stand out. If he thinks that makes me dull, why the hell am I here? I don't have anything I need to prove to him.

Coming to the conclusion, I think it's a good time to leave. I attempt to remove my arms from his neck, but he yanks me into him by pulling on my back. Normally the 'don't let go' thing is sexy, but this time it's just fucking annoying.

"See that, there you are, Red. I don't fucking get why you fade into the background." He continues to instigate me. "How can the same girl with the big hair, piercings, and bold outfits not see herself how others do? I don't understand how you can be so blind to it. Why do you try so hard to be perfect? It's like your friends don't test you, they don't *push* you. It's all I want to do; *I crave* it since you ran into me and gave me a verbal lashing."

"No one wants to be fucking tested," I hiss. "I am not a toy or game. You don't get to play with me because it's fun. I dress how I do because I like it. I don't try to be perfect; I'm just existing. Hiding who I am would require knowing who I am. And newsflash, I have no fucking idea."

"What does that mean?"

Is he joking, how dismissive of him. He is just going to respond to one fifth of what I say. I roll my eyes at him.

"What I mean is exactly what I said, I don't know who I am. My genetics are a fucking mystery because I'm adopted," I counter. "Every day I try to make sure everyone doesn't hate to be around me, all because I'm so obsessed with finding out where I come from. It's eating me alive. Everyone else has somewhat of an idea of what to expect in May and I have nothing, absolutely nothing to go off of. That's why my friends don't test me. None of them have any idea how to help me. They are just trying to be there for me. Basically, I have enough shit going through my mind."

When I finish unloading on him, he lets go of me and submerges himself completely under the water.

Great, let me just unload my baggage on this man and be ignored, *again.*

I start swimming towards the rocks so I can get out of this spring and back to reality.

"What if I helped you?" he asks from behind.

What? Not sure if I heard him right, I stop swimming and turn to face him.

"Help me with what?" I snap, feeling agitated.

"What if I help you try to get more information about who your birth parents are?" he repeats in more detail.

I have no idea where to even start.

"Why would you do that?" I ask hesitantly, taken back by his offer.

Zayn smirks. "Well, for me, it's entirely selfish. I'll get closer to you. But it will help you realize who you are and how I see you. Wait, no that benefits me too. Well shit, I guess it's just for me then." He shrugs both of his shoulders, laughing.

Is he oblivious to my annoyance, or is he just choosing to ignore it? I attempt to stop the rage fueling inside of me for a minute to figure out what this could mean for me. No one has ever offered to give me any information. He is a Founder, he has more access than anyone but...what will he end up asking for in return?

And for a moment, I wonder, what if I hate what I find? How badly do I want to know who I am?

"Okay," I mutter, begrudgingly.

"Okay?"

"Yes, Okay. I will accept your help. I want to know more, I *need* it. But my parents and friends can't find out what we're doing. I don't want to hurt my parents' feelings. They have done everything for me. I just need to know you aren't expecting anything in return. I don't have anything to give you. If you help me, it's only because you want to."

In seconds, he's breathing the same air as I am. He's so close when he grabs my face. "I am going to say this once, only once. I'm not doing this expecting something in return from you. I'm doing this entirely *for* you. And I won't tell anyone."

His eagerness to help me diffuses my anger.

Where did this man come from? Every single assumption I make, he proves me wrong. Every time I suggest his intentions are anything other than pure, he gets angry and shows me otherwise.

Zayn is proving to be a complex individual. I want to know why he gets so testy. He's always trying to push me to react, he wants me passionate. It's terrifying, but it triggers something in me I'm not familiar with.

My lip's part as my breathing picks up. His hand caresses my face and I want to push it further down; feel it wander my body again like on my birthday.

"Red, I want to kiss you," he confesses. "Can I?"

"Ye—"

His lips pounce on mine before I can finish the word. Hungry, needy. His hands drop down to the small of my back, completely aware of how close he is to touching my ass. I revel in the way his mouth devours mine. I need him closer to me.

He walks us back until we are on the edge of the spring where I was sitting before jumping in. In one swift movement, he grabs my hips to pick me up and sits me on the rocks once more. He uses his knees to part my legs around him and all the while, his lips never leave my mouth.

His kiss deepens, becoming rougher. He swallows my moan, humming in agreement.

He hasn't looked down, but his shirt is becoming dangerously close to baring my all to him. I can feel the wind against my core. My kissing slows, I'm so fucking nervous. My body tells me *more*. But my mind tells me I have no idea what I'm doing.

Of course, Zayn notices.

He releases my mouth from his. "What's wrong?"

I lean my forehead against his. Closing my eyes so I don't have to look him in the eye. "I have no idea what I am doing. I haven't done anything before."

"Open your eyes," he commands delicately.

I hesitate.

"Aurora, baby, I said open your eyes."

I do as he bade, lifting my head. My eyes finally met his.

"Do you have any idea how sexy it is that no one else has gotten to touch you? That no one's mouth has been anywhere near your pussy? That makes me absolutely primal for you. I want you, Aurora. I promise I'll take it slow," he continues on as his hands drift further up my thighs. "Can I touch you?"

I nod my head slowly. The further up my thighs he inches, I can feel myself soaking. His hands are large and dominate my body, owning me. Right as one of his fingers reach my pussy, the other pushes his shirt out of the way.

Just enough to expose me to him. He looks down and I watch the way his eyes darken. He sucks in his bottom lip.

Before he touches me, he asks, "Can I take this off?"

"Yes," I answer, breathy. He grabs the hem of the shirt with both hands pulling it over my head. It takes everything in me not to pull his hands back to my body. When it's off, he throws it behind me, smacking the ground with a wet thud. I feel exposed and yet, completely exhilarated.

He moves my bangs away from my eyes and arranges my hair to fall behind my back. His hands run down my shoulders and arms in smooth caresses.

He leans back, scanning his eyes over every inch of my body. "Fuck Red," he hisses. "Your body is fucking perfection."

My breathing completely halts when he reaches up to my chest and palms one of my boobs, his mouth moving to cover the other. I feel every swirl of his tongue, the bite of his teeth. My entire body jolts at the pain mixed with plea-sure so he bites down again.

"Holy fuck," I scream out. My upper body leans into him as I throw my arm down beside me to catch my balance on the rocks. He reads my movements and acts on it. He switches to my other boob as his hand rubs over my belly down to my pussy. As soon as his hand sweeps over my center, I'm basically done for.

He pushes one finger inside of me. I moan loudly, no longer embarrassed. I am taking what I want, and right now all I want is him. The cold water at my legs lowers my body temperature to keep me from overheating. He adds another finger, completely filling me.

"Fuuuck, you are so fucking sexy, Aurora. I need you to breathe. I can feel you holding your breath," he murmurs against my skin.

Nodding in acknowledgement, I try to hold my balance on the rocks. His fingers pulse inside of me and he keeps taking me right to the breaking point before stopping.

I should have known it's on purpose.

"You are not allowed to come until I tell you to. Try to hold off. I promise it will hurt but it'll feel so worth it when I am done with you. Okay, baby?"

"Yes, yes, yes," I repeat myself to him, feeling the pleasure vibrating through my core.

His fingers curl inside of me and his thumb reaches for my clit in precise movements. I'm going to come, I can't hold it.

"Zayn, I can't, I need to. Please," I beg him.

"Not yet," he growls in my ear.

His mouth gives me feverish kisses all over my neck. My head falls back with my eyes closed. He picks up speed with his hand. The other grabs my ass and pulls me forward to change my position.

Holy fucking shit.

"Come for me, now," he commands.

With his words, I come completely undone. I've gotten myself off plenty of times, but this...this is incredible. I didn't know it could feel like that.

When the final shock eases, my entire body sags. Zayn doesn't remove his fingers until the aftershocks end. He holds my body against him to keep me upright where my head rests against his shoulder, coming down from the high that he just gave me.

"Was it worth it, the wait?" he asks.

He doesn't need an actual answer to that. He knows damn well it was.

"Is it always like that?" I ask.

Zayn smiles wide. "I fucking hope so."

"Have you...?" Maybe this is too soon to ask.

"I told you I haven't had sex. I have done other things. But it's also been a while. I lost interest in women until you came along. But now, you are all I see. That means no one is going to touch you besides me."

"No one was touching me before, so the claim on me is unnecessary. But I don't want anyone else." I laugh nervously before my teeth snag my lip, needing to ask the question: "Is that...mutual?"

Zayn shakes his head. "Just so we are absolutely clear, yes, it is mutual."

As he pulls away, I realize I'm still completely naked and go to cover my chest with my arms.

"Oh, absolutely not. You will not be shielding yourself from me." He grabs both my hands and pulls me into the water fast. I can't fight the smile on my face when he pulls me up to him.

His hands explore every inch of my body before wrapping under my hips. "These fucking hip dips, I swear." He disappears under the water, kissing them.

"Ouch, what the fuck? Did you just fucking bite me?" I ask when he resurfaces. The huge smirk on his face is answer enough. I start rubbing my side to ease the sting of his teeth.

He chuckles. "It's getting dark outside, so I need to get you home. Let's get dressed before we continue what we started."

We reluctantly exit the water and head onto the land. He grabs a black cotton towel out of his bag. I reach my arm out, thinking he's going to hand it to me, but he just smiles.

Slowly, he drops to his knees. My breath hitches in my throat as I instinctively cross my arms.

He takes the towel in both hands and wraps it around my right ankle, drying all the way up to the top of my ass before switching legs. He skips my intimate parts and instead comes to a stand. He unwraps my arms before dragging the towel from my neck, over my arms, down to my stomach. He smooths it across my chest in a soft caress, causing my nipples to instantly react.

He circles me until he is standing behind me, he lifts my hair and places it in the towel, squeezing the water out before drying my back.

Reaching around me, he kisses my neck before sweeping it over my center. The touch sends goosebumps prickling over my skin, again.

I feel the heat of his mouth on my ear as he whispers, "Spread your legs."

I swallow the lump in my throat as I part my legs for him. The only thing distracting me from the discomfort of a man drying my intimate parts is the way his mouth layers kiss upon kiss to my skin.

When he's finished drying me, I'm practically panting. He grabs my panties from my clothes pile and pulls them up my legs. Just as they're almost completely up, he lowers a kiss to my pussy. I release a sound of shock, instantly slick between my legs.

If he notices, he doesn't say or act on it. He just continues to pull them up the remainder of the way. He finishes getting me dressed but shoves my bra in his bag instead of putting it on me.

Once he's dressed, forgoing his soaking wet shirt he let me wear, we get in the car. He throws his bag in the back seat and our drive back to my house is relatively quiet. His hand is resting on my thigh but my eyes roam every muscle and line of his body on full display.

He grabs my phone to play music since I left it on the

charger. When he grabs it, I see his face clench. He hands it to me and I read the message on my screen.

> Oliver: What the fuck are you doing?
> Why is Zayn Everett driving you home?
> Don't do something you can't take back.
> Not with him.

Shit, of all messages for him to see.

I have no idea why Oliver is so upset. I saw the way he was looking at Zayn by my car, but I thought he was just being protective. I have to talk to him when I get home.

I press play on my playlist and set the GPS for my house.

"Hey, I'm sorry. I don't know why he sent that, but it's not his business what I do," I say.

Zayn grips the steering wheel tighter. "You're mistaken. It is his business. He is your brother, and he is trying to protect you. I don't blame him. I'm just sick and tired of people thinking they know who I am because of my father. I am not him."

We don't talk the rest of the car ride until his car comes to a stop. He parks down the street instead of parking at my house. I start to overthink; he must be embarrassed to be seen with me. So, he isn't even bringing me to my house. He doesn't want to be seen dropping me off.

"I can't drop you off half naked, we also both have soaking wet hair. It's not the kind of impression I want to make when I meet your parents," he says, facing me. "I do have something to ask you though. Would you come with me to the Halloween party? It's a masquerade, so my father won't know who I'm with. I understand if it's asking too much from you. I don't want to hide you, it's just complicated with him."

My mind is completely reeling at the idea of him inviting me to a party. I wasn't expecting that at all. I get why his dad can't see us even if it hurts a little. It opens an entire can of worms. Especially if we start digging around together about my birth. My parents normally don't make me attend the events even though they are required to. But it may just be fun this time.

"I'd love to, I'll have to find a mask." I tilt my head, my mind instantly spinning as to where I can find one.

He looks surprised by my acceptance, but excited. I don't think he was expecting me to say yes.

Making a bold move, I lean over and kiss him. He reciprocates by grabbing the back of my neck to pull me in deeper.

When I pull away from him, I reach in the back seat to grab my bra from his bag. I shove it in my book bag so no one sees it.

I grab my phone and exit the car, turning around before closing the door.

"Bye, Zayn."

"Bye, Aurora."

I walk down the street to my house. He doesn't start the car or pull away until I open my front door. I swear to Lina, he is nothing like I expected. I shut the front door and check to make sure no one is around before I lean my back against it. This entire day feels like a dream.

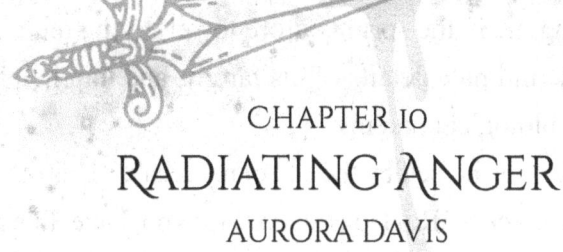

CHAPTER 10
RADIATING ANGER
AURORA DAVIS

Oliver wasn't home when I got back from being out with Zayn. His attitude will just have to wait until tomorrow.

As soon as I open my bedroom door Jade leans forward from sitting against my headboard. I approach her annoying grin with caution as I reach for the remote on my nightstand to turn down the TV.

"Do those braless baddies tell me Zayn loosened you up?" Her smile is wide with anticipation.

I turn to throw my bag down, ignoring her question. "I'm fucked Jade. Zayn is…incredible. Everything he does perplexes me."

I sit at my vanity and begin telling her about the car ride and his nickname for me. She still swears it isn't his mom's clip, I know I'll never hear the end of that.

"Jade, he literally stole my breath away with every

touch. He even made it clear what's going on with us is exclusive," I explain after giving her the sexual details of him fingering me in the spring before towel drying me.

I skip the intimate details of his family, and him helping me find my biological parents.

Jade is fanning herself by the end of my recap. "This man is the one who's fucked, Ro. He is starved for you, babe, like hot damn I need a good fuck to release the tension coiled from that. I swear, every time he is around you it gets hotter and hotter."

"You are so weird. All I know is he has me so flustered. I can't get enough of him."

I motion for her to scoot over. I plop down, face first, beside her.

"Please tell me you are staying, I am spent," I plead.

She scoots off the foot of the bed, changing into pajamas before throwing some at me to change. "Let's get you to bed, *Red*," she singsongs the nickname.

The next morning, I don't get to talk to Oliver before we leave for school. Ashton texted Jade that they got a ride this morning. I'm walking to fourth period on auto pilot when I hear, "Hey."

I spin on my heels to find Zayn leaning against the wall.

My smile brightens. "Hey."

"How are you?"

I laugh. "Why are you so awkward right now? This isn't the first time we've spoken? Pretty sure we did more than talk last night. Let's go, walk with me to class."

"Yeah, sorry," he says peeling himself from the wall. "Hey, did you talk to your brother yesterday?"

"No, I never had the chance. He wasn't home and didn't have me take him to school this morning."

"Hmm."

We get into class and sit in our seats. Daniel and Jade follow shortly after, one behind the other. When Daniel walks by my desk he leans down, "You better not make him regret this." *What the fuck?*

I look up at him and he's smiling as if he just made a joke. I turn in my seat to see Zayn narrowing his eyes in question at his friend.

When we are split into groups, I'm quiet, trying to figure out what that was supposed to mean. Everyone else is so engrossed in conversation about the project, I throw in comments and questions when needed. I simply bide my time until the end of class.

When class ends, I swiftly exit without saying goodbye to anyone. When I get to my car, I am the first there, so I start the engine and wait inside. My pocket vibrates and I reach to remove my phone from it, finding a text from Zayn.

> Zayn: Why did you leave so quickly? I would have walked you out.

Jade rips open my passenger door. "What the hell, you basically ran out of there. Are you okay?"

I jump at how fast she opens the door. "I'm fine. Just feeling a little overwhelmed by everything."

"Okay, but you better text Zayn because he looked pissed you ran out," she responds.

"He already texted me. I'll talk to him," I say, trying to appease her. I just want this conversation to end.

Oliver and Ashton get into the car right after. As we head home, I try to think if I should say anything to Zayn about what Daniel said. I don't want to cause drama between them, I just don't understand. I don't bother to tell Jade because she's just going to say that Daniel is looking out for his friend.

I have this feeling in my gut that it's more than that.

Once I drop off Jade and Ashton, Oliver hops in the front seat.

"What's up with that text you sent me yesterday?" I asked, keeping my eyes on the road.

"Aurora, don't act so oblivious. Zayn is one of the Founding families, he will be a Founding Four one day. The last thing you want to do is be stuck with one of them for the rest of your life," he scoffs. "What are you going to do, let him fuck you? Then what? He tosses you to the side the second his father arranges his marriage. You have a few fun years? What if you get pregnant? You aren't this stupid. Unless you are under the impression it will actually work out, which would be comical. You are just a tally on his list of conquests."

My brother is an annoying little shit, but I am not about

to take this from him. If he had made a comment like this a few weeks ago, I probably would have believed him. But now, I know better.

Zayn has proven he isn't what people think he is. The thing is, it's not just about what he thinks of Zayn that makes me so angry. It's how little he thinks of *me* by making that entire statement. I have déjà vu back to when he found out I was adopted. The way he spoke to me reminds me of a shitty time between us.

I slam on my brakes and turn to him.

"Don't you ever speak to me like that again. I don't care if you think this is you being protective. You could have tried to warn me to stay away respectfully and maybe I would have listened. But inferring I'm in this just to be fucked and thrown away, fuck you," I spit, "I will do as I please. You know nothing about him."

"It's not about being protective, it's being realistic. Do you really think you're going to defy the odds? That you will be special enough to change how they treat people. That you will fuck him into a trance of respect. Maybe they will make an exception for you being unpure? Think with your head, Aurora. You aren't this fucking stupid."

He is really starting to piss me the fuck off. "Actually, I know the rules. No, I don't think that I have some magical pussy that will 'defy the odds.' But again, you know nothing about him, or the situation, so why don't you try minding your own fucking business."

"I thought you were smarter than to trust a boy after

knowing him for only half a minute. Obviously, I gave you too much credit." His blow strikes true.

I turn back onto the road, blaring the music as I hit the gas. It takes me about two minutes to get home. I am so beyond livid with Oliver right now. I want to break something. I pull into our driveway in a rush to get him away from me.

"Get out now," I demand. He listens, slamming the door behind him like the brat he is.

I sit there for a second, a futile attempt to gain control over the war waging inside me. I have never been so angry in my entire life.

My blood is boiling, causing me to sweat profusely. I crank the AC, trying to find some relief to cool me down. It doesn't help in the slightest. My hands wrap around the steering wheel and I squeeze my eyes shut, fighting to breathe.

I smell smoke and my eyes shoot open searching for the source.

I remove my hands from the wheel to open my door and try to find where the smell is coming from. As soon as I let go, my blood cools and my breathing settles, my sweating ceases.

I've gone *cold.*

Handprints branded into my steering wheel stare back at me. Panic flares as I realize I've somehow burned clean through the leather. The smell of the charred material fills the air of my car. In a desperate attempt to air it out, I fumble for the door to put the window down.

I could be killed for this. What the fuck am I supposed to do? How am I going to hide the evidence? I don't understand how this is even possible. We shouldn't have any access to our powers before the ceremony.

Wracking my brain on who I can call for help, I realize I can't risk putting my friends in danger. I fucking hate Oliver right now, even thinking about asking for his help makes me furious.

Then, *he* comes to mind. If he was willing to help me find my parents at risk to him, would he help me with this?

Is that stupid to even think? What if there is any truth to what Oliver said. I need to consider it carefully.

Option 1: He turns me in immediately. Which would suck for obvious reasons. But realistically, if anyone else were to help me and be caught, they would be in a significantly worse position than him. If they found out he did something, it would probably be swept under the rug. He doesn't have another brother to take over his position. If one of my friends helped me, they would be butchered alongside me.

Option 2: He helps me and I owe him.

Option 3: I continue to sit here with my hands up my ass and I get caught by Mr. Gordon on his afternoon walk.

My gut says that I can trust him, even if I don't know why.

With shaky hands, my fingers begin dialing. As soon as

I hear the other line ring, my stomach drops, I want to hang up. Who am I to risk his life for mine?

He answers on the second ring; leaving me no time to figure out what to say.

When he is met with my silence, he tries to get me to talk to him. "Aurora?" More silence "Red, what is it?"

I flinch at the use of my nickname. I can't do this, I can't. What if he immediately goes to his dad?

"Where are you?" I can hear his voice growing agitated.

"I am at my house, I didn't mean to call. I'm fine seriously. I'll text you later," I rush out, trying my best to keep my voice level.

"Do not hang up on me, I will be there in 10 minutes. Can you get to a safe place?"

"Wait, what? I'm in my car. Oh no, Zayn I didn't mean…" Oh shit, he must think something way worse is going on. He's going to think I'm in danger the entire way here. "I'm safe. I just need your help."

"I'm on the way. Just stay on the line with me."

CHAPTER II

HOT HANDS

ZAYN EVERETT

W hen I got her call, I was so eager to answer, hoping she was calling to tell me why she ran out of class. I saw she read my text and…nothing. I figured it had something to do with what Daniel said. She was quiet all class but she was fine in the hall with me, joking even.

As soon as she ran off, I turned to Daniel. "What the fuck did you say to her? She's been upset all fucking class."

He was taken aback by the question. "Man, chill. I made a joke about you guys being a cute couple. I have nothing to do with her mood. Get off my dick."

I don't respond to him and head home. Daniel is probably the best liar I've ever seen. He is so used to having to be two people all the time: who he is at home versus who he is to the world. It's not his choice, it's the result of having a father like his.

He is my best friend and I trust him with my life, but I don't believe him; he said something to her and he's lying.

When I answered the phone, the only sound I could hear was her ragged breathing. I tried prompting her to answer but she wouldn't respond. A wave of dread washed over me, thinking something was happening to her. Was she hurt, was someone forcing themself on her?

I panicked and immediately grabbed my keys, heading for my car. I had no idea where she was. She wouldn't answer me. I just knew I needed to head to her side of town.

When she finally made it clear she wasn't in immediate danger, the relief that crashed through me was palpable. Whatever it was though, she was raddled enough that she called *me*. I don't know if I find comfort in being the one she called, or if that worries me more.

I made her stay on the phone with me. I floored it all the way there, needing to make sure she was okay.

I park right in front of her house this time. I turn off my car and throw my keys in my pocket. I hear her car running so I go straight to the drivers side. She's inside with the windows cracked. I try to open her door, but it's locked.

"Aurora, unlock the door." She looks up at me with bloodshot eyes, tears soaking her flushed cheeks. It takes her a few seconds, but she does as I ask.

I crouch down with the door open, my knees hitting the grass on the side of her driveway. I immediately reach into her car to pull her into me and she leaps into my arms, nearly halfway out of her car.

"What is it, what happened?" I look over her body, searching for injuries. It doesn't seem like she was in a car accident.

She's not answering me, she can't. Not with the rate her tears are flowing and the way she's hyperventilating.

I wait for her to calm down enough to respond when my eyes catch sight of the steering wheel. It's been burned. I try to get a closer look, that's when I see the outline of fingers wrapped around the leather.

She starts to talk quietly, her head still buried in my neck. "I got so angry. Oliver and I were talking on the way here, he was hateful, making accusations, and questioning me. As soon as we got here, I made him get out of the car. The more I thought about what he said, the angrier I got. I don't know what came over me, or how it happened."

She unlatches from me and leans back into her car. Her mascara smears when she wipes her tears. She looks at the steering wheel. "I burned it, Zayn. How is that even possible?" She looks down at her hands in shame.

What could he have possibly said to make her this angry? I shouldn't have been testing her so much yesterday, did I help provoke this?

This isn't the time for me to think about that. I need to console her. I reach out to grab her hands and she recoils from me. I need to show her that she doesn't scare me.

So, I reach for them again. This time she lets me. I hold

them tightly in mine. I lean down and kiss both of them softly. I may not know what or how this happened, but I trust that she won't hurt me. I have no idea yet if she is in danger of hurting herself.

"I'm so sorry, Zayn," she murmurs, eyes on me. "I know the risk helping me carries. I just need help with changing this steering wheel before anyone sees it. Do you know how to do that? I swear I will leave you alone after, if you promise not to tell anyone."

"Red, I am not leaving you alone. Yes, I know how and I will help you. But I need to know if you can trust Oliver. I know he made you angry, I won't let him near you. I just need to know if you trust him to keep this a secret."

"I can't talk to him right now. Idiotically, I do trust him, but how can I ask this of him? Especially knowing how he feels about us."

I will find out what that means later. "I will handle Oliver. He won't bother you, but I need his help to do this quietly. Is he home alone?"

"Yes, my parents are at work, Abigail is at after school."

"Wait here. Keep your door closed and locked. Cover the marks with your hands in case anyone walks by. I will be right back. Call me if anyone comes home," I instruct.

She is scared but ultimately agrees. I close the door behind me, waiting for it to lock. I walk straight into her house and at first glance, I notice it's small. But, unlike mine, it feels like a home. I glance around the first floor, checking the dining room, kitchen, living room, and bedroom I realize belongs to her parents. I take the stairs two at a time, hoping to find Oliver up here.

I hear a TV on in the first room, hoping it is his. My knuckles rap on the door.

"Leave me alone," he shouts.

I reach for the door handle; it isn't locked so I push it open. I fill the doorway of his room, staring him down as he lays across his bed with his arms behind his head.

When he realizes it is me, he jumps up quickly.

"What the fuck are you doing here?" he questions.

I push down the anger I feel for him. At least for now. "Shut the fuck up and listen to me for a second. Your sister called me because she needs help."

His eyes flash with hurt and worry.

I continue, "*We* need your help. She didn't give me specifics, but the look on her face makes me want to grab you by your throat for whatever you said to her. Unfortunately, that will have to wait because I can't do this on my own. I don't trust involving anyone that doesn't have her best interests in mind. You cannot tell a fucking soul, if you do, I will kill you and whoever you tell. Even if you are her family. Do you understand me?"

He nods in response. "What's wrong, is she okay?"

"No, she is not okay," I remind him through clenched teeth. "She got so angry with you she somehow awakened her powers. She burned through most of her steering wheel and I need to replace it before anyone can see. But I need to move both of your cars. You have your permit, right?"

He answers quickly, "Yes."

"Okay, I need you to drive her car. I will follow behind you in mine and take her with me. But Oliver, she doesn't want to talk to you right now. Do not fuck with her, just help us. When she calms down, I will get her to talk to you."

His face has paled since I told him what happened.

"Do you know something?" I ask. He doesn't answer me. I get closer, "If you fucking know something, spit it out. She is waiting down there scared as fuck by herself."

"All I know is that I shouldn't have provoked her. I never would have said anything. I thought you were just out to fuck her." He pauses. "But she called...you...for help. She must actually trust you. Shit man, I'm sorry."

Why shouldn't he have provoked her, what does he know? Shit, this just got so much more complicated.

"We will discuss this later. Right now, we need your help. Do not approach her yet, got it?"

"I got it, let's go." He turns his TV off and snags his phone to shove his sneakers on before walking out of his room.

We rush out of the house.

"I need her keys to lock the door. Our parents will freak if it isn't locked when they get home."

"Hold on." I find her exactly how I instructed. "Baby girl, I need your keys to lock the door. Can you hand them to me and then go get in my car?"

"But, my car, Zayn! We have to move it now." She unlocks her doors in a panic.

"It's okay, I promise. Oliver is going to drive your car and I will follow him in mine. I just need you in my car with me. I have a place where we can bring it." I can't have her getting angry with him again, we *cannot* risk it.

Without answering me, she opens her door and gets out. She hands me the keys and looks up at her front door to Oliver, whose face is filled with regret. He looks down trying not to make eye contact with her. She walks to my passenger side and climbs in while I reach in her car and grab her phone.

I throw the keys to Oliver. He swiftly locks the door and gets into her car and starts it. When I get in my car, Aurora is leaning against the window. She seems to have stopped crying, which is a relief. I hate seeing her in pain. It makes me sick. I need to take care of this and then get to the bottom of what Oliver knows.

I keep my hand on her thigh so she knows I'm here for her. I text Oliver the address for our family's cabin, no one goes there this time of year. The Founders have so many events through the holidays, they're too busy planning to step away. I wait until I see he read it to set the phone aside.

We drive in complete silence the entire way. Thankfully, we make it there without any issues with him driving. I pull into the driveway beside him and we exit the vehicles at the same time. Aurora fell asleep about halfway here, so I go to the passenger side and open the door gently.

"Aurora, baby it's time to get up. We're here."

She opens her eyes, scanning her surroundings. "Where are we?"

"We are at my cabin, I swear you are safe. There are no cameras. No way for anyone to know we are here."

She gets out of the car, staying right behind me as I walk up the steps to unlock the door. Oliver keeps his distance.

As soon as he passes through the doorway, I tell him, "I am going to take her upstairs and get her to take a shower and hopefully sleep. Can you wait in the living room? I will be down in a few minutes, and we can talk." I shut the door behind him as he walks straight to the living room and sits down, scrolling on his phone.

I grab Auroras hand for her to follow me but make a quick stop in the kitchen to grab her a bottle of water first.

Upstairs, I guide her to my room. "This is my room, there's a bathroom attached. Why don't you take a shower and try to get some rest? Just grab anything to wear from my closet. I'm going to go talk to Oliver then run out to get a replacement steering wheel. It may take me a while, but I will be back as soon as I can. I'll leave your phone here on the nightstand. If you need anything, call me. Oliver will be downstairs the entire time."

"I'm just going to stay up here," she murmurs, clearly indicating she isn't ready to talk to him yet, which I don't blame her. I kiss her on the forehead before leaving the room.

I find Oliver exactly where I left him.

CHAPTER 12
UNLIKELY ALLIANCES
OLIVER DAVIS

Zayn comes down the stairs and sits directly across from me on the coffee table.

"So, what do you know?" he asks.

"Well, this is going to take a minute. I guess I'll start at the beginning.

"When I found out Aurora was adopted, I felt lied to. My big sister was my hero. I was proud to call her my flesh and blood. Of course, I was young and just being childish about the entire thing. None of it matters now. But I took it out on her. I said some awful things to her every time I would get mad at her," I explain with regret.

"I still remember the time she told me I couldn't go with her somewhere. I was so upset with her, I yelled 'you don't get to tell me what I can't do. You aren't even my sister.' She ran to her room crying. A few hours later my parents sat me down. They must have overheard.

"They told me how mean I was being to her, that it wasn't fair to her. Her real parents were bad people, so we took her in to save her life," I pause taking note of Zayn's expression, one of understanding. "I didn't understand the specifics. I just thought about how miserable it would be for her not to be a part of our family. They told me I needed to change how I treated her. So, I listened, terrified that if I didn't, she would hate me."

"Understandably so." Zayn's eyes narrow in on me.

"As I got older," I drawled, "I started to question things more. If they knew her bio parents were bad people, that must mean they know who they were. I began to worry if they would hurt her if they found her, or if they would take her from us. A few years ago, I confronted them while Aurora wasn't home because I was scared for her. When I asked them if her birth parents could take her from us, they looked at each other like they were trying to figure out what to tell me.

"My mom said, 'It's complicated, Oliver. The more you know the more you are in danger. All you need to know is that your sister comes from two extremely powerful people. No one knows who Aurora really is or, yes, they may come looking for her. We keep her away from the Founders, so they never find out her identity. It is our job as her family to keep her out of harm's way. We won't know until the Awakening Ceremony what her future holds.'"

Zayn's mouth thins and his shoulders go rigid. I can't say I look any differently.

"I questioned why her identity would be such a secret," I continue. "It finally clicked, if she turned out to be powerful the Founders would question her lineage. Exposing her to whoever her birth parents are. I wished what they told me was enough for me to stop asking questions but, unfortunately, it wasn't. I searched everything I could to see if there was anything about who her parents were. I came up completely empty handed."

I sigh, sinking into the sofa in defeat. "The only thing that makes sense is what happened today. As crazy as that may sound. Ever since we were kids, when Aurora would get upset, my parents did anything to calm her down, they would have bought her an ice cream truck to stop a tantrum. I just thought she got favoritism because she was their first. I truly didn't realize it was to avoid her getting *upset*. She was always quick to anger, but my parents knew how to distract her.

"When I snapped at her today, I was just trying to make sure she stayed as far away from the Founders as possible, i.e., you. There has to be a reason they are so desperate to keep her away. I rather have her hate me than be in danger. If it comes down to choosing her or choosing anyone else, I will always pick her. If anything, I owe it to her."

Zayn has been silently listening to every word. What if he decides this is too much for him? I will protect Aurora, even if that means from him. I rub my hand across my face, why isn't he saying anything?

"Questions, comments, concerns? Can I trust you will protect my sister?" I ask, prickling with irritation.

"I'm here, aren't I? With no information, I came to help her," he says.

That's what I am scared of. "Exactly, meaning her life is at your mercy. Something I don't feel entirely comfortable with."

"You clearly know I have a little sister, for whom I would die. So, let's stop the 'I will defend my sister at all costs' melodramatic lecture. I have fallen for your sister hard and fast. I won't let anything happen to her. I will protect your sister with my life as I would any woman." He continues, "We need to focus on learning how she can exhibit powers before performing the rite. I will tell you something to prove you can trust me. Which is never to leave this conversation." He raises his eyebrows in question.

"Okay, leverage and all. What is it?" I'm intrigued.

"I am trying to find a way to remove the Founders from power. To deconstruct the quadrumvirate in place. The Founders have done unforgivable things for the sake of power and need to be taken down. I aim to create a better system with checks and balances, where every seat of our government is controlled. Every person reports to someone. I've spent years creating plans. It will not be easy. I'm in no position at this point to do so."

I certainly was not expecting that. The idea of someone so high up who wants to deconstruct the Founders is slightly terrifying. I try to imagine how our society would function. Thinking through it, I cannot see a single con to having them removed. It also could mean that Aurora may be safer.

"I'll be waiting for when you need help," I offer.

With that, Zayn nods at me in thanks. He stands up and heads to the door. "I have to go get the new steering wheel. If I am not back before dark, can you bring her something to eat? There is a guest room upstairs, third door on the left. Daniel has clothes in there; they will fit you. Can you somehow let your parents know you two won't be home without them questioning it?"

"Yeah, I can do that," I assure him.

He leaves and I'm left trying to figure out how I am going to possibly apologize to my sister.

CHAPTER 13
STAY WITH ME
AURORA DAVIS

W hen Zayn left me in his room, the last thing I wanted to do was be alone. As soon as he left, I went straight into his bathroom. All I want to do is wash this day off of me.

I scrub my face, trying my best to remove the mascara that has dried under my eyes. I get it off the best I can before plopping onto the ground beneath me, tucking my head between my knees.

I have no idea how long I sat on the shower floor, but by the time I got out, the water raining down on me was ice cold.

I don't bother trying to do anything with my hair. Looking through his closet, I find a pair of dark grey sweats and a black t-shirt. I crawl under his expensive sheets and heavy duvet where I snuggle in the scent of him and let it carry me into a deep sleep.

A knock on the door wakes me sometime later. I sit up and yell, "Come in."

He is the one who opens it and I immediately become discouraged.

"I was sleeping, what do you want?" I snap.

He carries in a cup and a plate of food. "I come in peace, I swear."

He sets the food down on the nightstand, taking a seat at Zayn's desk. "I talked to Zayn and I'm sorry. I'm not just sorry for what I said, but how I spoke to you. We are going to work together to figure out how you have powers. In the meantime, I need you to be careful. I don't want something to happen to you."

"Maybe you should have considered that before you were so fucking hateful to me," I scoff.

Oliver shakes his head. "I'm sitting here trying to apologize to you."

I'm still angry, but I concede. It just doesn't feel worth it to sit here and argue with him. Everything he said had more to do with Zayn than me. If they were able to work it out, then I guess I can accept his apology.

"Can I ask you something?"

He nods and waits patiently for me to ask.

"You spoke to him…is he scared of me? Do you think he is going to say anything?"

"No Aurora," he doesn't even hesitate. "He isn't scared of you. I know this may seem like I'm lying because of everything I said before, but I truly believe he isn't going to say anything. He seems to want to protect you. Again, I am sorry for everything I said.

"If you need me, I'll be in the guest room. It's two doors down on the left. He texted that he got the steering wheel and should be back soon."

He leans in to give me a hug before walking out of the room. Once he shuts the door, I decide to check my phone.

Zayn: Hey, I got it, I'm sorry I have been gone so long. Is there anything you need on the way back?

Me: Any chance you want to pick up something to eat, please? Oliver brought me a sandwich and chips and I'm 99% sure this bread has mold on it.

Zayn: What do you want, Princess?

Me: I beg you to never call me that again. I would love a milkshake, the rest is dealers' choice. I prefer mint chocolate chip, cookie dough, or strawberry. In that order.

He doesn't respond, but he reacts to my message with a saluting face emoji.

About 20 minutes later, Zayn walks in holding a bag and two cups. One I really hope is a milkshake. He sets it on his desk before he looks at the plate of food Oliver brought me. As he evaluates it, both corners of his lips curl up in disgust. Which makes me giggle.

"Okay, I asked him to feed you. Not poison you with

145

bread that is green. There is so much food in there that isn't perishable. Does he not know how to cook?"

"Does mac n' cheese count?" I mock.

"No."

"Then no, Oliver does not know how to cook."

He laughs as he reaches for the plate, when he grabs it, he throws the food and the plate in the trash can by his desk. "That would have been a great detail for him to mention when I asked him to bring you food."

"Was that really necessary?" I ask pointing to the plate.

"Yes, yes it was," he answers unapologetically. He starts to open the bag of food he brought, causing me to unravel myself from his blankets. I'm eager to see what he brought us.

I reach around him for the bag, trying to snatch it from him. Unsuccessfully, I might add.

"Nice try. Snatching doesn't get you fed. You must wait your turn," he teases me, waving the bag in the air.

My eyes narrow at him, effectively annoyed. I'm absolutely starving. My stomach roars in the silence. Loud enough I look down at it before looking back up at him.

"Shit, I guess you really are hungry," he says, laughing his ass off at my discomfort. He reaches into the bag, avoiding eye contact with me. "It's normal for you to be starving."

My eyebrows furrow, not understanding. "What do you mean?"

"What I mean is, when someone uses their powers, it

146

exerts a lot of energy. Normally people are really hungry for a few months after the ceremony."

There's a brief moment that I forgot about everything that happened earlier. I was just so excited about the food and him being back. He hands me a burger or sandwich from the bag; I look at it and set it down on the desk. He notices and stops handing out the food.

"Are you okay with everything, that I called you for help?" I murmur.

He lets out a sigh, as if he is annoyed with me asking. "Aurora, I mean this with the utmost respect: I wouldn't have come if I didn't want to. Will you please stop questioning my dedication to you?"

With frustration, I throw my hands in the air. "You don't even know me. You shouldn't have blind dedication to someone. Today proved I don't even know myself. I had no idea what was happening until it was done. We don't even know what I am capable of."

"Even if I 'didn't know you,' we know your powers were triggered by anger," Zayn deadpans. "If they are related to your emotions, we should be able to control them. I will help you. Until then, I will just have to work really hard not to make you angry. I have a few ideas on how to make that happen." He winks.

He makes a show out of wiping his hands on his black jeans and walks right up to me, looking me up and down. I instantly feel insecurity flood my cheeks. I'm entirely aware I look like a hot mess. I have on his clothes that are about 3 sizes too big, my makeup is smeared, and my hair is a disaster.

"You never know, I may have to kidnap you and keep you here. Knowing you are in my clothes, fresh from my shower. My mind is playing out all the dirty things I could do to you right now." He purrs.

"As amazing as that sounds, absolutely fucking not. Oliver is right down the hall."

He laughs as if he wasn't serious about doing anything anyway. He fakes a pout, reaches for a fry and throws it in the air to catch it in his mouth. "Guess instead of eating you, I will just eat these fries."

As soon as he says it, I start choking on the burger I just took a bite of, causing my eyes to well with tears.

He holds his chest, laughing at me hysterically. "Oh, my sweet girl, maybe I will ruin you after all."

We eat our food and talk. He tells me about having to go to three different auto body shops to find the steering wheel we needed. I tell him about Oliver apologizing to me and when we finish eating, He gathers the trash into the bag. He walks into the bathroom to wash his hands.

I get back in bed and pull his blankets up to cover my lap. I sit against his headboard, waiting for him to come back out.

"I am going to step into the closet to change really quick," he states before closing the door behind him. It isn't long before he comes out and my breath hitches.

He looks like every girl's wet dream. He is shirtless and barefoot with light grey sweats, which are dripping in sin. I can practically see his entire dick outline. Which does nothing for the fact I can already feel myself getting wet in his sweats. He clears his throat when he catches me staring. I rip my gaze away from his junk to look at his smiling face.

"I am going to sleep in my sister's room, are you okay in here?"

His sister's room is next to his, I saw the door open on our way in earlier. I know it's just next door, but it feels so far away. I try to hide the disappointment coating my face.

"Yeah, that's fine."

Zayn looks at me puzzled. "Would you rather I sleep downstairs?"

"It's just, honestly, I would rather you sleep in here. It doesn't have to mean anything. I just feel more comfortable when you're close." On edge, I begin questioning why I told him the truth. But he walks right up to the side of the bed and leans in to kiss me, erasing any doubt I had. When he pulls away, he walks over to his nightstand and plugs his phone into the charger.

Zayn shuts the light off before he climbs into his bed on the other side of me, bathing the room in darkness. I watch the way he curls one arm underneath his pillow, his muscles flexing. He holds the blanket up in the air for me to come closer to him.

Anxiously, I roll on my side and begin to scoot back all the way until I feel his hard body against mine. He throws an arm over me, pulling me in tighter and my skin warms under his touch. Letting the weight of his arm swaddle me. His hand reaches up and sweeps the hair out of my face delicately. He continues to perform the motion over and over until I fall asleep in his arms.

When I wake up, Zayn isn't in his bed anymore. I check the bathroom, and he isn't there either. I can tell it's early, so I check my phone. It's only 6:00 AM, how did he get all the way out of bed without me waking?

I go downstairs and there is no sign of Oliver or Zayn there either. I start to panic. Please tell me they didn't leave me here. I rush outside in a frenzy and find they are both in my car, working on it. I instantly calm down. Zayn is walking Oliver through what to do.

"Hey, you were out cold. We are almost done. There is breakfast in the microwave for you." Zayn looks up at me.

"Thank you," I respond and turn on my heels to head back inside. I didn't have a chance to look around when we first got here. I decide to take this time while they are outside to do so.

It is beautiful. The cabin has a huge stone fireplace in the middle of the living room, it is so welcoming. The dining table is quaint for how big this cabin is, as if they choose not to have guests. It only seats four. All their furniture perfectly handpicked for the space and the only thing that stands out to me are the paintings. They are incredible.

I feel hands wrap around my belly from behind. "Do you like them?"

"How could I not? They are beautiful," I say while still staring in awe at the paintings that line the walls. They are all of nature, full of sunrises, sunsets, woods, lakes, mountains, etc.

"My mom painted all of these, it's her passion. My dad wouldn't let her work, so every few months she comes down here and paints as much as she can. Sometimes, she will switch these out, but otherwise, she donates them."

I turn to face him. "That's amazing. Oh, are you guys done?"

"Yes, everything is good as new. As much as I would love to stay here with you, I can't miss classes, or my dad will have my ass. I wanted to get your car done so you have time to go home and get changed before school. Did you eat?"

"I didn't, I'm sorry. I normally eat with Jade at school. Thank you, though, for cooking." I really do need to get going, so I can get ready. I completely forgot about school. I run upstairs to collect my things and change.

When I get back downstairs, Oliver is ready to go. I

thank Zayn for everything and head home. Being back in my car feels strange. The evidence may be gone, but when I look at my steering wheel, I still see the burn marks. I try to completely avoid touching where they were.

I don't have much time once I get home to get ready before school. I forgo the shower and get dressed, throwing my hair up in a bun for the day. There is no fixing this unless I was to get it soaking wet and use a gallon of conditioner. Mental note: the next time I decide to have a breakdown, bring my shower bag with me.

Oliver is showered and ready downstairs by the time I make it down. There is a first for everything. I have no idea what he told my mom, but she never texted or called me. The eerie quiet tells me she must have already left for work.

"Are you ready to go?" I ask my brother.

"Yeah," he answers, getting up from the table.

Neither one of us says anything to Jade or Ashton about last night. The entire car ride, Ashton hasn't stopped talking about a test he is going to fail—wasting our time because we all know he isn't.

The first half of the day goes by fine, nothing out of the ordinary. Then, at lunch, I'm eating my words. Our group of friends sit together like normal, when all of a sudden Zayn walks up to our table. Followed by Elijah and Daniel.

"Mind if we sit here?" he asks in my direction.

I become mute and lose my words.

Thankfully, Jade covers up my silence with her normal

sarcasm and wit. "These aren't assigned seats. If we are worthy of your presence, please, sit." Performing a royal sweeping movement with her hands to showcase the open seats.

Maybe *I* should have responded.

Zayn sits directly across from me.

I just shared a bed with him last night, and I'm acting like a schoolgirl with a crush right now.

Elijah breaks the ice, he stands back up and reaches his hand across the table for mine. "Aurora, I presume, I have heard great things about you," he says diplomatically before undercutting it with a wink. When my hand extends to take his, he shakes it delicately.

I look at Zayn in question. What has he told him?

Zayn answers my look. "He's just fucking with you, Red. He will flirt with anything that has tits and an ass." He turns to Elijah and shoots him a disapproving glare. "Keep your hands to yourself."

Elijah laughs and holds his palms up in surrender.

Realizing I completely forgot about the rest of the table, I turn back to them. They are all engrossed in a conversation, except for Austin who keeps sparing looks at our new table mates.

Lunch is over quickly. When I go to stand, Zayn grabs my tray. "I'll see you in class," he says before walking away.

Before we exit the cafeteria both Ruby and Jade stop me.

"Please tell me he is always like that," Ruby spits out first.

"Like what...?" I respond needing her to be more specific.

"Dominating, 'don't touch my girl,' taking your tray. I have a massive hard on right now."

Jade cuts in, "Ruby, imagine if Josh heard you. But I'll answer for her. Yes, yes he is. He has the whole sexy golden retriever thing going for him."

Ew, "I'm not enjoying any of this conversation, can I be excused?"

They both laugh at me. The awkward thing is, I'm entirely serious.

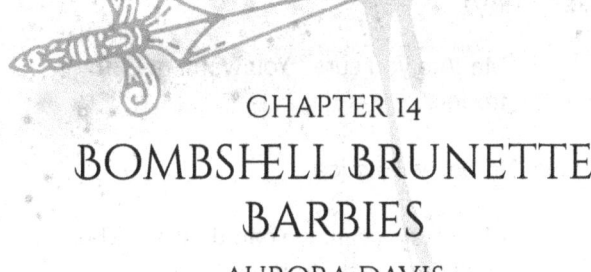

CHAPTER 14
BOMBSHELL BRUNETTE
BARBIES
AURORA DAVIS

The rest of the school day went by quick after Zayn joined us for lunch. Things in class with him were nice. Thankfully, Daniel skipped making any more comments to me.

When school was over, Zayn walked me to my car. Shortly after I got home from school, we began to text back and forth.

> Zayn: Hey, are you home yet?

> Me: Yeah, I'm just watching TV, you?

> Zayn: I'm at my dad's office. I have to help with the planning and set up for the Founders' day party. I wanted to ask if you were planning on going to it?

> Me: No, I normally don't. My parents go, but we stay home.

Zayn: What if I meet you after? I only have to stay for a couple hours and then I can get away.

Me: Are you sure? You won't get in trouble?

Zayn: No. No one will notice.

Me: Okay, yeah, we can do that. Where would you want to meet though?

Zayn: What if we go to Lancer Woods?

Me: Yeah, I can do that. What time?

Zayn: The party starts at 5, let's say we meet at 8?

We agree we will meet at Lancer Woods after the Founders' Day Party. I'm ready to finish this week so it can be the weekend.

I have to meet Zayn in an hour. I made sure to pack a blanket, drinks, and snacks in my trunk. When I finish getting ready, I let Oliver know I'm leaving. My parents are still out at the party, so he is going to watch Abigail for me.

I arrive at Lancer Woods with 10 minutes to spare and decide to wait in my car until I see him pull in.

It's 8:30 PM and he still isn't here. I try to call him but…no answer. So, I send him a text.

> Me: Hey. I'm here. Where are you?

It's been 15 minutes, and it still shows delivered, as if it hasn't been read.

I start to wonder if he ditched me or if something happened.

I don't know if I feel more embarrassed that I've sat here waiting for a guy to show up, or angry that he couldn't be bothered to answer.

The gearshift slams into reverse and I pull out of the lot with the intention of going home, getting into bed and forgetting this day existed. I waited for over an hour for him to show up and I have no intention to wait even a minute longer.

The next morning, I wake up to several messages and missed calls. None before 10:30 PM. The last one reads:

> Zayn: I'm so fucking sorry. I forgot my phone at the house. I tried to leave twice, but my dad knew I was up to something and kept pulling me into conversations with his friends. Please call me.

Feeling frustrated with the entire situation, I choose not to answer him yet. I don't care about being petty. Not with the shit he pulled last night. He can see what it feels like.

Closing out of his messages, I scroll social media. That's when I see a bunch of pictures from last night's party.

I freeze when I find a picture of Zayn dancing with a tall, beautiful brunette. I have no idea who she is. She has on a long pastel sundress and her huge tits are tucked in so tightly, you can practically hear them screaming for help. Her silky straight hair is slicked back into a long ponytail.

She has on silver strappy heels. The exact kind I hate. No one dances in those without being covered in blisters by the end of the night. She's stunning. I think I might hate her when I don't even know her.

So, this is why he ditched me? He was too busy dancing with some bombshell brunette who probably comes from money. Maybe she's the perfect candidate for him for marriage.

I look to see who the account holder is and find out her name is Eliza. Her entire personality seems meticulously curated.

Her feed is nothing like mine. I just take pictures and post them. I don't care if they match some "aesthetic."

Fuck this. I slam my phone back on my nightstand. I'm spending the morning after being ditched staring at the girl I was seemingly ditched for.

Everything between Zayn and I happened too soon.

Between my birthday party, the spring, the cabin...what the fuck was I thinking?

I put my life in the hands of someone whose life is not his own. I don't think he will tell my secret, but I should have thought through what I was doing more. Maybe, to a small extent, Oliver was right. I need to step back.

How did I fall for a man so quickly? It's been what? A little over a month since we spoke for the first time?

I shake my head, thinking through everything.

I decide to take the rest of the day to organize my room. I shut my phone off, I don't want to see if Zayn tries to reach out to me again.

Well, at least my closet looks amazing now. Pretty sure it looked like someone died in there before. When I'm done there, I decide to go take a bath. I skip dinner. I think my body has finally returned to normal after eating everything in sight the last few days. By the time I'm out of the water, my skin is pruning, but at least all of my muscles are relaxed.

I go back to my room and plop down on my bed, towel still wrapped around my body.

I can't run away forever. Unfortunately, I need to set my alarm for school tomorrow which requires turning my phone back on.

When it finally turns back on, I don't have any more calls or texts from Zayn. Just one from Jade.

> Jade: WTF, have you seen this??

Attached is a screenshot of the unfortunate picture I stumbled across earlier. I roll my eyes and text her back.

> Me: I have. I'm really not in the mood to talk about it right now. We will catch up tomorrow. I'm going to sleep.

The next day, I catch Jade up on Zayn's absence. She tried to text and call me a few times after I said I was going to sleep, but I chose to ignore my phone in case it was him.

Of course, as soon as we arrive to school, he is waiting by my parking spot for me.

Jade turns to me. "You got this?"

I nod my head, even though in reality I'm not entirely sure. What I do know is we agreed we would be exclusive, and this feels a hell of a lot like the opposite.

I exit the car to see Oliver whispering something to Zayn before walking away. Zayn's face unreadable to whatever Oliver said.

"I need to get to class." I rush out in an attempt to dismiss him as I grab my things from my car.

He grabs my bicep as I am leaning into my car, forcing me to turn in his direction. "Aurora, I texted and called you over and over trying to apologize to you. You wouldn't even answer me. I had to drive by your house Sunday to make sure you were at least there. Will you tell me what happened?"

Is he joking? My eyes narrow at him. "What happened? I waited an hour for you. You couldn't bother to borrow someone's phone to send me a message letting me know you wouldn't be able to make it? On top of that, I see a picture with your arms wrapped around a busty brunette Barbie. Don't try to act like you don't know what I'm talking about either. What was this to you?" My voice quiets as I say the last part. "I trust that you won't discuss what happened with anyone. But, just leave me alone. I was perfectly fine before you came into my life."

With that, I haul my ass into the school, as quick as I can without looking like I am running from something. I've missed breakfast by the time I make it inside.

I decide to go to the vending machine, needing some kind of substance to at least make it to lunch.

You have got to be fucking joking. The vending machine eats the last $2 I have in my book bag. I was in such a rush I didn't even grab my wallet from my car. I kick the vending machine and rest my forehead against it.

"What did that poor machine do to you?" I hear Austin's voice come up behind me. We haven't hung out since my birthday party. Life has just been...busy. I turn around dramatically, leaving my back rested up against the glass.

"Long story short, my wallet is in my car. This stupid thing ate my money. I didn't get to eat breakfast. Can this day be over with?"

He smirks. "Aurora, scoot over. What were you trying to get?"

Reluctantly, I move from the machine, crossing my arms in front of me. "I was just trying to get a bag of chips, A12."

He uses his card, avoiding his money from also being hijacked. I release a sigh of relief when the chips bounce into the dispensing door. He reaches in and grabs them out, handing them to me.

"Thank you, Austin, seriously."

"Anytime, Ro. I have to get to class, but can we please catch up later? I feel like we have barely spoken lately. I miss you."

"I miss you too. Let's catch up soon. Get to class before you're late." I do mean it, we haven't seen much of each other and I can feel his absence. In this moment, Austin feels safe, predictable. Why does that also feel so... unexciting?

Compared to the other man who has infiltrated himself into my heart, more than I would like to admit.

He feels like an impulsive thought. It's like you know you shouldn't do it deep down, but then your mind reaches for it without your approval.

162

We go for these guys that make us question everything. Sometimes I feel so little next to Zayn, but then moments like at the spring, he awakens every single part of me. I thrive under his gaze.

How can it be so fucking exhausting and yet so exhilarating? I eat my chips and walk to class, asking questions I don't have any answers to.

Lunch rolls around and surprisingly, I'm not that hungry. Jade and I grab our food and walk back to our table. Zayn and the guys are already there. As well as Austin, Josh, and Ruby.

I turn to her, stopping her before we get too close. "Can we sit somewhere else?"

Jade acts like my question is insane. "You're joking right? This is *our* table. They will be the ones who leave it, not us. Come on."

As we approach the table, Jade starts on Zayn before she even sets down her tray. "Now, I know you aren't this stupid. Go back to where you came from. We want to eat in peace. You shouldn't have sat here. You can't take a hint? I'm sure there's a whore around here that you can eat with."

Elijah replies before Zayn, "Hot damnnn girl." He looks amused and impressed as he rips a bite of his bread off.

I glance at Zayn, and he is radiating anger. His eyes

burn into her. "Now, I'm going to watch my mouth because I am trying not to piss off Aurora worse than I already have. But, you will not speak to me like that again."

He is 100% threatening her and yet, she doesn't seem remotely scared of him, but she backs down anyway. As she sits down, Zayn's eyes turn to mine. "Can we talk? Actually talk, where you don't run away from me?"

"There is nothing that needs to be said. Jade is right. You should eat elsewhere," I respond, clipped.

I can feel 3 sets of eyes on us to my left.

"Why do you always leave me no choice in doing this?" He motions at the table of people, as if I'm the one telling him to talk in front of them. Last I checked, I told him to leave. So, this is on him.

"She wasn't anyone, Aurora. Eliza is a power-hungry bitch. She is at KAE and comes from a powerful lineage. Our fathers parade us around at these events. She is an 'option' as they like to put it. One I would rather cut my dick off than be chained to. We don't get to say no to entertaining them. It was just a dance. If you look at her page, I made her take it down. She must have had someone take the picture when I wasn't paying attention. Because I wasn't, Aurora. All I was trying to do was get away from there to come meet you. I'm sorry I couldn't do that. I wanted to."

Everyone is staring at Zayn now. Daniel and Elijah look at him as if he shouldn't have said anything about Founders' politics. I get the feeling Zayn doesn't care about that. Why is he so concerned with apologizing to me if we never have a chance? What is the point in all of this?

"I think its best if you wait for one of your options to become available to you. Let's face it, there's no point in waiting for the inevitable. Before we both regret it." I say the last part as cold and heartless as I can looking at Daniel, who shrinks in his seat.

Even though inside all I want to tell him is, *please fucking figure it out and choose me.*

He looks at me with a pained expression as he stands up. He lifts his tray and slams it back on the table, sending his food up into the air before it lands partially on the tray and the table. I try not to jump when the tray makes impact, which causes the entire lunch table to vibrate. All eyes in the cafeteria now on him.

"Damnit, Aurora! Why won't you just fucking listen to me? I tell you the same shit over and over and you don't actually hear what I am saying. Even if I could have you, you would sabotage it. You doubt everything I say and then call me when you need me—"

"I think you've said enough," Austin stands. "It's time for you to walk away. Before you fucking say something you can't take back."

Everyone in the cafeteria is staring at them. I'm beyond embarrassed. My eyes are welling with emotion. I cannot cry in front of everyone right now. I push and push the tears back.

I'm in shock he just threw that in my face. I feel ignorant about calling and trusting him. Now, what's to stop him from telling everyone what happened? Did he even get rid of my steering wheel yet?

Zayn storms off, throwing his entire tray in the trash on his way. Daniel and Elijah follow behind him. They never stepped in or said anything.

When it's just us 5 at the table, Ruby turns to me with sad eyes. "Ro, are you okay?"

"No, no I don't think I am," I mumble back to her as I push my food around on my plate wishing for lunch to be over.

Josh dips his head around Ruby. "Clearly, he's hot but a total piece of shit, right, Austin?"

Austin doesn't respond, nor does he remove his eyes from staring at me. Burning through me.

"Thank you," I say to him. "For defending me."

He dips his head in a curt nod but doesn't verbally respond. So, I turn my head back to my untouched food.

The rest of lunch is extremely awkward. I don't think anyone knows what to say to me. I prefer the silence over having to explain myself or Zayn's actions.

I rush out when the bell rings and decide I'm skipping the next two periods. I don't want to run into him or sit in front of him. I wait in my car until the end of the day.

Jade didn't question me after school. Neither do Oliver and Ashton. We drive home in silence. I'm sure it's all over school that Zayn Everett got into it over a commoner.

It's around 5:00 PM when I hear the roar of an engine in our driveway. Neither of my parents are home yet. I go to look out the door and it's Austin.

"Hey, what are you doing here?" I ask surprised to see him as I step outside the front door, barefoot.

"Can we talk?" He looks angry and disheveled.

"Yeah, let's go to my room," I offer, weary. We head up the stairs, him behind me. We pass by Oliver's closed door, I know he's home still because I can hear his TV on.

When we enter my room, I close my door behind us. Austin begins pacing in long strides.

"Austin...what's wrong?" I try to coax it out of him.

He stops in his tracks. "Did you fuck him?"

"What?" I tip my head to the side in confusion and anger at the accusation.

"Aurora, I asked you a question. A guy like Zayn doesn't just become so obsessed with a girl he barely knows that quickly if there is nothing going on," His tone grew more menacing as he repeats himself. "Did. You. Fuck. Him?"

"You can't be fucking serious right now. You know me, Austin, how dare you come to my house throwing around heinous accusations? Under the assumption he couldn't possibly like me without me spreading my legs for him.

You have got to be shitting me right now. I think you need to leave."

I throw my arm out pointing to my bedroom door. He needs to get the hell out of my room. His eyes narrow, darting from my face to my wrist.

He grows angrier. His hand shoots out, clamping around my wrist in an unyielding grasp. Way fucking harder than he should be touching me.

"Austin, let go of me," I demand. "What the hell has gotten into you?"

My voice cracks as I continued to beg him to stop, but he remains silent with his fingers locked around my wrist. My other hand scratches at his fingers for him to release me. He is completely unresponsive to my voice or touch.

Fear and confusion flush through me. I didn't even do anything! The same question echoes in my mind, what is going on right now? The echoes turn into screams when I hear and feel the sharp pop of my wrist.

The pain shoots through my arm switching my fear for rage. My blood is boiling, no longer able to control my emotions. He needs to let go of me before—

A switch flicks inside of my brain, despite my consciousness screaming *NO*.

I stare at him. Angry. How dare he? Accusing me. Hurting me. He needs to let go of me, *now*. I feel the heat swivel down my arms in ribbons.

Then, I smell burning skin at the same time he yanks his hand away. He latches onto his wrist, staring at it in agony. He screams deep from his chest and I watch as the skin of his palm burns. It melts, peeling away from his fingers.

"I told you to fucking let go of me." I relish the way the power feels flowing through me. Feeding me. I feel alive, more than I ever have before.

Within 30 seconds, the door slams open and Oliver barrels inside. His eyes scan between us and in the time it takes me to blink, he grabs my lamp from my vanity and smashes the bottom of it into Austin's head, causing his body to thud onto the floor. The ground vibrates beneath my feet.

Reality smacks me in the face. I look between them and drop to my knees. "Oh no, oh no, oh no. What did I do? Oliver, what did I do?" I stare at Austin's limp body on the ground and sobs wretch from my chest.

Oliver crouches down onto one knee behind him and touches two fingers to the side of Austin's neck. Dear Lina, is he looking for a pulse?

He rushes over to me, dropping both knees to the floor. He holds both sides of my face in his hands. His eyes lock on mine, like he's searching for a sign my awareness has returned. When he realizes I'm in control he tucks his head, breathing heavily, before he speaks softly.

"Aurora, he's fine. I need you to go take a cold shower, you are burning up. Can you do that? Can you walk? I will tell you when to come out. Please."

I don't move so he scoops me up, cradling me to his

chest. I tuck my wrist into my lap so he doesn't touch it, the pain is still very present. He sets me on the shower floor in my clothes and turns the faucet to cold.

As the water pierces my skin, all of my muscles tighten, and my breathing stays erratic. I shiver so hard as the chill slices straight through me.

"Stay here," Oliver demands, and he rushes out of the bathroom.

CHAPTER 15
LAMPS AND MIND SWIPES
ZAYN EVERETT

Oliver's name illuminates my screen. I let it ring until it reaches voicemail, honestly I have no desire to explain myself while he yells at me for how I spoke to his sister. My phone dings an alert almost immediately after the call ends.

> Oliver: Get the fuck over yourself, this isn't what you think. I need you. ASAP. Our house.

I dial him immediately, panic rising in my throat.

"Oliver, what happened?"

"Come straight up, I have something funny to show you," he says, completely monotone and hangs up the phone.

What the fuck was that about? I try to call him again

and he doesn't answer, his phone goes straight to voicemail.

Well, it's safe to assume he wouldn't have told me to go all the way to their house for something as stupid as being pissed off, so I grab my keys and leave.

When I get to their house, the first thing I see is an unfamiliar truck parked outside. I hesitate before going into the house, but Oliver told me to come straight up.

I find him sitting on the top step of their staircase. His face is buried in the palms of his hands. When he hears me approaching, he drags his hands down his face and props them under his chin as he looks up at me.

"I don't know what the fuck to do here, Zayn. I'm out of my depth. I heard shit is going on with you two, but we don't have time to worry about that. My parents will be home soon. Follow me." He stands and walks down the hallway. I skeptically follow behind into Auroras room.

Where is she? My eyes fall to the floor, to Austin with his wrists tied to the foot of Aurora's bed frame with rope. I scan over his body and find one of his hands is mutilated. Completely shredded. It's fucking disgusting. Blood is running down his wrist and pooling onto her carpet.

He also has a gash on the side of his head, I'm guessing from the lamp lying beside him.

"Is he...dead?" I ask hesitantly.

"No he's alive," Oliver leans over the body. "I knocked him out and tied him up so he couldn't run."

"Where is she?" I finally ask out loud.

"She's in the shower, I put her in it with the cold water on to cool her down."

I turn to the bathroom to check on her. I don't know if she even wants me here. We haven't talked since lunch, but I need to know she's okay.

"Wait," he doesn't yell but says it loud enough to stop me in my tracks.

"I don't know exactly what happened," he says as I face him. "I only heard bits and pieces, but it was enough to cause me to rush out of my room. Austin was screaming. I rushed in and heard her say, 'I told you to fucking let go of me.' But, it wasn't what she said, it was *how* she said it. She was cold, emotionless, she was just staring at him as he was screaming. It was as if something took her over, Zayn. I was terrified. I didn't have time to think; I needed to act fast. So, I hit him. I don't know how much longer he'll be out. What do we do?"

He is scared, understandably. I am going to need Elijah's help to cover this up.

"Oliver, you did the right thing," I try to ease his nerves. "I will fix this. But I need to check on her. I'll be right back." My gaze flickers over Austin again. "If he wakes up, just fucking hit him again."

I turn down the hall in the direction of the running water. Quietly, I ease the door open and closed behind me so I don't frighten her. When I get to the shower, I peel back the curtain. As soon as I find her, I want to rush in and hold her. Instead, I evaluate her, I need to know she isn't hurt.

Fuck, how long has she been in here? She shivers so hard her teeth are chattering.

I notice the way she's circling her wrist, in a soothing motion. When she moves her hand slightly, I catch the angry red handprint marking her soft skin. A possessive need bangs on my chest to run back into her room and finish what she started. It takes everything in me not to surrender to the impulse. She pulls me from my anger when she releases a quiet gasp at the temperature dropping colder.

Her clothes are sopping wet, sticking to her body. Her bangs are hanging over her eyes.

I reach in to cut the water off. Looking around for a towel, I spy a purple robe hanging on the bathroom door. *Hopefully this is hers.* I grab her out of the shower, careful not to soak myself, and set her on the bathroom floor. She hasn't said anything to me since I came in.

I need to get her out of these clothes. I don't think twice before I begin to peel them off. Each article of clothing one at a time. When I am done, I wrap the robe around her body.

The fabric starts to soak from her hair dripping all over it, so I look around the counter for a hair tie. When I finally find one, I collect all of her hair into a bun. *Man, she has a lot of hair, this is a lot easier on my sister.*

Once I have it all up, I lean down to talk to her. "It's all going to be okay. Stay here, I'm going to grab you something to wear, I'll be right back."

She doesn't answer, still cradling her wrist. I press a soft kiss to the top of her head before stepping out of the bathroom.

When I walk into her room, Oliver isn't here.

Since I have no idea where anything is, and I need to be quick, I start rummaging through her drawers. I find one that is full of pajamas and grab her a set and some undergarments from another.

I rush back to Aurora and hand them to her, delicately placing them in her lap. "I just grabbed what I could find, can you get dressed for me? I will be back for you in just a minute."

I step into the hallway, closing the door behind me and begin to dial Elijah; he answers me right away.

"Hey brother, what's up?"

"Hey man, can you meet up?" I ask.

"For what and where?"

"Cabin, oh and I forgot my notebook in your book bag."

Finally catching onto why I need to meet him, he agrees. Talking in code becomes extremely annoying but is absolutely necessary.

When I walk back into her room Oliver is sitting on her bed with his shoes on, ready to go. "Can you get something to wrap his hand in?" I ask while I start untying the rope.

He comes back with a long-sleeved shirt, quickly ties it around Austin's wrist, and glances up at me for approval. "Good enough, help me get him into my car."

We carry Austin downstairs, pausing inside the front door before we take him out. I quickly move my car into the driveway so the neighbors can't see us and run back inside to help Oliver get his body in the car. We lay him across the floor of my backseats and tie the rope around the frame of my passenger seat.

Oliver waits by the car as I go inside to get Aurora.

"Aurora, you are going to go with Oliver in your car. We are going to the cabin for a bit," I say as I bring her to her feet.

"But, but Austin?" she asks through heavy eyes.

"Baby that's why I'm here, we're handling it. All you need to do is get in the car. Oliver has your phone. I will be down in a minute."

"Zayn, I didn't mean to. He wouldn't let go of me. I just reacted," she fumbles out.

"Why was he even here? What happened?" I ask harsher than I should have.

She sniffles. "I don't know. He was so angry. He assumed we slept together because of our argument. I have never seen him mad before, he just snapped."

I knew he liked her; this confirms it. But even if she did fuck me, why would he lose control like that? You get hurt and then get over it. I don't know if I am more pissed off that he snapped on her, or of him accusing her as if it isn't her choice. It just doesn't make sense, why would he be this angry? She didn't cheat on him or something.

She takes my pause as if I am upset with her. She instantly reaches up grabbing my shirt in her fists.

"I'm sorry. I was so pissed off at thinking you ditched me for someone. I didn't give you a chance to explain. I sat in the shower thinking, welp this is it. Just another thing to cover up. How long can we do this, Zayn?"

Her eyes well with tears. My hands find the back of her arms rubbing them up and down. I lean in and kiss her forehead, pressing my lips to where her bangs are for several seconds before removing them.

"We will do it for as long as we need to. This won't be forever. We will learn how to control your powers. But, lunch wasn't on you, I shouldn't have caused a scene. I was so angry at my dad. Angry at the Founders for these standards we have. But you didn't deserve me to take that out on you, and especially not in public. Now, as much as I know we need to work this out, we really need to go. Can you please go get in the car with Oliver? I promise we will talk about this more after."

She reluctantly releases me and heads downstairs. I check her room, needing to clean up so it doesn't look like anything happened. I try to find something to hide the blood by her bed and opt for a sweater from her hamper to throw over it, as if she just took it off and left it on the floor. *Hopefully the blood comes out.* I straighten the few things that were knocked down and go back downstairs.

I step outside the door to lock it and when I turn around, I see Austin's truck. *FUCK.* My head falls back in annoyance.

This needs dealt with. I tell Oliver and Aurora to hold on, climb into my car, and dig in Austin's pockets for his keys. I move his truck down the road and walk back. Just so it isn't directly in front of their house when her parents get home. They shouldn't see it coming home from the entrance of the neighborhood.

I drive all the way to the cabin with this asshole still out cold in my back seat. Oliver must have really hit him for him to still be out.

The whole thing has me setting a mental reminder to stay away from Oliver and lamps. When we get there, Elijah is waiting. I step outside of my car and hold up a finger to Oliver, motioning for him to give me a minute to talk to Elijah.

Elijah meets me halfway, the gravel crunching beneath his sneakers, "Dude, what's going on? You're lucky I understood what you were saying. Did you hurt someone?"

I don't have time to explain this delicately or sugar coat it. "It's a really long story. Austin tried to hurt her, and she burned him. She's started showing signs of powers. I'll explain more later, but we need to get him inside before he wakes up."

Elijah has already started following me to my car when

he mumbles, "Man, I'm really going to need a drink after this."

We get Austin into the house while Oliver takes Aurora right upstairs.

Elijah has been learning from his mother since he started talking on how to make elixirs. They can be extremely dangerous in the wrong hands. He could make them blindfolded, with his hands tied behind his back at this point. His mind is more dangerous than anyone truly knows. He could never receive powers, and he is still one of the few I would want to fight by my side in this world.

He always keeps the main potions needed in case of emergency in a bag hidden in his car. Not that his mom or dad knows that.

Since we got to Austin in enough time, the healing elixir should provide a full recovery to his hand. The second drink is to make him forget.

I stand behind Austin and hold up his head as Elijah pours both down his throat.

"I didn't use one of the normal batches," Elijah says as the last drop falls. "I didn't know what I was walking into, so I made one before I left that was strong enough he'll forget the last few hours as well. It will keep him out for a couple more."

Which means I need to get him back to his truck or house before he has a chance to wake up.

In no time at all, we are all sitting in the living room with an unconscious Austin, Oliver and Aurora included.

"We gave him two elixirs," I explain. "He won't remember what happened and the other will heal his hand. Everything is going to be okay."

Red lets out a deep breath. "I'm sorry to bring you into this," she says to Elijah. "I don't know what Zayn told you. I swear this isn't me. I don't know what's happening to me."

Elijah stares at her with a look of sympathy and concern. "You are safe with me. I wish Zayn told me sooner." He shoots me a disapproving glare. "But you don't need to explain yourself to me. Do you want some help with that?" He motions to her wrist.

"Thank you, but no. I think I need to keep this pain as a reminder to keep myself in check," she murmurs.

He shakes his head at her, not accepting that answer. "A reminder to keep yourself in check from a man trying to hurt you? I don't think so." He gets up and twists a cap off another healing elixir, handing it out to her. "You are going to drink this, love and if a man ever hurts you, you defend yourself and ask questions later."

I can't help but cringe at his use of 'love' towards her, but knowing he doesn't mean it in any other way then helping her, I let it go.

Once she drinks the elixir, I can see the immediate relief washing over her face. Giving me peace of mind that at least her physical pain is gone, I begin to instruct Oliver on what to do next.

"You will drive Aurora back home and I will follow

behind with Austin. We can get him into his truck and move the truck to his house. Then, you will follow me in my car, so I have a ride back. I will drop you off at home when we are done."

Oliver nods his head. "Works for me."

I turn to Elijah. "Thank you for helping us. I'll come by later and talk to you."

I hug Aurora tightly in my arms before we walk outside of the front door. Thankful she was able to protect herself. "I need to say something, and I need you to truly hear me, okay?"

She nods her head against my chest. "If you ever need me, ever, you call me. I don't care if we are fighting, not on speaking terms, whatever the case may be, you call. I'm not here only for the blissful moments; I am here for you. That means protecting you in any way I can. You never need to apologize to me as if you are a burden, because you are not. Promise me that you will remember that?"

She sniffles, holding back tears as she looks up at me. "I promise. Zayn thank you for this, for being you."

I hold her cheek in my hand as I lower a kiss to her lips. "Always, Red."

By the time I get back to Elijah's, it's late.

I text him and tell him to meet me outside, leaning on

my car as I wait, letting it take the weight off of my legs. I'm absolutely exhausted. Both from carrying a man up into his truck and mentally from trying to make sense of everything today.

"Seriously, her secret is safe with me. I feel bad for the girl," Elijah says as he approaches. "But fuck, dude, is she a danger to us?"

"No, it has only happened when she's been angry, to the point of rage. From what I can tell, it's only been one other time." I sigh. "I don't know for sure if it ever happened as a child, but from Oliver's stories I think it may have. Her powers had to have been dormant for years. I don't know what's causing them to suddenly flare. I'm trying to find out more. All I know is I need to keep her safe."

"She could fuck up our entire plan, Zayn," he hisses. "This is our life. We cannot risk anything changing what we have to do. If you are out there protecting her and get caught in the crossfire, we're fucked. You cannot choose her over us. She's a great girl, but we need you."

"Man, don't you think I know that!" I throw my arms in the air. "My entire fucking life I've been the one making plans and sitting back quietly, observing the shit around us. I work with the monsters every damn day. I know more than any of you what is at stake. So, don't switch shit up now. My goal has always been the same, *nothing* will change that," I spit.

Elijah takes a moment of silence. "I see it now. I didn't before, but I do now. You know, don't you?"

"Know what?" I ask, scared of what he might respond.

"You know who her parents are. That's why you have been so fascinated with her, but why?"

When I don't respond, he questions me again.

"Does she know?"

CHAPTER 16
WHISK ME AWAY
AURORA DAVIS

The last several weeks things have gone quiet between Zayn and I. Since the incident with Austin, Zayn has distanced himself from me.

The next day, he sat with us at lunch again and I had warned my friends to be nice. I told them we talked about what happened and we were okay. Austin and Jade both haven't been Zayn's biggest fans.

I was scared shitless for how things would be with Austin. But thankfully, the elixirs Elijah gave him worked amazingly, it's like nothing ever happened.

The phantom pain in my wrist lingers, especially when Austin is around.

Zayn and I haven't hung out once since that night. He claims he doesn't want his dad to get suspicious, that he can't risk shining any light on me. If that was the truth, then

I would understand, but I can't help feeling like he's holding something back from me.

We barely talk anymore and even his texts are dwindling down.

The Halloween party is tonight, but Zayn hasn't said anything to me about it since he asked me to go.

I never bought a dress because I have no intention of showing up somewhere unwanted. If he wanted me to be there, he would have said something.

I hate that I miss him. His smell, his touch, *him.*

I'm lying in bed when I hear someone running up the stairs. My door whips open to an idiotically smiling Jade.

"Why the fuck are you so happy?" I ask as she jumps up on my bed holding a box half the size of her body.

"Get the fuck up! Get up now. You will never guess what I have."

I sit up, eyeing the box. It's beautiful, all black with a delicate design, wrapped with a red bow around it. But the bow is all sloppy?

"What is it?" I ask, curious.

She jumps off my bed and stands beside it, placing the box on the comforter and unwrapping the bow. She practically screeches as she opens the lid.

I lean in to see what's inside. On top sits a stunning rust

colored velvet dress. I run my fingers across it. It has off the shoulder straps and looks so expensive. Above it sits a matching velvet, lacy mask. But there's something underneath it...

"This one is mine, wait until you see yours," Jade says, bouncing in one spot. She gently picks up the dress by the straps and lays it across the bottom of my bed. As she does, I look back into the box, audibly gasping.

"Holy shit," I say out loud. This can't be mine. I don't wear flashy, revealing stuff like this. It's a golden slip dress with spaghetti straps for sleeves. Pulling it out of the box, I walk with it over to the mirror and hold it up to my body.

The neck hangs delicately and a slit runs high up on the side. The dress drapes all the way down to the floor, stopping perfectly at my ankles. I flip it over and hold it out in front of me to look at the back. It laces all the way from the neck down to the small of the back. The solid fabric doesn't start until right at the hips.

I spin around. "Jade, where did these come from?" I know the answer, but want to hear it anyway.

She walks over to her purse and starts rummaging through it. Once she finds what she is looking for, she holds it out to me.

A black envelope.

Before I have had a chance to look at it, she speaks. "You didn't even see your mask yet! Oh, and he also has a cover up in here for you."

No wonder the bow was a mess; she already opened the box before she came over. Nosy bitch.

I look in the box again and she's right. Beneath the dress sits a black silk shawl, it's so simple yet perfect for this dress. The mask is black too with specs of gold. It has layers of lace, flowers, and gems.

"These can't be real right?" I question.

Jade scoffs. "Do you think he would give you a mask that's been bejeweled with toy gems?"

There's no way. "Jade, it's a mask, no one spends that kind of money for something you wear once."

"I can't with you." She laughs. "You just don't get it do you? They have all of the money, all of the power. The things Zayn could do—let's just say, he has more than enough money to spoil you."

I take another look at the dress draped over my arm, then at the envelope I have sitting on my bed. I lay the dress down, careful not to risk wrinkling it and open his letter.

Red,

I'm sorry. I know things have been off lately. I hope you find this letter better than the last. I will explain more tonight. I want you at the party by my side. In this envelope, there are two invitations to bring with you. I sent the dresses to Jade's, so your parents wouldn't find them. Yes, the gold dress is for you. I cannot wait to see you in it. There will be a car to pick you up at 8.

See you soon.

-Z

Jade stands over my shoulder reading it with me.

My parents will be leaving by 7, he must have scheduled it for later on purpose.

"You heard the man. Now hurry up. We have 3 hours to be ready. Get your dirty ass in the shower."

She smacks my ass as I walk out of my room. I shake my head as I close the door behind me, laughing.

I get a text to my phone from an unknown number as I'm almost done getting ready.

> Unknown: Good evening, Ms. Davis. My name is Christian. I have been sent by Mr. Everett to pick you up. I just wanted to let you know I have arrived. Please don't rush, just come out whenever you are ready.

"Well, he sure is punctual," I state while putting on the heels Jade brought me.

We go to head downstairs when Oliver's door swings open. He is dressed in a maroon and black suit with a mask in his hands. *Wait, no.*

"Is the driver here?" he asks looking at both of us. "Stop looking at me like that. Zayn told me to come. He took me to get this suit the other day. Does it look okay? A bit much isn't it?" He runs his hands down his pants, looking at his loafers.

Jade eyes him up and down. "You look good, kid, let's go."

"Wait, do you even have an invite?" I stop to ask.

"Yes, *Mom.* I have my wallet and phone, too," he responds, sarcastically.

We greet Christian at the car, and he opens the door for us. Oliver sits up front with him. The drive is longer than I expected. My palms are sweaty. Why am I so nervous right now?

"What is wrong with you?" Jade asks, eyeing me suspiciously.

"I'm just nervous," I lie. "I've never gone to anything like this before. I don't dress up like this. I feel like an impostor." I fiddle with the mask in my lap, running my fingers along each delicate stitch.

Okay, maybe not a total lie. Truth is, I do feel like an impostor. I'm wearing something provided by Zayn to a party thrown by the Founders. This isn't me. I don't need handouts to fit in with the 'right' crowd. Not to mention, I'm trying to stay off the radar. I can't risk my magic making an unwelcome appearance here.

The more stressed I feel, the more worked up I get. When I realize it, I try to distract myself. I breathe deeply in my chest and out, trying to calm my nerves like I've been working on.

"Hey, stop. You look beautiful. Zayn is lucky to have you here. He wouldn't have invited you if he didn't want you to come. If you are uncomfortable, we can go," Jade tries to reassure me.

Oliver turns in his seat to see us. "Ro, everything will be fine. You are going to have fun. If you aren't, Christian here is on strict instruction to bring us home immediately. Right, Christian?" he asks him with a smirk.

"Yes ma'am, I'm at your service tonight. Just text me at any point and I will pull the car around. That being said, we are here."

I look out the window as he pulls up to a mansion filled with light. It's breathtaking. There has got to be 60 cars lining the street and the driveway. The staircase could seat an army. I count four floors of windows and balconies lined with flower arrangements.

We all place our masks on, Jade and I checking each other to make sure they sit okay against our hair.

"Wow." Is all I can say.

I watch as people line up to at the main doors with their

masks. Dresses worn by beautiful women sweep the ground, all of them on the arms of men in suits and ties.

We exit the car and walk the black carpet up to the door. For Halloween, there isn't gore or anyone jumping out at you.

Once we hand our invitations to the guard at the door, we are granted entrance. A beautiful woman stands just inside the door checking coats, I hand her my shaw and she gives me a ticket. Jade takes my ticket and phone and places them in her purse.

My eyes automatically scan the house in awe. It's incredible. We edge deeper inside, past a large entryway with a grand staircase to the next floor. It is chained off to block people from going up. Once we reach the main hall, there's a huge dance floor. People sway with the slow, sultry music.

Golden light reflects off the mirrors lining every wall, and the marble beneath my heels. Curtains fall from the tall cathedral like ceiling. Expensive paintings and portraits of past Founders, I assume, surround us.

The tables are lined in black tablecloths where platters of food cover every inch. There are masked, well-dressed waiters, circling around with trays in their hands.

"Can I move here?" I jokingly ask in amazement.

They both look at each other quickly and then look back at me. Oliver goes to open his mouth to speak when I feel a presence come up behind me.

I spin on my heel at the same time *he* speaks. "Maybe

one day you can," he says, curling the side of his lip into a grin.

I almost check to make sure there isn't drool pouring from my mouth. The sight of him immediately takes my breath away. The way he looks absolutely divine in his all-black suit. His dress shirt is unbuttoned by a few buttons, skipping the tie. He has on gold cuff links to match the gold accents on his loafers. His gold mask covers one half of his face and goes up above his right eyebrow, exposing his right side.

He is perfection. He towers over me, taking in the dress he sent me. My nipples instantly harden under his stare. I forget how thin this dress is and don't realize he can see them. His eyes roam down at the same time he lets out a rugged clearing of his throat before stepping closer to me. He leans in just so he can whisper loud enough for me to hear him over the music. "Aurora, I'm going to need you to behave before I take you upstairs and rip this dress off of you."

My pulse races, wanting to get a reaction out of him. He has barely talked to me lately, maybe he deserves to regret that. I grab for his dress shirt, snaking my fingers into the space between a couple of the buttons to ease him closer, grazing his toned stomach underneath.

"Maybe you should," I invite him with a raise of my eyebrow.

His eyes glaze over, darkening. The rumble in his throat

barely audible above the music. He licks his lips which sends Oliver over the edge.

"Get a room or at least dismiss your bodyguards. I don't want, nor need to see this. Disgusting," Oliver says loudly to get our attention. When I turn around, he is shaking his head and shoulders as if he is trying to perform an exorcism on his mind from what he just witnessed.

As we walk further into the dance hall, Zayn leans into my ear from behind me. "You will pay for that," he says, sweeping all of my hair over one shoulder. His fingers trace all of the straps on my back as we walk. He is so close to me I can feel his body heat.

His hand sweeps right underneath the fabric on the small of my back where the dress hangs. He growls in my ear. I smile knowing he can't see my reaction.

Jade and Oliver stop abruptly at a table, checking out the food. I halt, causing Zayn to run right into the back of me.

He snakes his arm around me, splaying his fingers across my stomach.

"Watch where you are going, huh?" I tease him over my shoulder. I'm going to love this game of cat and mouse tonight.

Daniel and Elijah approach us. Both looking gorgeous. Daniel hugs Jade and whispers something in her ear when a flush cascades over her cheeks.

Guessing from her reaction, he wasn't threatening her. He then shakes Oliver's hand. When he gets to me, he looks at Zayn and then back to me. "You look beautiful, Aurora, truly." He doesn't hug or touch me, he just moves over to the side.

Elijah's greeting is the complete opposite. He walks up to me with a wide smile. I notice he isn't wearing a mask, I look down to see it is tucked in his pocket.

"What don't you like masquerades?" I ask jokingly.

"Love, everyone enjoys a masquerade, but I can't keep this gorgeous face hidden for too long." He shoots me a wink and wraps his arms around me for a hug, keeping distance between our bodies. As he releases me, he whispers in my ear, "It's itchy." I laugh and he continues, "You're looking stunning, lady, Zayn has practically been waiting by the door for you to get here. He won't leave you; you are safe here. I will be keeping an eye out close by." He kisses my cheek before stepping back.

I instantly feel Zayn circling to the front of me. I reach out to press on his stomach to stop him.

Elijah laughs. "Relax, man, you've already pissed on her." Both Jade and Daniel chuckle in response.

I drop my hand from Zayn and curl my lip up in disgust. "Gross."

My brother chortles at my distaste.

Ignoring them, I browse the table of food, grabbing Jade's hand on my way. I'm starving. We leave the guys standing there talking while we search for something resembling normal food.

Once we have small plates stacked to the brim, we

begin to scarf everything down. Even if I have no idea what most of these things are, they're delicious. And, well, I never actually ate today. I laid in bed for so long when Jade showed up. It's not like I ate after that; my nerves were a mess.

But, seeing Zayn and everything feeling normal between us again, it has me feeling relaxed enough to eat.

My stomach thanks me as the food begins to settle. Deep down, I know I should probably starve myself in this dress, but right now, I don't give a fuck.

I look over and see the guys all sharing a very serious look, totally engrossed in a conversation.

"What do you think that's about?" Jade murmurs.

"I wish I knew," I answer honestly.

Lately, it just feels like people are talking *about* me, not *to* me. What else would Oliver have to discuss with the 3 of them?

We grab champagne flutes on our way back over to the guys. Zayn watches me as we approach.

"Dance with me?" he asks, holding his hand out for mine. I don't respond or grab his hand.

"She can't dance, not formally," Oliver says, harsh and blunt. I angle my face to the side to give him a dirty look. Thanks, bro.

"Okay, so come step on my feet then," Zayn offers with a smile. Jade reaches around me, grabbing the glass from my hand.

I grab his hand hesitantly. We slowly walk onto the

dance floor right as a new song is about to start. I look around trying to figure out how everyone is dancing.

When Zayn notices, he grabs my arms and wraps them around his neck. They barely reach around him when he is standing tall. He pulls me in and wraps his arms around my waist.

"Just sway back and forth. No one is watching us."

I look over to our friends to see if they are still there. Jade is dancing with Daniel. Elijah has some random girl on his arm. But where is Oliver? I don't see him anywhere.

"Trust me," he says gently.

"I do trust you," I reply.

He sighs. "You do, but you don't. Anytime I say something you need proof, or to see it for yourself. That's why even despite me telling you no one is watching, you had to check. You trust me to keep you safe, but not at face value. What do I have to do to make you take me at my word?"

I look down at our feet. "It's not about you; it's *all of this*." I glance back up, circling my head to motion where we are. "All of this isn't me. This dress, this life. I can't help but feel like we have an expiration date. Maybe I'm just trying to not fall too hard. I want you, Zayn, trust me I do. But I also want to stand on my own, be powerful on my own. Not people looking past me at the man standing behind me. Or looking at the man who has to stand in front of me to protect me."

"Baby girl, no one—and I mean no one—in this room is looking past you and looking at me." He spins me around fast, swaying behind me as he presses into my back. One hand grips my stomach, the other on my hip. He rocks our bodies to the music.

My eyes close and I press my head back into him. This kind of dancing I can handle. Both of my hands instinctively search to intertwine with his. I let the music take control, moving our bodies in sync with one another. I let his hands roam the silk of my dress and one of the straps begins to slip off my shoulder. He sweeps it back up and I twist my arm behind me to wrap behind his neck, losing myself to the beat of his body.

Right as the beat slows, Zayn leans into my ear. "Your body is hypnotic, Red. Each curve is on full display in this dress. That's why I picked it for you. I wanted to watch you dance in it, feel almost nothing between us." He pulls my ass back into him forcefully, grabbing my hip by my pelvis.

When the song ends, I finally open my eyes, looking around. "Now people are watching you," he whispers as I drop my arm from his neck, my instant reaction is to walk off the dance floor. I'd rather stand off to the side than be the center of attention for the scrutiny of strangers.

Seconds feel like hours as he holds me still in their gaze. As my eyes roam around, it's clear they aren't just staring at the grey eyed man over my shoulder; they're staring at me. Focusing in on the way our bodies rock together, at where his hands are placed.

He finally spins me back around and I'm panting. The next song starts and people return to their dances. That was mesmerizing. My eyes find his, the heat crawling up my skin.

Suddenly, he grabs my hand and drags me off the dance floor. Each stride long and powerful, fueled by passion. He holds my hand as he pulls me behind him. My heels skid across the floor, nearly tripping over my dress as I try to keep up with him. I try to gather it into my open hand so I don't fall.

He rushes up to a door and pushes it open, dragging me in and then slamming it behind me.

I look around the room before turning to face the door. I stand in the middle of what appears to be an office. It's huge. The desk is bare except for a couple of books. Every wall is hidden behind floor to ceiling bookshelves. Wait, maybe it's a library?

Zayn doesn't face me at first, he leans his forearms on the door on each side of his forehead. I can see his chest rising and falling in sharp bursts. I start walking forward to touch him, reaching one hand out onto his upper arm closest to me.

He shivers at my touch.

"Zayn, why did you rush off like that. What's wrong?"

"I'm fine, I just need a minute. I needed to walk away," he dismisses me, yanking off his mask as if it's suffocating him.

I take mine off in response and try to pull him off the door. "You want me to trust you, talk to me. Don't distance yourself like you have been."

He spins around abruptly nearly knocking me off my feet. His hand reaches out to stabilize me. His eyes darken as he stares at me and he exhales a heavy breath before he begins to speak.

"You make me lose all my fucking common sense," he says as he throws his hands in the air. "I'm so desperate to get you to see how I see you. I'm addicted to you. When I spun you around on that dance floor, I wanted to prove something to you. When I saw the eyes on you, it only made me crave you more. You don't even notice when people look at you. You're actually oblivious to it. Everyone on that floor wanted to take you home with them. Meanwhile, I want to throw my fist through their faces for thinking so inappropriately about you. I'm trying not to draw attention to you and then I am flaunting you on the dance floor like a fucking pet."

As he talks, he walks me backward to the desk until my thighs hit the side of it. I throw my arms out behind me to stabilize myself as he prowls forward.

I inch my legs open, ready for him to take what's his. I want him to realize that craving isn't one sided.

His voice drops, wrapping in smoke. "Want to know why?" He eats up the remaining distance between us, towering over me. "Because seeing how other people look at you makes me murderous. *You are mine.* Watching Elijah kiss you? Knowing Austin wants you so bad, he completely snapped over it? What am I supposed to do with that?"

He talks as if it isn't only him and I in the room. As I

lean against this desk throbbing for him and only him. My heart is pounding, my temperature raising. I part my lips to shut down his notions of other men, to tell him what I want, but he continues.

"I want to fuck you in there with everyone watching, I want to *own* you. Not in the way all these sick fucks own their women. I want to fucking ravish you until you are screaming my name so loud that these men go home knowing I have what they can't get. My head between your knees with you begging for more. I can't fucking take it, Aurora. My attraction to your mind and body is making me go crazy. Damnit, I am the cool and collected one, the one who thinks things through. Then I see you and I want to pounce on you like a fucking animal. I don't know how I'm supposed to find an in-between. It's like I am a puppet and someone is controlling me, but my brain says more, more, more." he chants as he stabs his pointer finger into his temple.

He turns around trying to steady himself, but it's not working. I can hear his erratic breathing, breathing that matches my own, just before he walks back over to the door and punches it. I don't flinch, but my breath hitches. His need for me pulses through my bloodstream, fueling years of missing desire. His want doubles into my own.

Despite the control he is searching for, all I want is for him to lose it. I want this man more than I've ever wanted anything. I imagine us out there just like he said. The idea of him taking control for everyone to see has my thighs soaking wet with desire.

Zayn wasn't just honest, he laid out a fucking private, explicit diary and said, 'read me.'

Quietly, I remove myself from the desk and stalk towards him until I stop only a few feet from him.

I reach behind me and untie the straps of my dress quietly, loosening it enough to drop it from my shoulders. It falls, pooling at my feet.

I step from it, leaving myself standing there in only my heels. My arms wrap around his body, reaching for the front of his shirt where I begin unsnapping the buttons with my nails.

One by one. "Zayn, turn around."

"Just give me a second. Please, I need to calm down," he says, trying to stop me from unbuttoning his shirt the rest of the way. But I don't allow him to, smacking his hand from mine as I finish what I started.

"No you don't, turn around," I command again as I undo the last one.

He doesn't move. So, I walk around him to his side. I wrap my hand around his belt buckle and yank on it to *make* him face me. My fingers line the inside of his slacks, against his briefs.

When he turns around, his eyes roam every single inch of my body.

"Aurora," he rasps in warning.

He isn't going to scare me away.

"You said you wanted to make me scream your name, do it. Make every woman out there wish they were me. Make them know it's me who gets you, not them."

The battle is clear on Zayn's face as he struggles with his deepest desires against whatever it is causing him to keep pushing me away.

Something clicks into place, allowing him to give in.

He rushes me, slamming his mouth onto mine. His hands grip my legs to scoop me up, pressing my pussy against his rock-hard body. I push the sleeves of his shirt down so it falls to the floor.

He sits me down on the desk as he reaches behind me, swiping the books from it so they clatter to the floor. His palm splays on my chest, throwing me back. It makes my spine ache at the same time as a rush of adrenaline floods through me. I raise my arms up behind my head gripping the edge behind me.

His hands sweep over every crevice I have. His mouth presses hot kisses all over my body.

"Are you sure?" he stops kissing me to ask.

"Yeah, I'm pretty fucking sure, Zayn."

His mouth finds my pussy immediately. His tongue diving between my lips as he wraps my legs around his neck.

"Ohh, fuuuck," I moan. He holds one thigh so tight it makes me grind into him harder. His other hand goes towards my pussy, diving two fingers inside me, which aches at first until he stretches me to fit them. Angling them just fucking right, he pounds in and out of my body. His tongue makes my clit ache with the need to come. I don't give a shit who hears me right now. Heat swirls to my core way too fast.

"Fuck, I need to come, Zayn, please," I beg. He pushes his long fingers in deep at the same time he picks up speed with his tongue before returning to a steady pace. Between the swirls of his tongue and the pressure of his fingers, only seconds pass before my body begins to spasm with release.

Forever the gentleman, he waits to remove his hand until the aftershocks are done and sets my hips gently back down onto the desk. I lay there panting as my legs shake.

He walks up beside my head and kisses me deeply. I return it with passion, tasting myself on him but not wanting to stop. When he stops kissing me, I groan.

He smiles and smooths my hair out of my face. My skin is slick with sweat, I feel disgusting and he is just staring at me.

"I am going to have so much fun with you, Red," he says, kissing up my chest to my neck. He reaches his arm behind my back to help me up. I flinch. "Did I hurt you?" he asks nervously.

I look at him trying not to laugh. "I'll only say yes if you promise that you'll hurt me again?"

His eyes challenge mine. "Did you like when I pushed you down on the desk?"

I swallow the desire I have for him to take me again. "Yes," I respond, chest heaving.

He growls; his hands roam up both of my thighs stepping between them. "You may just kill me, do you know that?" One hand reaches for mine and he presses it on his dick. I can feel moisture through his pants. "I almost came in my fucking pants at the sound of you moaning. We need to stop, or I'm not going to be able to hold back from fucking you."

Deep down, I care but in this moment I don't give a single shit about saving my virginity. All I want is him.

"Stop looking at me like that," he demands.

I don't.

He yanks me to the edge of the desk, where my ass partially hangs off. I wrap my legs around him to keep me from falling, sliding my hand out from between us.

He presses his covered dick right against my pussy.

I practically hiss at him from the immediate need. I grind my hips against him in shameless desire. He throws his head back in pleasure, eyes closing for a brief second.

He reaches behind my head gripping my hair, spinning it in his hand until it is wrapped around his large hand. The hair at the base of my neck is tight in his grip. He pulls me back so that my head is angled up to him, reaching between my legs and rubbing my clit as I grind against his dick until I come a second time.

He releases his hold on my hair, my curls fall back down and Zayn snakes both hands around my neck and rubs from the bottom of my scalp to my neck, soothing the tension.

My head rests on his chest as he continues to massage down my back. Both of us are breathing heavy.

"I'm never going to let you leave if we don't go now. I need you to walk out first, so my dick can recover before I walk out there hard as a rock."

I nod slowly before my selfishness escapes me. "What about you?" I ask realizing his entire focus was on me and he is left standing here untouched.

He leans in pressing kisses to my neck between his words. "It is best my pants stay on, if they come off, I won't be thinking clearly. I am not taking your virginity here. It's nothing a cold shower won't fix later."

He wraps around me to help lower me from the desk. I stand there as he retrieves my dress and mask. Zayn falls down on one knee as he holds it out for me to step into. Without hurrying, he pulls it up my body and then slips my shoulders into the straps. His hands spin me to lace up the back of the dress before tying it and he smacks my ass when he's done.

"Oh, and how dare you show up to a party without underwear on," he throws at me.

"How dare you pick a dress that shows every single nook and cranny of my body! I didn't own anything I could wear underneath this!" I snap back in response.

"I will be sure next time to send a special box from Allure," he winks and kisses me fast and hard for a few seconds before pulling off again. "Fuck, damn it you have to go. I will be out in just a minute, okay?" He says as he smooths my hair down the best he can to slip my mask over my face.

I offer a smile before stepping back into the hallway and closing the door behind me. I feel like I am on a cloud right now.

As I walk to the bathroom, Jade rushes over to me, eyeing me up and down suspiciously. "No, you didn't, did you just rush off to have sex? I have been searching for you everywhere. You are a mess!" she accuses.

I just smile at her deviously. When her mouth falls open, I laugh. "No, I wasn't off having sex." I admit.

She yanks me hard into the bathroom where she locks the door, demanding I give her the play by play.

Normally, I am one who severely lacks details, but right now, I am in a different atmosphere. I word vomit.

"He just ate me out and then made me come again. That man is perfection, like I wish I was exaggerating. Every move he makes, praise Lina. Jade, he is rough. Like, throw you down, but then asks for consent before touching you. When I'm around him, I can't get enough, like I'm drawn to him. A couple months ago, I hadn't even made out with someone, now all I want him to do is fuck me. I don't know if this is a good thing or if I am losing it."

"Hot damn. I think if a man slammed me against a desk, I would come on the spot."

"Jade, be serious with me," I groan.

"Well, I was being serious, but okay. You're allowed to feel alive. He is opening you up to something you haven't experienced and by the sound of it, doing a damn good job. Enjoy it, Ro."

She helps me fix my hair and straighten my dress before we make our way out of the bathroom and head back into the dance hall.

The guys are all standing at the drink table. As we walk up, Zayn holds a lemonade out to me.

"Thank you," I say almost blushing.

He leans in. "No. Thank you." His tone suggestive.

We all have a few more dances and then the party begins to file out.

Zayn and I decide to have one last dance before we go. When I feel his entire body tense, I only have time to peer up at him but I hear a deep voice behind me speak.

"Zayn, I haven't seen you all night, who is this beautiful lady?"

"I have been here the entire time," Zayn says motioning to the dance hall, all too defensive.

He towers before us, a murderous smile twisting his lips. I don't need an introduction to realize who he is. I feel myself shrink in his presence.

Deep lines fanned from the corner of his dark gray eyes —an unmistakable mark of someone who narrows their eyes often. His eyes are missing the light Zayn's carry. His hair is as dark and thick as Zayn's, besides the singular strip of gray in the front.

He is handsome, and pictures don't serve him justice.

But, the energy that radiates off of him is enough to churn your gut.

"Excuse my son's lack of manners," the man says. "My name is Terran. What is yours?" He reaches his hand out in front of him to shake mine, with one arm tucked behind his back. The way Zayn freezes up has me nervous. I hesitate and don't immediately reach to shake his hand. Zayn steps closer to his dad, trying to put distance between us.

"Her name is Pen. She was just leaving," he says before turning to me. "It really was nice to meet you. I'll call."

I go along with it knowing he has a reason.

"I'm sorry." I try to mend my reaction to his father. "I didn't mean to be rude. It was a beautiful party. I'm thankful to have been invited." I reach to shake his hand.

"Thank you, you are welcome in our home any time."

Schooling my face as I nod. I release his hand and say goodbye. I take this as my chance to leave.

I hear them whisper shout behind me as I walk away.

Their home? This is Zayn's house? Why wouldn't he say that? Now the way Oliver and Jade looked at each other earlier makes sense. Not to mention Zane's comment, *"Maybe one day you can."*

I stand in front of his house, looking to see if Christian is anywhere to be found. I didn't have time to look for Jade, so I don't have my phone to text anyone.

Zayn runs outside after me. *Thank Lina.* "I'm so sorry. I lied about your name because I didn't want him to have any of your information. I hated to do it. I just didn't want you to leave without you knowing that."

"It's okay, really, with everything going on its probably for the best, for now," I reassure him.

He smiles and grabs both sides of my face. "You're right, he will know your name one day."

"Can you please text Oliver that I'm waiting out here? Jade has my phone."

"Of course." I hear the swoosh of a message being sent before he turns to me again. "I had a great time tonight. Thank you for coming."

"Thank you for the dress and mask." I smile up at him, grabbing the sides of my dress in a mock curtsy.

He kisses me. "Bye, Aurora."

"Bye," I say smiling as he walks backwards to the front door.

CHAPTER 17

FATHER DEAREST

ZAYN EVERETT

I walk back into the house hoping I can escape to my room before my father finds me. I unlatch the rope blocking the stairs. As soon as my foot hits the first stair, I hear my mother's voice, "Was that her?"

I spin around at her question, stepping back onto the main floor. "Who?" I question her.

She tilts her head at me with a knowing glare.

Her bright blue eyes stare at me with disapproval. Her chestnut hair that normally falls to her hips is pulled tight into a bun. She tilts her head, waiting impatiently for my response.

"Yes." My eyes fall to my feet in shame. I know she won't be happy with me. I have gotten too close.

She shakes her head at me, "I had a feeling. She looks just like her mother. I watched you two dancing; you are infatuated with her. It's clear she isn't just a means to an end. Do you have any idea what you are doing?"

I don't respond, at a loss for words. This was never a part of the plan, getting close to her, touching her.

Her voice grows quieter as she responds to me. "She's absolutely beautiful."

My smile brightens as I look at her. Her mask is still on her face, but her smile is completely visible.

"She really is," I agree.

"You have to be careful with beautiful women, Zayn. Don't let your dick distract you from your plans, your future."

"I won't," I promise and mean it; Aurora is a part of those plans.

She reaches for my face, tapping my cheek softly. We spend a few more minutes discussing the party and who is left in attendance. She walks away, so I try to make my way up the stairs again.

I'm almost all the way up when I see my dad standing at the top of them. *Fuck, I was so close.*

"Come with me," my dad commands. I follow behind him as he leads me to his study. I know the routine.

He rounds his desk and sits in his chair while I close the door behind us.

I wait for him to speak as I sit down in one of the two chairs in front of his desk. He uses the study downstairs for guests, the one I took Aurora to earlier. This is his private study. No one else—even the housekeepers—can enter unless he is with them.

He pours a glass of whiskey before finally acknowledging my presence. "You left me no choice. Your little show tonight caused a lot of attention. I have made the arrangements and you are to marry Eliza after completion of the academy."

"That is not fucking happening," I raise my voice.

My dad stands up and presses both of his palms into his desk. "It is and you will. Now, I suggest you don't raise your voice at me again boy. Maybe I will have to go out and find your pet. She sure did look delicious," he says with a menacing grin on his face.

I launch myself forward. Before I even reach his desk, he suffocates the air from my lungs. I scratch and rip at the bands he has wrapped against my throat. He throws me against the wall with them, pinning me there. He laughs with callous amusement as he deprives me from oxygen. Right when I stop fighting, he releases his power, and I drop to the floor. I pant and cough trying to allow the air to be restored to my lungs.

"Watch yourself, son. That is the only warning you will get. Where did you think that was going to go, hmm? Were you going to hurt me?" he mocks. "That's a fucking joke. Get the fuck out of my study. If you lift a finger to ruin the arrangement in place, I will kill your pet and leave her in your bed for you to find. The question is, what would I do to her first?"

He has a grin plastered on his face as he sits back down and lifts his glass to his lips.

I don't say anything, I can't say anything. If I do, he will know she means more to me. My plan has to work, which means 'marrying' Eliza. I won't let it get that far. I just have to tell Aurora that the girl she almost ended everything over is now my future wife. *Fuck me.* I step out of his office and the door slams behind me, rattling the walls.

The idea of him touching Aurora, the things I know he would do...I run to the closest bathroom and throw up all of the contents of my stomach. I flush the toilet and rush out of the house, passing by the stragglers on my way.

My throat is hoarse; I cough trying to clear it. In desperate need of something to drink.

I hate my dad. When I was young, he was barely around. I had no idea who he was. As I got older, I started seeing the real him more. I don't know how much my mom knows, but I know my sister idolizes him.

There is nothing I can do to protect them. He's right, I'm powerless. I have seven months until the ceremony. I have spent every day counting down. Most may be scared of the ceremony, but I'm not. I need it, I need to be one step closer to dismantling our fathers. I can't do that when I'm weak. I'm so fucking sick of waiting.

Daniel, Elijah, and I have been waiting for years, for any piece of information we can find to figure out what it will take. We have come to the conclusion we will be stuck in this never ending loop until we graduate and are set to take over. From what we have heard, our grandfathers stayed involved in decisions for a few years after our dads were appointed. Then, they only appear every now and then.

If we can just get through until they think we can be trusted to operate how they would, we can react.

I get to Daniel's and text him to meet me outside. When he does, I fill him in on what happened, and we agree we need to meet up with Elijah and Oliver and see if he has found anything yet.

We stayed at Elijah's last night trying to strategize what to do next. We barely got any sleep before the sun came up. None of us are any closer to figuring out how Aurora's powers are forming or if there is any way to bind them until the ceremony is performed. They won't think twice about her having access to fire at that point.

We leave early in the morning and Elijah drives us to pick up Oliver. We wait down the street for him. Oliver not being able to drive is incredibly fucking inconvenient. It's not like I can show up at his house without Aurora asking questions.

Once we pick him up, we head to the diner down the

street from their house. We don't go inside, that would bring too much attention to us.

"Did you bring it?" I ask.

"This is all I could find. I have to get it back immediately before they notice it's gone," he says, handing me a manila folder. I flip it open, reading through the documents. There's a birth certificate with Aurora's name on it and John and April are listed as her parents.

There are no adoption forms in here at all. I keep sorting through, finding nothing out of the ordinary. There are doctor and dental records, copies of her license application—

I stop when I find a copy of their home insurance paperwork. In 2011, their house was severely damaged in a fire. It looks like the damage was primarily to the living room and kitchen. The insurance claimed it originated from the stove being left on.

"Oliver, are you sure you read through this?" I ask.

"I mean, I glanced at everything, but it was just a bunch of paperwork. I didn't see anything stating an adoption. I thought that's what we were looking for."

I try not to roll my eyes at such simplistic thinking. "Do you remember anything about your house needing to be rebuilt after a fire?

"No? When?"

"In 2011, your living room and kitchen had serious damage from a fire. There's insurance paperwork in here." I show him the pictures that were attached to the claim.

"My parents have never said anything about it," he says with worry on his face. I can tell he is thinking the same thing I am. Was this the incident that made her parents start being more careful? But what happened?

"Okay. Maybe try and see if you can notice anything at home about it. We know that she wasn't formally adopted. Meaning, your parents forged the birth certificate as if your mom gave birth. We need to find out how they ended up with Aurora."

I place everything in order of how I found it and close the folder before handing it back to him.

CHAPTER 18
HAPPY NEW YEAR
ZAYN EVERETT

I t has been weeks since I have been able to touch her, to hold her. Halloween has played on an endless loop in my head.

Every time I close my eyes or rest my head, I think back to two moments.

The first being the moment Aurora forced my hand, she didn't let me sulk in my own mind. I tried to stay away from her, worried in that moment I would hurt her. But, she pulled me into her, as if she wanted my pain.

It clicked in that moment, that's just who she is. It made my desire for her grow, still. My head between her legs was pretty fucking awesome, too, but it's the emotional connection that keeps replaying. The distance between us is eating me alive.

The second being that I'm fucking 'engaged,' the rage I feel for my father has never been greater.

Every event I am told to attend with Eliza, I want to slit her throat. She's relentless, trying to seduce me every chance she gets. I think she may have forgotten the virginal promise behind a Founders wedding.

She even had the audacity to tell me that I wasn't allowed to date anyone until we marry. She clearly needs to seek a therapist if she actually thinks I am going through with this wedding. She's barely even in town because she is at the academy. Since we have been 'arranged' she has received a pass to come to events. I gag at the idea of seeing her.

The little I do talk to Aurora, she always asks how Eliza is. No matter how many times I say that it's nothing.

Since the semester ended, Aurora and I don't have a single class together. I considered putting in for a transfer for one of my classes to be switched, but I can't draw attention to her. At least we have lunch together.

But, it kills me that I haven't seen her since Christmas break started.

Daniel, Elijah, Oliver and I have been relentless in our search. Aurora has asked Oliver so many times if we have gotten anywhere and he keeps telling her, "Not yet."

It's not exactly a lie, but I'm not sure how much longer she will buy it.

Some kid from school is throwing a New Year's party tonight. I told her I couldn't go so I could surprise her.

I can't stay away from her much longer. I can't wait until the day I can make it up to her for all this shit.

There she is. I have been searching for her for almost half an hour. What the fuck is she doing? I watch as her, Ruby, and Jade dance on a table. Aurora is wearing a short black dress that barely covers her ass.

Her and Jade look wasted, but Ruby seems fine. Josh is standing at the edge of the table laughing and cheering them on with a bottle of vodka in his hands.

Daniel walks up beside me. "What the fuck are they doing?"

"I just asked myself the same thing."

"I'm going to kill her," Daniel says narrowing his eyes at Jade across the room before stomping off towards her.

"Good luck with that."

He rushes up to her and I follow behind. He yanks on her wrist yelling something into her ear. Her face pales before she is ripped out of the room.

I look up at Aurora. "What are you doing?"

"Oh, me? I'm dancing, Zayn. That's what people do at parties." she says before she takes a chug from the bottle of beer in her hand.

I huff in annoyance. "Obviously. Why are you wasted, causing a scene on the table right now? Wearing barely anything? Aurora, its freezing outside."

She leans down so she is closer to my face, her ass poking out into the air. "Zayn, don't worry about me. I am a big girl. You have Eliza. I am here to have fun. We aren't fun anymore. Come back for me when you aren't engaged." she slightly slurs.

How many fucking times do I have to say that it won't happen, that I am not going to marry her? I am so fucking over this marriage talk, it's all bullshit.

"Aurora, get down please," I ask through gritted teeth.

She drops down, sitting on her knees on the table. She spreads her legs, just enough for me to see the tiny scrap of black fabric covering her slit. I huff a deep breath.

"Or what?" She tilts her head to the side, testing me.

I lean in. "Or, I am going to take you to the closest room I can and make you really fucking regret coming here. I'm going to show you that it was a big mistake to come to a party, wearing something so short that anyone can see up it while you dance on a table."

"So fucking make me regret it," she spits out.

I grab her by her hips and throw her over my shoulder. Using one arm to hold her in place, and my other hand covers her ass so no one can see up her dress.

There's an open room a few doors down the hall. I kick the door shut behind me and lock it before I throw her down on the bed.

She squeals as she bounces up and down before her body settles into the mattress.

"I can't fucking contain myself with you. The distance I've created between us is only to keep you safe. Don't you get that? My dad will kill you if you get in the way of his plans." I throw my arms up in annoyance, needing her to understand the reality we're facing.

She is leaning up on her elbows, one knee bent the other straight down. "I'm not scared of your dad," she says nonchalantly, unfazed by the potential threat.

"I'm scared of my dad, how are you *not*?" I raise my voice, almost yelling at her.

"While you've been running scared, I have been practicing. You have been so focused on creating distance, you haven't once asked me how I wanted to approach any of this. Did you consider that?"

I stay quiet.

"Didn't think so. I'm not worried about your dad, Zayn. I want you. No one will hurt you, and no one will hurt me." She pauses. "I have been spending my time reading every single book I can on controlling my magic. I have repeatedly gotten myself so angry I could blow up everything around me, just to learn how to control it. It was pretty easy given the material I have had to work with lately. Do you trust me?"

That isn't even a question. Of course, I trust her. She raises her eyebrows at me waiting for an answer.

"Yes, of course I do."

She stands up from the bed and closes her eyes. I watch her as she raises both arms out beside her, bent at her elbows. Her palms face the ceiling and she tilts her head back as both hands engulf in flames. I step back from the heat. She doesn't stop there. The fire crawls up both of her arms wrapping around them in a spiral of orange and red.

The flames dance in the air, heating up the room. They continue to grow higher until she suddenly suffocates the fire with a snap of her fingers, everything gone in the blink of an eye.

I stare at her in awe and confusion. People attend KAE for two years, focusing every ounce of their energy on controlling their powers. She can cease a fire that fast while drinking. She shouldn't be able to do that.

She stares at me deeply, the glowing embers of her eyes dimming, losing their energy. What was pure confidence a few minutes ago has turned into a look of terror.

She drops to the ground, slamming her head on a bench that was in front of the bed on her way down.

I rush to her side, dropping to my knees. "Aurora, Aurora, baby girl answer me." She doesn't, she's passed out.

Panicking, I call Daniel and tell him to get in here immediately with cold towels.

I'm pacing the small room when I hear a knock on the door. "Who is it?" I demand.

"It's me, open the door." Hearing Daniel's voice I open it quickly.

"What is she doing here?" I move to block the crack in the door as soon as I see Jade behind him.

"What the fuck do you mean, what am I doing here?

What are you hiding? Aurora, are you in there?" She slams into my chest with all of her strength.

Daniel looks apologetic at the same time Jade pushes the door hard enough for her to duck under my arms into the room.

CHAPTER 19
ANGRY BEST FRIENDS
ZAYN EVERETT

J ade sees Aurora lifeless on the floor with a pillow under her head. "Oh, my L—" She stops talking, "Is she okay?" She caresses Aurora's face and checks for a pulse.

I share a glance with Daniel, I don't know what the fuck I am supposed to do here.

"Why the fuck are you guys staring at each other? Eye fuck each other later. What the hell happened to her?" she yells at both of us.

"Tell her," Daniel says calmly in my direction.

"Daniel," I whisper-hiss.

Jade gets more and more agitated by the minute. "I'm going to punch both of you, tell me *what*?"

Aurora opens her eyes and clears her throat. "What did I miss?"

Jade slaps her across the face. I step forward, ready to

remove Jade from Aurora if need be. With one step Daniel whips his arm out, staring at me with silent warning that I better not touch Jade, while Aurora holds her hand out to me, telling me to stop.

She looks to Jade for answers.

Jade demands, "You better tell me what the hell is going on before I hit you again."

"Fuuck fine, damn it." Red says as she rubs her face.

I lean down to help her up, bringing her sit on the edge of the bed.

"What I say cannot leave this room. I didn't want you brought into this. I have purposely kept you out of it," she murmurs as she settles on the mattress.

"Go on," Jade motions her hand in a circle for Aurora to explain.

"I started showing signs of having access to my power the day after I went out with Zayn to the spring. I got so angry at Oliver and I burned right through my steering wheel. Zayn and Oliver helped me change it to cover it up. Then, it happened again a few days later." She hesitates before continuing with the story. The part that is a lot more damning for her, and for Austin.

Once Jade is told everything that happened with Austin, Aurora has to hold her back from leaving the room to go find him. Her anger is barely tamable.

"Everything was going great until the Halloween Party. Zayn's dad basically threatened him to leave me alone. Then, told him an arrangement was made for him." Her eyes fall. "When I found out, it kept every fiber of my being to hold back the anger. I have had a lot of time lately. Every time I felt the heat start crawling up, I focused on it. I allowed it to happen how I wanted it to. I have been studying, that's why I've spent so much time at the library. Also, to see if there were any answers on why this is happening to me. The passing out only happens when I haven't eaten. I forgot to eat since breakfast. I swear I'm okay. It was a stupid mistake that I have made before."

We all stare at Aurora when she finishes, waiting to see what is going to happen next.

Jade turns around, spinning her neck slowly. "Did you know?" she asks Daniel, her voice cracking.

"Yes, I knew most of it. I didn't know she had been testing her powers. But J, you have to understand, telling you meant that you weren't safe. It would make you an accomplice, we have enough people involved in this."

She walks over to him, stabbing him in the chest with her pointer finger. "You knew my best friend was alone, that she was suffering through it. With a couple of you idiots who have barely even been around her lately. It should have been my fucking choice; don't you get that? Fuck you, Daniel," she curses.

"J, please. We can talk about this later."

"No, it's not a discussion. I'm so fucking sick of people making decisions without talking to the other people it affects. See how it feels!" She whips her head back to Aurora. "That goes to you too, how dare you? I don't give a shit about my life; my life is fucking pointless if I don't have you in it. I live for you and Ashton. You are selfish, and you didn't care about what I want. That really fucking hurts. When have I ever given you the impression I wouldn't be there for you?" Tears pour from her cheeks in frustration.

"I'm sorry," Aurora murmurs through watery eyes.

Jade sits down beside her. "Are you okay to go home?"

Aurora nods her head in response.

"Okay, whichever one of you drove is taking us home," Jade demands, scrubbing her face with the back of her hand. "We clearly drank too much to drive. So, get over yourselves and take us back to Aurora's. We will talk to you when we feel like it."

Daniel and I don't bother arguing, we both know this is more between them, than about us. I can't help but feel bad for Daniel though, he seems genuinely hurt. It was Aurora's decision not to tell Jade, and now, Daniel is taking the blame for it. Even though I believe her not telling Jade was the right choice, that doesn't seem to matter right now.

The girls grab their coats on the way out, saying goodbye to their friends as they pass.

I drive them to Aurora's. Daniel follows behind us in Aurora's car. We didn't want her to have to leave it there and find a way to pick it up.

I quickly get out and circle the car. I open the door for Aurora so I can talk to her before she goes inside.

"Give us just a minute please," I ask Jade.

She squints her eyes at me. If she stands in the way of me talking to Red, I am going to lose it. I stare back at her, not standing down. She huffs and turns towards the front door, completely ignoring Daniel on her way. I watch her cross her arms in annoyance as she stands by the door, waiting for Aurora.

"I'm sorry I wasn't there for you. I should have asked how you were and what you needed. But Aurora, you should have told me about practicing your magic. I could have been there to make sure you didn't burn yourself alive," I say.

The night air slashes through us, sending a chill down my spine. I wonder if Aurora is cold, if she wants my jacket, but I don't say anything yet. I don't want her to mistake my kindness for charity. She is pissed off enough at me and I don't want to make it worse.

Instead, I reach my hand out for hers. She is warm to the touch, comforting me. I'm thankful when she doesn't pull away. She looks down at our hands but doesn't interlace her fingers with mine. They just sit there, together but not connected.

When her eyes meet mine again, she responds, "Yes, you should have asked. I don't owe you anything. I want to tell you things, but not when we are barely speaking. Am I supposed to update you on everything? Like you do me?" she counters. "That's right you don't, because you haven't updated me on anything you guys have found. I don't even care anymore why I have them. I needed to be able to get through the ceremony without anyone detecting them. That meant I needed to learn control, so I did. I'm okay, Zayn. I still have work to do, but I can keep the fire at bay even when my emotions are heightened. I'm not a risk to myself."

I forfeit. "I'm sorry, I really am. I have been so pissed off at things with my dad. I should have considered how you felt. For what it's worth, I am really fucking proud of you. What you showed me today...you were remarkable. I don't know if anyone has ever been able to self-train themselves, let alone this fast. Will you please call me tomorrow?"

A hint of a smile crosses her face, but she tries to hide it. "Yes, I will. Goodnight, Zayn."

I kiss the top of her hand before releasing it. I look up to Daniel and motion for him to throw me her keys, reaching my arms around her to catch them.

I hand them back to her and watch as she heads to the front door and they enter the house. The car ride home is quiet, neither one of us want to discuss tonight's events.

CHAPTER 20

BREAKING BREAD

AURORA DAVIS

W hen we're finally in my room, I turn to Jade. "Let's drop my shit for now. Daniel is who you've been with, for how long?"

"We've been seeing each other since way before school started back. We agreed not to tell anyone, so his family wouldn't find out," she says. "It's not like I could ever be with him. It will be over one day and that's it. Might as well end it now, he clearly doesn't trust me."

I can relate to her having to keep it a secret and the frustration that holds. "It was never about him not trusting you. I wanted as few people brought into it as possible. I didn't want any of my friends or family to know what has been going on. You can blame me, but you can't blame him."

I may not be Daniel's biggest fan, but this isn't his fault.

"Actually, I can," she announces leaving no room to argue. "He should know me, he should know that you were just trying to keep me safe, that I wouldn't give a shit about any of that. He should have told me anyway. Is his loyalty to Zayn more important than me? Never mind, don't answer that. Clearly, it is."

"Maybe you should talk to him?" I offer "Explain why it hurt you that he didn't come to you?"

She begins getting undressed. "Maybe, but for now, I want nothing to do with them. Can I stay here?" She doesn't give me any time to answer as she crawls under my covers.

Jade and I knew we needed to talk to the guys at some point. We called them and asked if we could meet up so there's no secrets between any of us anymore. We all clearly have shit we need to figure out.

We meet a little further into town where—hopefully—we won't be bothered by anyone. Jade and I grab a booth all the way in the back of the restaurant.

I'm starving and all I can think about is bacon. I would love to say that the hunger has gone back down, but I have been eating almost three times as much as I normally would in a given day since practicing my gifts. It's becoming extremely time consuming and expensive.

After we order our drinks, the guys keep telling the waitress they need more time. As soon as she walks away, *for the third time,* I snap at them. "Please, please figure out what you guys want to eat. I'm going to die."

Everything has been so tense. I can handle it, but not like this, not on an empty stomach. They finally figure out what they want to eat and when she comes back, they order right away. I let out a deep exhale of relief.

She takes our orders, collects our menus, and walks away. Zayn decides to speak first, attempting to break bread with Jade.

"I don't know where to start. I just know that a lot of things were said last night. Jade, you don't have to like me, but I am trying to do what is best here. Aurora is my priority, and I will do what she wants. Now that you know what's going on, I will let you know if something happens with her. If Aurora and Daniel trust you, I will too."

"About time." She rolls her eyes.

"Why don't we all just enjoy the meal together. We can't really talk about the heavy shit here, and there's no point in trying to tiptoe around it," I offer.

"When did you become so grown up?" Jade asks, jokingly.

"I'd say it was life or death, but that seems a bit drab." Everyone laughs except for Zayn, whose eyes bore into mine.

No mention of death, got it.

CHAPTER 21
BRIDGES AND QUESTIONS
AURORA DAVIS

Before I can make it to my car, Zayn stops me.

"Hey, can we please go somewhere? I miss hanging out with you."

"Where do you want to go?"

"I have an idea." His eyes fill with mischief.

"Just us, or *all* of us?" I ask.

"Let's all go, it looks like they have some things they need to work out."

We glance over at Daniel and Jade who are fighting across the parking lot. They are a lot more serious than I realized. She loves him, and from the looks of it, he clearly loves her, too. I hope they can find a way through it.

Zayn tells me to leave my car here at the diner, I don't argue. Riding with him means being closer to him. Daniel and Jade both climb into the back seat, so I get into the front.

I pause when I go to grab the seat belt because Zayn places his hand on my thigh. I stare at it, thinking about the way his touch makes me feel. Things between us have essentially dissipated, but that doesn't mean the feelings have, at least not for me. Being close to him makes sense to me. I feel calm in his presence.

"It's going to be a bit of a drive, but it's worth it." Zayn announces before looking in his rear view mirror at Daniel who gives him a knowing smile.

"Wow, this is incredible." Jade says in awe as she looks around. We had to take a hike to get this far up, but it was well worth it.

In front of us is a large bridge overlooking some of the highest mountains in Kyrosia. I have never been this far up before. It is absolutely breathtaking.

A thick layer of white snow covers the mountains, blanketing their dark rock. The jagged peaks beyond are tucked away behind a wall of fog, just enough that you can see the white outlines like a shadow.

I love the snow. Chunky clothes keeping you warm, fixing a bad hair day with a beanie. The joy of sitting on your couch, cuddled under a blanket, sipping hot chocolate. Oh, and your family huddled in front of a fire watching movies, pure bliss.

Don't get me wrong, I do love the way the sun coats my

skin, but I have always enjoyed the colder months when the snow is here. I am too warm of a person to prefer the heat.

The guys walk up to a large bridge and step onto it as if it is nothing out of the ordinary to them. We watch as it sways under their weight, screeching as the boards rub together.

Jade and I look at each other in shock, our eyes wide in horror at this historic bridge they're expecting us to trust and cross. I would estimate that it's about a mile long. It has to be spelled because there is no way a bridge would be able to withstand the elements for this long.

"Fuck me," I hiss under my breath before we both step onto the bridge simultaneously.

As I feel it rock beneath my feet, I let out a deep breath. Trying to ease my nerves and get across in one piece. I hold onto the rope for dear life.

Zayn and Daniel stare at us from safe land on the other side with humor crackling through their smirks.

Each step we take across the bridge, it creaks, the sound making my heartbeat faster. I'm nauseous by the end, physically needing to be off the damn thing already.

I listen to the world around me for a minute, taking it in. Birds chirp and the wind rushes through the trees. It would almost be nice, if I wasn't so terrified that I could fall off it at any moment.

Finally, we get to the end and step off the bridge.

"I would very much like to not do that again," I quaver.

Jade looks like she's about to piss her pants, hands on

her knees as she tries to slow her breathing. "Can I second that?"

Daniel pats her back in fake sympathy, but she shrugs his touch away.

"It's safe I promise," he says. "As kids, we would run across the bridge for hours. My mom would take us here to get our energy out. Whenever she would want some peace and quiet, she would come sit against the mountain ridge and read while we played."

He continues, "I remember one day, Zayn cut his knee and my mom said that the fresh air would heal it. He yelled at her and said it wasn't true, that she was lying to him. He was still bleeding when we got in the car. We both passed out on the way home. When we woke up his knee was completely healed. She would say, 'magic is most powerful when it is at its purest. When you need to heal, come here. Breathe it in. Feel it carry you away.' I never did know what she meant by it. She hasn't come here in years. I miss seeing her sit there, she looked so at peace."

I imagine what that may have been like. I see a version of Zayn, Daniel, and Elijah running around, playing tag and falling so close to the edge of a mountain. I would be a nervous wreck.

Each step I take further from the bridge, I feel weird. Almost sick to my stomach. My skin tingles everywhere.

"Guys, I don't feel so good," I say.

Zayn rushes to my side. "What's wrong?"

"I don't know, I can't explain it. Ever since we got off

the bridge, I've felt sick. I was listening to Daniel as we walked around and it just got worse. Maybe it's the food from breakfast? Do you guys all feel okay?" I ask.

We ate primarily the same things, I can't imagine why I wouldn't feel good. They all tell me they are fine, making this even more odd.

"Why don't we head back?" Zayn suggests to me before turning to Daniel and Jade. "You guys can stay here, and I'll take Aurora back for now. If she feels better, we can come back."

I nod in agreement. Jade is hesitant but ultimately agrees with the demand that we don't go past the bridge without telling her so she can come with.

We start heading back over the bridge and as soon as we are halfway over, I turn around to face Zayn.

"Zayn, I'm fine."

"What do you mean you're fine, are you feeling better?"

"Like, I'm fine. As if it didn't happen. I feel completely normal like I did before we went over the bridge." I don't understand what's happening, but nothing is wrong with me now.

"But, how?" he asks, puzzled.

"Hold on, wait here." I run back to where we just came from, no longer holding onto any fear of the bridge. Once I reach the end, I turn around and face Zayn who hasn't moved. I close my eyes for a minute.

Everything returns. Except this time, I don't feel sick. I

feel strong, like my senses are heightened. Keeping my eyes closed, I focus in on the sounds around me. I can hear every noise as if I am standing right next to it. If I focus hard enough, I can hear Daniel and Jades footsteps and whispers.

My eyes shoot open, staring at him across the way. He comes running without me saying anything to him.

When he reaches me, he grabs my shoulders. At his touch my heart races. I'm in tune with him. I can hear his heart beating, the way his breathing picks up. I start to shake. The realization hitting me like a brick wall.

"Zayn," I say, my voice shaking.

"What is it, are you okay?" he demands in a panic.

"I'm not sick. I can't explain it. It's magic. I can feel it. Not like I can at home, or when I draw from my powers. It's natural, like there's a line. I didn't feel it the first time because it was new, I didn't know any better. Now that I am paying attention, it's strong. I can feel every ounce of power in my body. The fire...I can feel it flowing like a river through me. Do you feel the magic?"

"No, I don't feel anything at all," he answers, sounding disappointed.

I turn around fast. "Daniel, Jade!" I yell, trying to get their attention.

"Hold on, we are coming!" Jade hollers back.

When they reach us, I ask, "Do you feel any different, even at all?"

They look at each other in question and both shake their heads no.

"We are completely fine. Why are you asking that again?" she inquires.

"I need to talk to your mom." I turn my attention to Daniel. I don't ask, I state it.

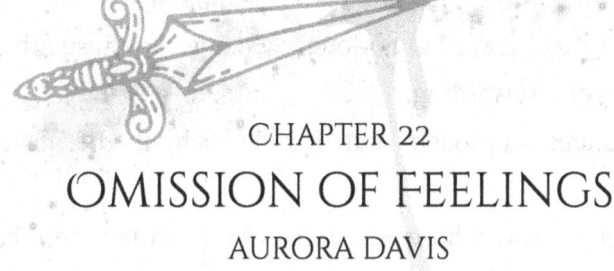

CHAPTER 22
OMISSION OF FEELINGS
AURORA DAVIS

I t has been two months since I told Daniel I needed to meet with his mom. I have tried my best to give him time to approach her about it but I'm sick of waiting.

Jade has been distant lately. Her birthday came and went, and she refused to do anything. All of us begged her to have a party or allow us to do something for her, but she wouldn't.

I keep trying to get her to talk to me, but she only gives me a few sentences at a time. I know it is something with her parents because even Ashton has been around the house less.

With her hardly over, I've been spending most of my time here at the bridge. I feel more myself here. I can also control my powers better here since they're stronger. Although, I never push it, the only thing I try to do is start and stop them. I allow the fire to grow and then snuff it out.

KAE will teach me how to grow my powers in a healthy way. I don't need to learn anything else on my own, the relief I feel that I am no longer a danger to those around me is beyond rewarding.

Footsteps approach and I hide behind the nearest alcove.

When I know who it is, I come out. I can feel him, hear him, smell him. I have become so in tune with his body and soul lately. It's as if he is an extension of me. Even when I'm over the bridge, I'm aware of him before he enters the room. But how do I explain that to him without sounding obsessed or creepy?

"What are you doing here?" I ask.

"I would ask you the same question, but my messages haven't been going through for hours. I figured you were here and decided to come join you." Zayn and I have talked constantly since we were here the first time. Sometimes he joins me when he needs time away from the noise.

Being here, I can breathe easier. When I leave, it's like a film is over my chest, restricting me.

The snow has stopped. It's started warming up as spring approaches. I've been bringing a blanket with me lately to sit up here and write or draw.

We sit down on the blanket where he curls me into his side. "I need to tell you something," Zayn states, ominously. I scoot out from under his arm to look up at him.

"Daniel's mom has agreed to come here and meet you next Saturday."

Finally! I feel like I've been waiting forever just to hear something from her or Daniel.

"Why don't you sound happy about that?" I ask.

"It's just that things have been so good between us. I feel like we're finally at a point where we can come here and it just be us. Like, here, I'm not a Founder and you are just *you*. I don't know if I'm ready to let go of that just yet," he admits.

Instead of responding, I walk on my knees closer to him. I throw my leg over his hip, lowering myself onto his lap. He leans forward wrapping both hands around my butt. I move one of my hands up to run it through his hair where I scratch his scalp like he enjoys. I practically lose myself in his eyes.

"Zayn, don't you realize that this is what we need? I've been killing myself trying to understand why I feel so different here. That must be why Daniel said his mom seemed so peaceful here." I sigh. "I think I can feel the difference because of my access to magic. I think that some tether is loose that allows me to reach into it."

"I'm just worried that maybe she doesn't have the answers you are wanting," Zayn says. "Or she knows less than you think she does and you'll just be let down. I don't know how else we will get the information you are searching for."

I think how best to explain this for a moment. "It's not

just the why. There are also a few things I haven't told you yet. I know I should have, but I've been trying to understand everything."

Zayn arches a brow.

"The first being that I can feel something else. The fire is there, but it's not all I feel. There is something powerful but frozen inside of me. I can't focus on it. I've been trying to sense what it is, but I can't pinpoint it. I think it may be another power lying dormant."

When I finish explaining he doesn't look remotely shocked.

"Why don't you look surprised?" I ask.

"Elijah thought you may have a second specialization. He didn't think it made sense that you would be granted this gift, then nothing happen at the ceremony."

"Why wouldn't you tell me that you guys thought that?"

He rubs his hand over his face. "I didn't tell you because we have no idea what to believe. No one has ever experienced something like this. No amount of research would tell us anything. None of us will know until the ceremony. You have been stressed as it is, why would I give you another thing to worry about?" He sounds like he is pitying me. He should have told me. You think the recent battles of non-disclosure would have been enough for him to talk to me. I shake my head, changing the subject before it becomes a useless argument.

I roll my eyes. "Okay, moving on. The second thing I need to tell you is a bit more complicated..."

"Elaborate, please," he says, waiting for me to continue.

I've been wanting to tell him for weeks. It just never feels like the right time. I just need to spit it out.

"On the first day we came here, do you remember when you touched me when I ran back over the bridge?"

"Yes?" he answers in question.

"When you touched me, I felt something click for me. I don't really know how to explain it. It was really strong. Since then, it's like I can't be away from you for too long without feeling as if I am missing something. Like you're a part of me? I know it sounds crazy. It's just this over-whelming feeling of needing to be with you. I can sense when you are close. Something is screaming in the back of my mind that you are *mine*."

Zayn doesn't say anything at first, he reaches behind my head and pulls me in for a passionate kiss. In one swift motion he flips me over so I'm on my back. He leans over me, holding himself up on his elbow. His opposite hand makes slow movements over my shirt up to my neck.

"Well, either you love me, or I'm your mate," he says with complete confidence.

CHAPTER 23
MATED BY FATE
ZAYN EVERETT

The second she started explaining how she felt to me, I knew. I've heard about people having mates in the past. It's one of those folklore stories you hear about, the 'lucky ones.' Fated mates are *extremely rare*, I have heard the Founders talk about it before.

No one in the last several generations has been mated.

It makes so much sense when I think about it. The way I've felt pulled to her since I met her. The loss of control I experience in her presence. The primal need I have for her. I never realized she was my mate because I don't have any powers.

I smile, thinking about the moment I see her once it hits me. Man, now I can't fucking wait until the ceremony. The idea offers something positive instead of needing powers to survive.

This girl will be my wife. There is no way I'm letting

my mate slip through my fingers. I always planned to find a way free from the grasp of Eliza, but now my motivation and determination to be relinquished from her is greater.

"What do you mean—mate?" Red looks up, biting her lip and scrunching her eyebrows in confusion.

Is that why she is nervous or because I brought up love?

Still leaning over her, I start to explain. "Mating is extremely rare. It almost never happens. It only happens when two people who are meant to be together, meet. It's fate. An arrangement or love can't hold a candle to it. Those two become incredibly powerful together. It's said that mates can intertwine their powers. I have no idea if it's true or not, this is just word of mouth. But from what I've heard over time, less and less people mate."

She doesn't respond. Before she has a chance to over-think, I tell her, "Oh, and Aurora, I love you. I just thought you should know that before the ceremony. Once it hits that you *are* my mate, I don't want you to think that me loving you has anything to do with that. I have no expect—"

"I love you too," she cuts me off before I can finish.

"You do?" I ask, maybe I just need her to say it again. So I know I'm not imagining things. My heart races with anticipation.

"I do, I love you. When you said it was either love or I was your mate, you scared me. I didn't want to tell you first. Things have been so on and off since we met. My feelings for you have never wavered. Life just hasn't been on our side."

252

Her voice is soft, barely above a whisper. As if she is telling a secret she didn't mean for me to hear. I want to reiterate to her I never wanted to be apart from her, I have been obsessed with her, I would crawl on my knees at her demand. I have spent so long running in the other direction, for years I sat and watched.

I lower my body so I am pressing into her so she feels my erection. Leaning into her face. "Aurora, I will never be away from you again. You're stuck with me now."

"Damn it," she says as if that's such an inconvenience as her eyes flame with heat.

I grab her hands to sit her up. I start by removing her shirt. Peppering kisses on all of her exposed skin, leaving behind angry marks as I suck and nibble on her skin.

Her bra is next to go, slowly. I lay her back down and feast on her breasts, taking each bud between my teeth gently, causing her to hiss in pleasure.

Between kisses I voice my love for her, my desires. "Red, I love you. I intend to keep showing you my love. Whether that is devouring your pussy on my knees at your command, or standing by your side, I will show you show just how much you deserve."

I continue kissing down her body until I get to her jeans, unhooking her button. She leans her hips up so I can pull them down her legs. Before pulling them off completely, I remove her boots. Throwing them to the side.

All that's left are her panties. I leave them on for now, pushing them to the side I check to see if she's wet. I push a finger inside of her warm pussy but she reaches to stop me. "Wait, I'm sick of being naked and you being dressed. I want your clothes off now."

"Are you sure?"

"Will you stop fucking asking me that?"

I let her take the lead. She sits up on her knees, so I lean back on mine. She grabs the hem of my shirt and pulls it up over my head. When she gets to my belt, her hands shake. I hold my hands over hers and help her undo the buckle, ripping it off. I kick off my boots and remove my jeans and boxers in one swipe as I come to stand.

She's still on her knees in front of me, staring at my dick. She has never seen me naked before. I have purposely kept everything slow, restraining myself to the point of jacking off in cold showers thinking about her. But, having her in front of me? *Fuck*. Seeing the way her red curls lay over her back and chest, all messy and frizzy. I love her undone like this, knowing I'm the only one to see her like this.

My dick aches for her to reach out and grab it, to shove it down her throat and make her gag. *Easy, Zayn, Easy.* I close my eyes to breathe through the temptations when her touch makes me jolt.

She has her hand wrapped around the base of my dick, making slow movements until she reaches the head.

"Aurora," I pant in warning. She doesn't stop, looking up at me to read how it feels. I wrap my hand around hers and squeeze a little to let her know she can put more pressure. She takes note and grips harder and picks up her speed. I grip the back of her hair in my hand. I don't pull it, despite my impulses telling me to.

She opens her mouth and slides my dick down her throat. Removing her hand, she takes it all the way in.

"Holy fuck, baby girl." I look down at her in absolute awe. She is so fucking sexy. She keeps moving in and out, I use the hand wrapped in her hair to push her head forward. She moans deep with her lips still wrapped around me.

No gag reflex, I've died and gone to heaven.

I don't stop, getting rougher as her moaning becomes louder. Right when I feel like I am going to come, I slow down. Red apparently doesn't agree with me as she reaches up and wraps one hand at the base and picks up speed.

"Aurora, I'm going to come if you don't slow down," I growl. She takes this as a challenge to keep going and before I can process anything else, I come hard, straight down her throat. She swallows every drop, like the good girl she is, and the second she releases me I lay down on the blanket.

She takes this opportunity to jump onto my lap, I quickly reach to adjust my dick so it isn't near her. When she realizes she scoots further up my stomach where she lays down on top of me. "How was it?"

"Ask me tomorrow, I need a nap," I say, joking with her as I close my eyes.

She grabs my hand I have resting on my chest and moves fast, sitting up and covering her pussy with it.

"No way. You aren't sleeping yet. You have work to do, it's my turn."

I gladly get to work making her feel good, knowing that I will make sure this is what my future holds. This woman who isn't scared to take what she wants. She excels in every single thing she does without trying. I cannot wait to see where the world takes her and sit by her side as she dominates the presence of those around her.

Honestly, finding out I am her mate might be the best thing that will ever happen to me.

We lay there on the blanket completely exposed, her head on my chest and my arm wrapped around her. Both of us are soaked in sweat. Turns out, she may still have a hard time controlling her body temperature. I pull her leg over me, my head resting in her hair as it flows over us.

"That was amazing, but now I can't stop thinking about fucking you." As soon as I say it, I realize maybe I shouldn't have. Especially when she doesn't respond right away.

"I don't know how this works." She clears her throat. "If we are mated, can we?" she asks hesitantly.

I sigh. "Unfortunately not. Even if we are mated, that doesn't change the policy that a woman shall remain pure for marriage."

"I hate all these rules, what purpose do they serve? Why can't we just be together? If we do get married, what difference does it make if we fuck before or after?"

She's right, it makes absolutely no sense. "Not *if* we marry, Red, *when* we marry. It shouldn't make a difference; it's just a way for the Founders to show control. They need their women entirely at their mercy. It's sick." I kiss her on the head. "Just hang tight, we'll be alright."

What I don't say, is that one day, I will make sure no man has any right over a women's body. Especially not my woman.

We lay there, talking and laughing for what feels like forever. Before we know it, it's getting dark. We have to head back before we end up hiking in the dark.

CHAPTER 24

MOTHERS AND PROPHECIES

AURORA DAVIS

I wait for Daniel's mom at the entrance of the trail. She's supposed to meet me this afternoon at 2:00 PM. I wait anxiously when I hear a car door shut. Finally, she turns the corner and I realize she's alone. I expected Daniel to be with her.

Not that I'm complaining about having to spend less time with him.

She's beautiful. She has the same fair, beige skin as Daniel and blue eyes. Her hair is rich with volume and blonde highlights, styled in loose waves, hanging over her workout jacket.

"Aurora, I presume?" She reaches out to shake my hand.

I hesitate. I'm not sure why I'm nervous, Daniel would have had to tell her who I am to get her here. But, I still find myself uncomfortable because Zayn's dad doesn't know my real name. Her being a Founder's wife has me questioning if this was the best idea.

I nod my head, reluctantly.

"It's okay, dear. Dan has told me everything. My name is Madeleine, why don't we walk? Sitting still makes me anxious these days." We merge onto the trail, my boots crunching over the leaves on the path.

"I know you don't know me," I start, "I'm thankful you agreed to meet with me. I need to make sense of things. I'm not sure if he told you 'everything,' but when Daniel brought me here, I felt different as soon as I crossed over the bridge. I've been coming here ever since. It feels like my body has been sleeping, then I reach that point and everything feels awake."

She nods her head in slow movements. "I know that feeling all too well. Dan told me you felt it. It took some prying, but he finally told me about your powers. When did you first exhibit signs?"

"After I turned 18. It's only happened a few times before I learned to control them. I've been working really hard to practice so my emotions don't trigger them."

"And how has that been going?" she asks.

"Honestly, at first it was hard. My body felt exhausted, and I lived in a constant state of starvation. Now, I don't even feel anything unless I forget to eat." I don't mention the time her son caught me passed out.

"I can't believe you have been able to do that by yourself, it's truly extraordinary. I'm sure you know this already, but it's really important you keep your powers to yourself. Don't tell anyone that you don't absolutely have to. Even after the ceremony, I wouldn't offer that information. You being able to take control over such a powerful specialization without training could make you immediately deemed as a threat."

"I know," I admit, feeling defeated. It's been hard. I feel like I am lying to everyone around me. Those who do know, primarily keep their distance.

I didn't realize though, that it was so difficult for people to train themselves versus having instructors. I mean it wasn't easy, but I would imagine plenty of people could do what I've done.

When we get to the bridge, she motions her hand forward "Shall we?"

As we walk across, I feel that familiar breeze of power rush through me, raising the tiny hairs on my body.

I turn around to look at Madeleine at the same time that I feel it. I watch her tip her head back in ecstasy. Her smile widens.

"I have truly missed this."

"Can I ask why you stopped coming?"

She sweeps her fingers along the bridge as we reach the end of it. "It feels like forever ago. It was one afternoon, we had just gotten home, and Dan was so hyper. I tried to tell the boys it was our 'private time', so they would keep it between us. But, one day he runs inside and tells daddy about how Zayn fell by the bridge and hurt his knee. How it was magical, and that it was heeled when he woke up. When I went to bed that night, Levi told me I had no business coming here. It wasn't safe and that I better not bring his son back here again. I tried to come back a couple more times by myself, but every time I did, I became more anxious that he would find us here. So, I stopped coming, it was easier than dealing with him if he found out I went against his wishes."

"I'm sorry," I offer as we step off the bridge.

"Don't be sorry. I've accepted it. I had no idea the boys had been here since that day until Daniel told me about your experience," she continues, "I want to help you with what it is you want to know. But I'm afraid I need to ask you something before we continue. I wouldn't say anything if it wasn't crucial to what comes next. Are you aware of who your parents are?"

"No...I don't," I say, swallowing the lump in my throat.

She stops walking and stands in front of me.

"This isn't going to be easy to hear. I wish I didn't have to be the one to tell you this. But unfortunately, it's time you know so you can make decisions about what your future holds. You may not know me, but I did know your mother."

I still, every muscle rigid as I wait for her to continue. I don't respond, unable to.

"Angela, Zayn's mother and I were best friends with her. We grew up together. You carry yourself just like she

262

did, and you look so much like her. Dear, your mother was Leanne Ariti."

"No." My stomach sinks.

"Yes. It's true. I confirmed it with Angela."

"But. How would she know?"

"I told Dan they needed to tell you—"

I don't hear anything else she says, my mind completely lost. She said 'they' needed to tell me. Obviously referring to Dan and Zayn. Zayn has known who my parents are? For how long?

Is this why Oliver and Zayn haven't been telling me anything, practically avoiding the subject as a whole?

I stay silent for a few minutes, running through every question in my brain when Madeleine interrupts me.

"Are you okay?" she asks softly, placing a hand on my arm to console me.

"I'm processing." Processing is a nice word for it. I'm hurt, I'm livid. Zayn just told me he loves me. Now, I find out he's been lying to me.

Then, there's that other small thing, like my mother was Gabriel Ariti's wife. Meaning the most powerful Founder is my father. Meaning my mother, his first wife, is dead.

"I would love to let you take your time on this, I know it is a lot. I'm so sorry, but I have to be back in 45 minutes. We have a lot of ground to cover during that time."

Madeleine begins to tell me how close her and my mother were. They grew up best friends. Their lives were different though. Both Angela and Madeleine came from

Founding families, my mother did not. Her family was of commoner origin, so she grew up much different from the way they did.

As soon as she performed the rite in the ceremony, her powers almost consumed her. Her unfortunate display of power had been seen by Gabriel's family, and they realized her potential. As soon as the ceremony was completed, they commanded she be married to Gabriel.

She never wanted to be with a Founder. She had saved herself so she could be with someone she loved the first time. Had she not, she would never have ended up with Gabriel.

I don't have time to think about what all this means for me. Every time she finishes one story, she rushes into another.

She explains to me the history behind the mountains and finally, the thing I have been waiting months for:

I learn that the bridge was built to cross into Kyrosia. There's a glamour placed at the edge of the bridge so no one inside can see out and no one on the outside can see in. That is how they were able to build the city we live in without being detected by anyone else. If anyone was to pass by, all they would see is mountains. What they didn't realize when creating the glamour, was that it can only extend so far. The Founders knew they could never grow Kyrosia because they could never figure out a way to extend the range.

That is why anyone who has access to their powers can

feel them deeper over the bridge. The hex placed on the city doesn't allow you to feel them at full strength, but they are definitely stronger than anyone is made to believe. They don't want anyone to know that their powers are greater elsewhere, or they will search for a way to leave.

The Founders have no idea what is left of where they came from, Zylenia, since so much time has passed.

She explains, "Some of us, for generations, have tried to find a way to see past the glamour, but we have come up empty handed. We have no idea if the fae in Zylenia have made peace or if they have been wiped out. We have not seen anyone who is able to perform a glamour spell. But if it was done originally, there has to be a way to do it again. If the information has been passed down through the generations of Founders, we certainly haven't heard of such tales. We can't even tell the boys this until we are sure of what they will do with the information. Soon, they will be in a position of ultimate power. This information could only make them protect the truth even further."

I listen carefully to everything she is telling me, but my mind is still reeling about my birth mother, Zayn, the secrets.

Madeleine continues, "I know right now this may not make much sense to you. Why I would willingly tell you this information, trusting you won't immediately run to Zayn with it? But you need to understand that the day may come where the boys' movement could depend on you to lead them. I believe that you are the answer. You are already extremely powerful, I can sense it. I have a feeling Zayn will be too.

"He also trusts you; I know how that may sound given he has not told you the truth about your family. But you need to know that a Founder has never chosen a woman over his duty. Zayn protecting your secret, all of our boys protecting it, proves that caring about people is more important to them than having power."

I know she's right, but it doesn't take away the sting of their betrayal.

"Us wives, with the exclusion of Myra, have worked very hard to train our sons to take the correct path since their births. Unfortunately, their fathers always find a way to take the upper hand. When it comes time to do what needs to be done, all we can do is hope that we have done enough to show them the right way." She pauses, considering her next words. "None of this is something that can be done overnight. It is going to take years for us to get anywhere. The boys won't be able to take their appointment until all four have passed KAE."

Where do I fit into their plan? Was I just a pawn to him? I don't understand, it doesn't feel like a game between me and Zayn. But, why would he keep lying to me?

"We are developing a plan to help Connor on the right path. Which we may need your help with when the time is right." She checks her watch, "I'm sorry but I don't have much time left. Please ask me as many questions as you want, but quickly."

I rapid fire questions, of course. "Does Gabriel know I am alive?"

"No," she returns.

"Where does he think I am?"

"Dead, that's a longer question for another time, dear. I promise to answer when we have more of it. I'm sorry."

"Who knows who I really am?"

"Myself, Angela, Laila, your parents, and whoever you have told."

"*What?*" My parents?

"Your parents work for the Founders, Aurora, they have always known who you are. They have done everything they can to protect you. Please go on."

I have so many questions, the most important being: "How did my mother die?"

Daniel's mom sighs heavily, fighting to swallow the knot in her throat. "The rumors weren't a lie. She killed herself. I'm so very sorry. I wish it wasn't true. I miss her dearly."

For so long I wondered who my birth mother was, if I would ever meet her. My heart silently breaks at the truth that she is dead. I will never meet her, hear her voice, understand why she gave me up.

But the pain ceases when I begin to wonder, what made her kill herself? It forms into anger, hunger for information.

The questions I have asked thus far don't even scratch the surface of the things I want to know. I try to think of anything else of dire importance, and come up empty handed. My mind completely blank. She starts walking back to her car quickly, she has to be home soon before her husband questions why she has been gone for so long.

"I am sorry, Aurora, I have to go. I will see you again. I will try to answer what I can but I do think you need to talk to Zayn and your parents. Please don't mention me. No one besides you, Zayn, and Dan can know I was here. I'm giving you a lot of trust, I expect it will be reciprocated."

"I won't, I promise," I assure her. "Madeleine, thank you."

With that, she gives me a curt hug.

I slowly walk over the bridge, staring at the mountains in front of me. I wonder where the glamour starts and how it works. What binds the glamour, keeping in place? It's crazy to think that there could be people out there looking for us. If there are, is it with the intent to harm us or reunite the fae? Maybe they think we are all dead because no one has found us.

I've heard stories about Queen Lina, but only from my mom when I was really little. Most of the stories are jumbled in my brain with other nursery rhymes and books as a kid.

There are only a few parts that I can remember clearly. I know that she was the queen who ruled the original land of the fae. She was the most powerful fae they had ever seen.

She was adamant about peace between all species. It was all she ever cared about, a land of peace and serenity. Until one day, she was murdered by her husband at the start of the war, and some of our people fled. They created Kyrosia as a sanctuary for the fae. Over time, the Founders seized control.

Thinking of the Founders reminds me of what Madeleine said. Zayn knew who my parents were and chose to withhold that information from me. Why would he do that? I have trusted him with everything. I thought we were finally at a good place and then *this*.

I need to see him immediately. I need to hear why he would keep something so important from me, he has to have a reason. Especially knowing how bad I have wanted to know more about who I am before the ceremony. I leave the mountains in a hurry and text him that he needs to meet me at his cabin immediately.

I throw my phone in the center console, not wanting or waiting for a response.

CHAPTER 25
HOW COULD YOU
AURORA DAVIS

I wait in my car anxiously for Zayn to get here. After a while, I finally give in and check my phone, he responded to me immediately and let me know he was coming.

Zayn's engine roars as he pulls into the driveway of the cabin. He cuts off the engine and exits his car. I watch as he waits patiently for me to meet him. I'm so fucking angry with him, I try to take a second to calm down.

I get out of my car, slamming the door behind me.

"Aurora—" Zayn starts.

Oh, so he knows why I'm mad.

"No, you don't get to talk yet. I am here to ask questions and get answers. When were you going to tell me you knew who my parents were? When did you find out?"

His shoulders sag, leaning back against his car. "I've known for a while that Gabriel had a daughter, but—"

"*But,* you told me you would help me find out more about who I was? You offered? Then, you kept the information away from me this entire time. Was your goal just to get close to me?" My voice raises with each question I ask.

"I wasn't—"

"*Don't fucking lie to me!*" Flames erupt from the ground in front of me in warning as I scream. Emotion controls our situation and I realize I'm not allowing him to get a word in, but I trusted him and he betrayed me, for what?

My voice drops. "Was I just something for you to play with, an excuse to get revenge on the Founders? Leverage against them, one day using me to your advantage? Why?"

Zayn looks at me with pity, yet again. As if I am this poor girl who he doesn't know how to help. I am so much more than that. I'm not a weakling searching for a man to guide me. I am done being lied to.

His eyes don't show an ounce of terror at my flare in powers fueled by rage. He isn't scared of me. It's frustrating that he wouldn't dare fear me. My anger eases knowing he doesn't think that I would hurt him, proving he trusts me. Even if I can't trust him right now. I close my eyes and breathe through the fire, allowing it to settle. When I open my eyes, he's staring at me.

"Can I talk?" he asks.

I nod in surrender, motioning for him to go ahead.

"What I was trying to say was I heard a rumor about a Founder's child dying in childbirth. Daniel and I tried to investigate the rumors, but we were coming up mostly empty handed. All we were able to find out was that your mom was pregnant and there was no record of a birth or a death.

"I spoke to my mom, and she did not know if the child lived or died. All I knew was the date the child should have been born. So, I started to pay attention to everyone in school to figure out who it could be and one day, I heard someone say it was your birthday. After mentally sifting through what I knew, it started to make sense it could be you."

"It made sense it was me because my birthday lined up, do you realize how preposterous that sounds?" I ask.

"It was more than that, Aurora, I had been connecting dots. Paying attention to things. As time went on and I learned more about you, I became fascinated with you. I tried to stay away, I really did. Then, you quite literally ran into me, making it impossible. But knowing what I know now, I don't think any of my attempts would have made a difference. I wasn't pulled to you from mere curiosity."

I walk up to the porch steps and decide to sit down. He pauses before taking a seat beside me.

We sit in silence for a few minutes before I ask him another question. "How old were you when you learned about me?"

"I was 15 when I heard the rumor. It wasn't until later that year when I began to connect the dots about it possibly being you whom I had been looking for."

"You watched me for two years?" I ask

"Yes," he admits.

"And you didn't think to try to approach me?"

"I couldn't Aurora" he says, honesty dripping from his voice. "I was to keep an eye on you. My only intention was to make sure you were safe from Gabriel. I wasn't supposed to become attached to you. I didn't think it was part of the plan. Fate had other ideas."

"Why didn't you tell me?"

He turns his body facing mine, bending one of his legs at the knee until it's flat against the step. He grabs my hands in his, trying to hold my attention.

"When do you suggest I'd have done that? When I offered to help you, we had barely known each other. I told you my reasons were selfish. I spent so long watching you from afar, this was my chance to be close to you. Then, right after the spring, your powers started to show. It didn't feel safe to tell you then. Every time I considered it, I ultimately decided not to.

"I began to fall in love with you. I was scared at that point if I told you I would never hear from you again. I was planning on telling you until after the ceremony, when you would be powerful enough to defend yourself. Ever since we brought you to the crossing, I've regretted it. As soon as you asked to talk to Daniel's mom, I knew she would tell you. I won't apologize for trying to keep you safe, Red, I love you. Going after Gabriel and outing yourself is a death sentence. But mark my words, I will be by your side when you are ready for that."

I take in everything he's said. I understand that he was trying to protect me.

"What you don't realize is that I have been giving all of my trust to you. Asking you for help when I needed it, that wasn't an easy feat for me. On my birthday, you even pointed out I'm not the person who asks for help. Yet, I did.

"I expected in return to be able to trust you, not just with that, but in general. When everything as simple as the truth behind us meeting is a lie. If it wasn't for us finding out we were mates, I would question if there was even a point to all of this? But it seems like the world had planned this all along. If you ever expect me to trust you again, you can't keep shit from me. Especially something this big. I don't care who we are to each other."

"I had never originally planned to lie to you, but I know that isn't an excuse." Zayn says. "I truly am sorry. But I promise you, my feelings for you have nothing to do with me finding out who you are."

He pushes my bangs across my forehead with his thumb, running his hand down my face.

"You're beautiful, breathtaking. I am obsessed with every single inch of your body. Your mind is filled with love and compassion. You have a soul, a conscience. For most it is either beauty or intelligence, you have both and so much more. I watch the way you stare at things for too

long, trying to analyze them. Trying to see through someone's perspective. The way you always take pause to piece
together a picture. Aurora, Red, baby girl you are the light.
Being the son of a Founder is dark. Knowing I have been
bred to one day take over a position and expected to do
horrible things like those above me have...to force someone
into marriage and force them into children...it's disgusting.
To say a woman has no rights and then look at my mother
and sister and say 'I love them?'" he shakes his head.

"You give me hope," he continues. "Hope that we can
force change into this world for the better. I will spend
forever proving you can trust me. Starting today.

"I believe you are the key to everything. Why else
would magic provide you with a power before anyone else?
One that you can somehow control with such ease with no
formal training or guidance. I don't think that is a coin-
cidence.

"I think you are the *light* our world needs, that I need."

CHAPTER 26
RUMORS LED ME TO YOU
ZAYN EVERETT

(FLASHBACK)

When I was 15, I went snooping where I shouldn't have. Being a son of a Founder, you are always hearing rumors. People don't dare speak in front of our fathers but somehow have loose tongues when we're around. Which is ironic since we will one day be in their seats. But fuck, I was just a 'kid.' what did I know? Of course, you never know if those rumors hold any weight behind them. Until one day, there was a rumor I overheard and I had a gut feeling there was more to the story.

Rumor was, one of the Founder's wives' first child died in childbirth. The mother was so overcome with grief, she followed within a year by suicide. Those I overheard expressed how "unfortunate" it was.

This made me think about things. Suicide is very rare. There has only been a few over the last century. We don't get sick. So, normally people die of old age or an incident relating to magic. I wondered why a Founder's wife would commit suicide. Why wouldn't she just have another child? It was only a year since the death...I know child loss is devastating, but why did this loss haunt her so much? The Founders and their wives are supposed to display control at all times.

A few years prior to that, I walked in on my mom hysterically crying in her closet. I remember it so vividly, like a movie. She tried to hide it, quickly averting her eyes and wiping them dry. I wasn't stupid, she knew that. She motioned for me to sit next to her. So, I closed the door and sat down.

"Z, I need you to promise me something. In your life-time, you will be told a lot of things. How things should be. The proper way to handle a situation. When you question if what you are doing is right, I want you to remember this moment. You will one day be a very important person in this world. I don't say this to scare you, I say this to prepare you. There will be choices that have to be made, it is within your right to decide to follow all of those before you or, to do what you feel in your heart is right.

"Madeleine, Laila and I have been working very hard to make sure you boys understand that. Raising you to be honorable and respectful men. You will need to read people's intentions, ignorance will always be used against you. But none of us are ever fully prepared or educated. So, learning how to read people will allow you to see what others can't. Above all else you are to protect Rosalie. You, as her brother, will be the only one in her life to be able to protect her future.

"If one day, I am not here, I need you to know that I will be whispering in the wind to you. To trust your heart."

My mother shook with conviction. I was scared, she was talking as if I would lose her, it was unsettling.

"You will have an arranged marriage one day," she continued, "I hope and pray that it can turn into a marriage of love. But, if it doesn't, you are to treat her with the respect she deserves. You will not be any better than her. I understand how the public will view you. But you will treat her as your equal, or I will haunt you." Her laugh was watery.

"I love you more than you will ever know, Zayn. Your soul was hand crafted. You are wise beyond your years. If you ever feel yourself drifting, you will come to me, and I will help guide you."

On that day, I saw a side of my mom I had never seen before. My mom was always strong, never vulnerable. I had never seen her cry before and I hated it. I didn't want to see my mother cry. Half of what she said made no sense at the time, and I didn't know how to help her. We sat on the floor for a while, her arm around me. After almost an hour had gone by, she straightened her clothes and said it was time for her to make dinner. I went to my room and tried to analyze everything she said so I could understand.

At the time, my main take was to protect my sister. Which, I thought was pretty obvious. And also, to learn how to read people.

And be good?

When I was young, I thought my parents had the best relationship in the world since they never argued. Then, after watching Elijah's parents together over time, I realized my parents also never laughed, had conversations, smiled at each other or even showed an ounce of affection towards one another.

Over time, the more I discovered about our world, the more things she said clicked. I have used her words as a rule book in my head. I have become incredibly close with my mom. I felt her sorrow then and I never want to see her in pain like that again.

The things she said were why I questioned the rumor so much and why I had been determined to find out more.

It was easy to get what I needed; I had been training with my father for so long.

One day, he went out of the office and I'd been working on filing paperwork. This was a regular job duty of mine. Sneaking into a different cabinet wasn't too difficult, all I needed was my father's set of keys to unlock it. I lied earlier in the day claiming to have forgotten mine, so I needed his to lock up the office when I left.

To say he was disappointed was an understatement. A Founder is not allowed to fuck up. We are to always portray the definition of perfection. So that one day, when we take over, no one will ever question our position in charge.

I took his verbal lashing before he left. I knew anything he had to say wasn't going to change my mind about what I needed to do.

As soon as he was gone, I called Daniel to come help me. I always trusted him. His brother is the next in line for succession, so Daniel never felt the obligation to the Founders in the same way the rest of us do. He will have to have an arranged marriage, but he won't be held to the same regard.

As soon as I told him I was going to start investigating the rumor, he was all in. He never felt comfortable with how our fathers ruled. Despite him never having to rule unless his brother dies before providing an heir, his father has always been very demanding of him. Trying to mold him and change him to be more like his brother. Which has only made Daniel resent him and what the Founders represent more.

Once Daniel arrived, we started scouring the locked files. We went through each one of our parents files just in case. He was investigating the Ariti file when he found something, Gabriel Ariti was once married to Leanne Ariti.

He found records of a marriage certificate and pregnancy scans from the hospital. We dove further into the file where we found a death certificate of Leanne Ariti on

September 4th, 2009. We triple checked the folder, but there was no death certificate for the baby.

If anyone dies, they are to have a death certificate. It is the law. But this baby who died in childbirth on September 4th, 2008, there was no record?

Why would Gabriel and Leanne do that? The only logical explanation is that the baby didn't die, or the file is missing. But the filing is pristine at the Founders' office.

We decided we needed to look further into the case. See if there was any record of an adoption from that day. We found no record of any babies being brought in for adoption for over a month after the birth.

Feeling drained and defeated, we decided to try one more thing. We looked into our grandparents and ancestors for a few generations back to see if there were any other mysterious pregnancies. We were in utter disbelief when we found several other Founders over the years where ultrasounds were documented, and then there were no death certificates or birth certificates surrounding those dates.

The entire investigation left us hungry for answers. It was already getting late, so we needed to leave. We made sure to organize all of the folders and put them back exactly as they were. We locked up the office and headed out.

I told Daniel that I was going to try and find out from my mom if she knew anything. He was very apprehensive about bringing this to anyone else's attention, but I trusted my mom with everything.

When I got home, my dad was still not back yet. I waited until my sister was eating dinner and asked my mom if I could talk to her outside for a minute.

"Zayn, what is it?" she asked.

"Mom, I have to ask you something," I tried to warm her up to the subject and confirm her secrecy. "I realize what I'm about to ask you, I shouldn't know. I need you to promise me you won't tell Dad anything about this."

"It depends on what it is," she stated with apprehension. "I can tell something is eating you. What's going on?"

"I heard a rumor that didn't sit well with me. The more I thought about it, the more questions I had. So, I decided to look into it. I'm now more confused than before. So, I have to ask: Did you know Leanne Ariti?"

My mother's skin paled. She told me I needed to watch people and I can easily tell my mom knew her. What I can't decipher is if she's scared I brought her up or scared about what I've started digging into.

Her throat bobbed. "I haven't heard that name in a long time, Zayn. Why are you asking about Leanne?"

"Because there is no record of a death certificate of her baby. Hospital records clearly identify she was pregnant, but then everything just stops. Her ultrasounds go all the way until 39 weeks. If she had a miscarriage, there would have been a hospital admission, most likely, but if her son died during childbirth, there would be a death certificate. I looked throughout the generations and found multiple instances where Founders' wives have been pregnant and then suddenly, the file stops."

My mom took a deep breath and sat down on one of the patio chairs. She checked her phone to look at the camera in our driveway. My dad was still not home. Clearly satisfied with that, she set her phone down on the glass table.

"This is not something you should be digging into," she finally explained. "Leanne was a horrific example of what the Founders can do. She was my best friend in this world. I will forever wish there was something I could have done. The Founders have protected their lineage by ensuring that their seat does not end with them. Meaning, they have to have boys. They want to also make sure that there is no way a woman could one day take a male's place. To do this, they make sure their first born is a boy by any means necessary.

"I don't know what happened to their baby. But it wasn't a boy. Leanne was pregnant with a girl, she tried to hide it from Gabriel. Of course, he found out at the birth. I don't know if their daughter is alive today or not. I just hope that Gabriel never finds her if she is."

She wasn't going to scare me from searching into what happened, my mind was set. 'By any means necessary' the Founders sought it okay to abort and murder babies. How did the majority of these women survive? To have their baby ripped from them and killed simply because they were a girl?

Gabriel has no idea that his daughter was possibly out there somewhere? What would he do to her if he found her?

The only thing I knew was I needed to try and find her if she was. Better I find her and make sure she stays safe than Gabriel.

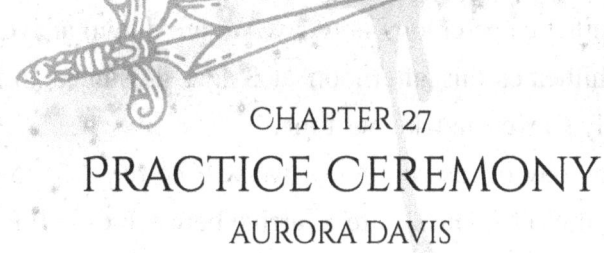

CHAPTER 27
PRACTICE CEREMONY
AURORA DAVIS

I sit in the back seat with Jade as I stare out the window. Watching the world as we know it fly by us. In a few months, we will be studying at KAE, away from everything. We will essentially be shut out from the outside while we're there. You're not even allowed to have phones, laptops, or any technology on campus.

How much could change in the two years we are gone?

I don't think I will ever completely forgive Zayn for not telling me, a part of me will always resent that he thought I couldn't handle it.

But as I sit here judging him, I'm a hypocrite myself. I still haven't talked to my parents. I can't help but feel like the second I tell them that I know, there will be a divide between us. They'll try to force me to leave it alone knowing I won't be able to do that.

I still have so many questions, and I can't help but feel like the answers likely died with my mother.

The practice ceremony is today. We are due to arrive at the amphitheater this afternoon at 3 PM. I wanted to be there early so we can take our time.

On the day of the ceremony, we will be required to be there by 5:30 PM. Guests are to arrive between 6-6:30 PM. The gates are locked and no one is to enter past that point.

The amphitheater is massive and the stone walls reach high into the clouds. As we pull through the gates armed with a guard on each side, I think of all the ceremonies that have been held here before. If you didn't know any better, you would think all of this was built prior to Kyrosia's existence. The homes, schools, businesses are all so modern, but here, nothing about this venue is new.

Zayn parks the car and we clamber out, looking ahead. Our classmates file inside, all identical in our ceremony uniform.

Today, the stone benches echo with silence.

The air hangs thick with pressure, weighing heavy as I take in every detail surrounding us.

Our class huddles nervously around the chasm totem.

In the center of the amphitheaters arena, the totem looms on the large stone platform. At 5 feet in diameter and 4 feet tall, it's made from stone and the outside is lined with etched copper.

The language carved within the copper is unknown to our people. Knowing what I know now, I wonder if it came from Zylenia. Did they speak the same native tongue as us?

Rumors have claimed the chasm is plumbed to the depths of hell, but the truth is unknown. You cannot see anything in it, blackness is all that stares back at you.

Some glance in while others are talking to peers. We make our way to the center where I see Professor Stratis at the registry table, setting up. He is one of the professors at KAE and he leads the ceremony every year.

The second the clock tower hits 3 PM, his voice roars around us.

"Welcome, class of 2025. You are here today to prepare yourself for The Awakening Ceremony. This *is* your graduation. When classes are done, that's it. Once summer ends, you will be joining us at Kyrosia Academy of Enchantment. There, you will spend every single day honing your powers. By the time you are done with your lessons, you should be able to channel all of your power.

"First year classes are specific to your specializations. You will strictly be learning the ins and outs of your gift. Second year, we place you in classes with opposite specializations who counteract your strengths and weaknesses."

He continues to project his voice with the use of magic. I watch him and it feels like he is staring at me. I look around and everyone's eyes are on him, no one noticing the way his gaze doesn't seem to leave mine. I begin to wonder if it's all in my head.

"All of the campus is spelled, so you can only use your

powers in the classrooms and designated learning areas. This is both so you can keep yourselves safe and the risk low to the campus," he continues. "Those who have received passes are able to leave campus as you please. If you leave campus without being assigned a pass, you will be under review with the Founders and not allowed to return until you receive a ruling. We will now go over exactly what will take place at the ceremony. Please line up in the following order."

He starts to list my classmates, name by name, as each student falls into line. It's not long before everyone is lined up and ready to begin practicing for the ceremony.

He calls each person to the front where they stand before the chasm and he explains what we are to say and how we enact the rite.

CHAPTER 28
AWAKENING CEREMONY
PART I
AURORA DAVIS

I pull the forest green tunic over my head, leaving the 3 buttons on my chest undone. I tuck my shirt into the matching cargo pants, fastening my belt. I lean down to put on my boots when my brother walks in my room and closes the door.

"Are you ready?" he asks, shoving his hands into his pockets.

I place my foot in my boot, pressing into the floor until it snaps into place.

"I think so." My gaze flickers to meet his.

"You've got this." I think he is trying to reassure himself more than build my confidence.

"Thanks. Can you please make sure to call Grandma so she won't be late?" I remind him.

"I just heard Mom talking to her on the phone, she'll be here in a few minutes," he responds.

"Zayn should also be here soon," I say, half asking Oliver to leave. I just want a few minutes to myself.

He goes to grab the door handle but releases it and takes large strides towards me. He picks me up for a hug, holding me so tight I can't breathe.

His voice is heavy, "I need you to be safe. Promise me that if at the smallest sign of anything wrong, you leave, you find a way to run?"

"Even if I wanted to Oliver, you know I wouldn't get very far." I sigh. "I have to live with whatever happens."

"That was a very non-comforting answer."

I laugh, releasing him to look at his face. "I promise I will try to find a way out if things go sour."

"Thanks, sis," he says, kissing my hair and finally walking out of my room.

My heart skips a beat seeing how scared he is for me. But I don't have time to be scared. I need to focus all of my energy on getting through this.

Today, the stands are filled to the brim with people. All eyes are on our class as if it's a game show. Who will fail and who will move on to the next level?

It's disgusting if you think about it. Using teenagers to mold generations of good little soldiers.

That's when I see *them*. In front of the rows are the

Founders. Their dais contains four executive chairs made of stone like the amphitheater's rows, but much larger and carved with intricate designs.

I take a moment to evaluate them. They are all seated tall with their backs straight and face cards planted on firmly. Expressions that scream commandment. Sitting from left to right is Gabriel Ariti, Terran Everett, Elijah Jackson Sr., and Levi Pierce.

I watch the way my birth father's eyes are scanning the line of students, too busy to notice me looking at him. My immediate thought is that he doesn't look like me at all.

I feel grateful for that.

When I tear my eyes away from him, grey irises meet mine. But they aren't the familiar grey I have found myself desiring. They are that stone grey, angry, cold.

I avert my gaze quicker than I have ever looked away from anything. Praying to Lina he didn't see me staring at Gabriel.

My focus is now firmly planted on the ceremonial stand. Josh approaches. He almost looks giddy? He repeats his oaths with pride and when he is done, he registers and exits the arena.

It eased my nerves to watch him perform the rite so effortlessly.

"AURORA DAVIS." My name is called forward. *Shit.* Yup, that previous ease is short lived. My heart threatens to pound from my chest as I walk on unsteady legs toward the chasm totem. My eyes find the audience. I try to search for my family but no idea where they may be.

Professor Stratis stands beside me and begins to perform the ritual, asking me the questions he has long since memorized.

"You are here today on the 18th year of your life to receive your powers. Confirm you are Aurora Davis," he recites, his voice full of power.

"I am," I answer, trying to stabilize the shake of my voice.

"Do you promise to uphold the laws of Kyrosia?"

"Yes, I do." In other words, to serve under the misogyny of our founders, of course, I would *love* to.

"Do you wish to receive your powers?"

"Yes, I do." This time my answer is honest, I'm ready.

"This ceremony will pronounce you as a full fae. You will receive your powers. Those powers are to serve the Founders, to bring value to Kyrosia. If you are called upon by the Founders, you will serve them proudly. With this blade you shall bleed, thus allowing your magic to be relinquished to you. Shall your blood forever remain embedded in our land."

He hands me the blade that has been cleansed from the student who came before me. I look to Zayn, who is a few students back from the front of the line.

Suddenly our world flashes in front of me. This blade marking my skin changes everything for us and the life we may possibly have. That is, if we can truly find a way for us to be together, before he is married to someone else.

He is my mate; I cannot allow that to happen. Working together to try to fix what has been broken in Kyrosia, it becomes reality that my future is to help our people.

I grip the handle of the blade tight in my right hand. Then, I run the tip hard and fast in a slit across my palm.

I whisper where no one should hear me, "Bleed for Kyrosia, I will."

I squeeze the blood from my palm into the chasm, it drips into the depths of darkness.

CHAPTER 29

AWAKENING CEREMONY
PART 2
AURORA DAVIS

A s the blood releases from my body, the blade falls from my hand in a scrape against the stone beneath us. My eyes drift shut as power rushes inside me, reining *free* and untethered. The embers beneath my skin floating around, sparking, seeking a way out. They are muted compared to when I am at the crossing, but they are here and awake.

That's when I feel the shadows creep around my brain.

Wrapping my mind in their dark silhouettes.

I keep my breathing still as I need to remain in control. My ears tingle and I reach my hands up to feel them. Gone are the rounded ears and now, they taper to a point. I smile. My entire body is waking up as if it's been in hibernation for 18 years.

Everything is heightened, my hearing, sense of smell,

strength. I was expecting to feel different, but what I wasn't expecting was the bond.

The bond between Zayn and I is infinitely different than ever before. I can feel and hear his heart beating from here. It's almost as if I could stop his heart or restart it. I can smell the people surrounding him, stepping into his place in line as if it was me there and not him.

My senses are overwhelmed with the newfound powers running through me. I feel his tension rise, becoming scared, realizing the fear he is feeling is for me. My eyes abundantly snap open. I look at him before glancing around at the countless eyes focused on me, as they are watching me cautiously. I'm incredibly uncomfortable knowing everyone is trying to guess what power I hold.

I reach down to retrieve the blade from the ground, noticing my hand has completely healed. As I come back up, I look at Professor Stratis, whose eyes are studying mine.

My brows dip just as his face falls, becoming unreadable. I move to hand him the blade and as he reaches for it, he turns his face from view of the stands.

"Mind, tell them mind," he whispers.

Scared, having no idea what that means, I give him a curt nod before stepping down, not daring to look up at where the Founders sit.

I approach the table inside of the arena to provide my information to be listed for the Registry of Powers.

"Name?" the man asks me in a commanding tone. I hear the professor performing the next ritual behind me.

"Aurora Davis."

"Power Group?" he asks.

"Mind." I do as I was told.

The gentleman turns to look at one of his colleagues standing behind him, he crooks his finger, beckoning for him to approach us. The man sitting whispers something in his ear before his counterpart returns to his flanking position. I watch him retrieve his phone and type a message, sending it before pocketing the device again.

I'm terrified, did I say the wrong thing?

"You may exit the arena," he instructs me.

"That's it?" I ask, confused.

"Exit, or you will be removed. The next student is approaching."

I scramble to exit quickly. I don't go to my friends; everything inside of me is screaming that I need to be with Zayn. I wait like a cat in heat by the gate for him to exit.

I count each person who finishes and exits, waiting eagerly for Zayn to finish his rite and meet me in the waiting area.

When I finally see him, I run up to him.

"What section are you in?" I rush out.

"Mind, you?" he answers.

Relief floods through me. I nod to myself, finally at ease.

"When I told them mind, the guy behind him sent a text to someone. Did that happen to you?" I murmur.

"Yes, the Founders want to know everyone who has mind powers. Mind can be extremely dangerous to them, so they want to be aware. I'm sure my dad is shitting himself right now." A smile tugs at the corners of his mouth, clearly proud of what he has received.

Without thinking, I lean in to hug him. His body swallows me in a deep, passionate embrace. I smell his cologne, his shampoo, the scent of his laundry detergent. I take it all in. Warmth floods through me at the familiarity of him and also, at these new abilities. I want to explore him. How can a person like him become even more attractive?

He pushes my hips back, creating distance. His eyes meet mine, tense and focused on me.

"What's wrong?" I ask.

Zayn answers through gritted teeth. "I think these powers are going to be an adjustment." His voice is strained, struggling to compose himself. "I can feel it now Aurora, the bond, I love you, but I can't be this close to you. Not here, not surrounded by all these people."

As Austin enters, I turn to head towards my friends, but they cluster together in a huddle.

"Zayn, what's going on?" I mutter.

As soon as my eyes clock Ruby's hand, I take off running.

"No," I say staring at the hand she has wrapped in front of her.

"Yes," she says, long lashes wet with emotion. Tears stream down her face. Josh is holding her from behind, his head tucked into her neck and shoulder trying to hide his tears.

"But, how?" I ask my voice cracking. "I watched your face as you entered the doors. You were smiling."

"Clearly we don't fucking know, Aurora. Are you done with the fucking questions?" Josh snaps.

Zayn steps up behind me, letting out a rumbling hum trying to warn Josh to stop. Josh shakes his head and squeezes Ruby into him tighter.

"She was trying to hide her hand until the ceremony was done." Jade breaks the silence. "None of us knew until Austin just finished." She hangs her head.

I look at everyone else's hands, needing to see if everyone else has healed. But when I look to Austin, he is staring at me with an uneasy expression. I feel an alarming pain shoot through my wrist, a reminder of before. I think to myself, *if anyone should have lost their powers, maybe it should have been him.*

We sit in silence, waiting for the remaining students to finish the ceremony.

Once everyone is complete, Professor Stratis enters and reads a list of names. Those who are on the list are to go back into the arena when the stands are empty.

We all know what to expect next. Not that hearing her name called makes it any easier.

We all hug her before she walks back into the arena. Even Daniel and Elijah wish her good luck, although they don't sound too optimistic.

We try to wait for her but we're told we are to leave immediately.

We say our goodbyes to each other and the second my arms wrap around Austin, his muscles stiffen. When I release him, his face seems void of emotion, distant. I try to ignore the nagging feeling that something isn't right.

Unease prickles the back of my neck as we are herded out like cattle.

As we leave the parking lot, I watch behind us in the mirror. Josh sits in his car alone, waiting for Ruby to be dismissed. We all offer to stay in support, waiting for her in the car, but he declined. He said he didn't want anyone to get in trouble for staying when we were told to leave.

The car ride home is silent for a while. Zayn reaches over and places his hand on my thigh to stop it from shaking.

Although, I can't help but notice how his face looks visibly distraught.

"Are you okay?" I ask.

"Yeah." He swallows hard, Adams apple bobbing. "It's the bond. You have had some time to sit with it, unfortunately, everything is hitting me all at once. I can feel your power."

I have noticed that now he has his powers, the bond is getting stronger. But I wonder how he can feel my powers? I can't feel his.

He continues. "I can feel your emotions. They are affecting me because I don't know how to push them aside yet. It'll get easier. I know this sounds insane, but right now, I can't be separated from you."

I know that feeling all too well, it's exactly how I felt as I waited for him to finish the ceremony.

"As much as I feel I need to be near you, I also don't want to leave you alone after everything that just happened with Ruby. Can I come in with you?" he asks.

"You mean into my house, to meet my family?" Surprise laces my tone.

"You say that like it's a bad thing?" His face falls in worry.

"That's not what I'm saying. I didn't think that is something you would want to do yet."

"Now is a better time than any. If they want me to leave, I will. I won't blame them," he explains.

"Okay, then yeah. Time to meet the parents." My hand covers his.

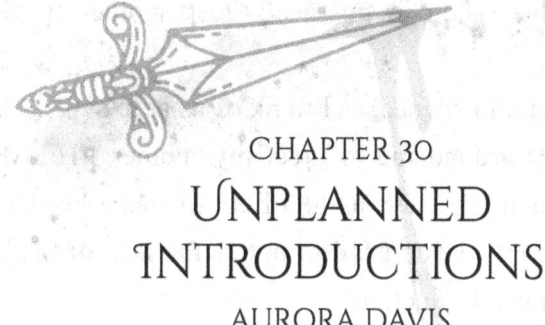

CHAPTER 30
UNPLANNED INTRODUCTIONS
AURORA DAVIS

Before I open the door, I take a deep breath. Zayn's hand finds the small of my back, signaling to me that he's here. With me. I don't know how my family will react to Zayn being here without so much as a heads up.

I walk in to my entire family in the living room. Zayn closes the door softly behind him. I unlace my boots and kick them off by the door where Zayn follows my lead, doing the same.

"Hey, guys," I greet awkwardly stepping into the living room, with Zayn behind me.

"Honey?" Mom asks in question as soon as she sees him.

I need to introduce Zayn, but as what? My mate? I'd rather die. It's not like we've discussed it. I mean, not unless you count him saying he'll marry me one day. I can't believe I'm standing in my living room having the 'is he or is he not?' discussion in my head. Just another fucking cliché.

I stand there, in silence, as I think of what to say.

Zayn steps around me to greet my mother. "Hi, Mrs. Davis. I'm Zayn," he says as he offers to shake her hand, which she accepts. I don't fail to notice the lack of his last name during his introduction.

My dad watches skeptically from his chair. Oliver and my grandma look like they're watching a movie, sans popcorn bucket. The former wears a big grin.

"I know who you are, Zayn," says my mother. "And excuse me for being blunt, but why are you here?"

Zayn glances at me for a brief second. "You may have heard, but Ruby was not granted powers during the ceremony. It was rather rough on them. I am sorry to intrude, but I didn't feel comfortable leaving Aurora alone." He steps back to my side.

"Well, Zayn, I appreciate you taking care of her. Even if it is unnecessary since she is in her own home. But this will not be the end of this conversation. For now, Aurora, breathe."

Zayn nods his head to my mom in understanding.

With that taken care of, I rush to my Grandma Louisa to give her a hug.

"I missed you so much," I tell her. "Thank you for coming to the ceremony. How are you?"

"I wouldn't miss it for the world," Grandma croons.

"Now, don't make us wait any longer. What section are you in?"

"Mind," I say, watching their reactions. My parents and grandmother look between each other and back at me.

Oliver tells Zayn to take a seat on the couch and then asks him, "What section are you in?"

"Mind, as well."

"Wow, what are the chances of that?" Oliver asks with genuine curiosity.

My Grandma Louisa scoffs under her breath. Causing me to look at her, but she shakes her head to no one in particular.

"What is that supposed to mean?" I ask at the same time Zayn shoots her a look of disgust.

"Nothing, just that the Founders have a way of getting what they want," she mutters.

"Are you suggesting he somehow interfered with the results of the ceremony?" I ask, appalled.

Grandma Louisa looks to Zayn. "Did you?"

"Enough," Mom snaps roughly to my grandma. She takes a seat on my dad's armrest, leaning into him.

Zayn laughs at her audacity. "Even if I did know how to do that, which I don't, I wouldn't have grouped Aurora with me. I would have given her a less powerful grouping."

Oliver elbows him at the same time my dad decides to step in. "You would make her weaker than you, so what you can overpower her?" he accuses, standing from his chair.

Zayn shakes his head, trying to explain. "No, not to overpower her. I would do it so she is less of a target."

"Target for what?" my dad asks.

His eyes find mine in question. We haven't discussed if I have confronted my parents yet or not.

I take a deep breath. "I know. We can stop the charade. I know who my biological parents are."

My family goes quiet. Oliver looks at Zayn. My dad takes his seat. Both my parents and Grandma look back and forth between one another again. Everyone in the room seems to be having silent conversations as I stand in the middle watching them.

Once again, here I am feeling present, but not a participant in the conversation. Everyone always seems to know more about me than I know about myself. I grow frustrated as the silence stretches.

That's when I hear a tendril of a voice starting to invade my mind. At first, it hurts as if my ears are ringing or popping. I try to hide the discomfort, unsure of what's going on. I reach up to rub my left ear when the words become clear.

"Red, can you hear me?
Red."

It's Zayn, I can hear his sultry deep voice sweeping through my mind, barely above a whisper as if it is my internal dialogue.

I ask myself how I'm supposed to respond. Do I just talk back as if I am talking back to myself?

His voice is clearer, louder now. *"Yes, you do."* He looks at me smiling. I furrow my brows at him in confusion.

"All mind wielders can speak between each other. I needed you to know I was here for you, only for you. I am not sure how this conversation is about to go. I had to at least try to say something to you. If at any point it isn't going how you want, tell me and we are gone. Or, let me know and I will step in. You cannot tell them we are mates though, not yet. If they can't sense it, then we need to wait. Otherwise, I am letting you handle this. And Aurora, I love you."

With which I respond, *"I love you, too."*

"If anyone would like to say something, now is probably a swell time," I say, finally sitting down on the couch and curling my legs underneath me, between Zayn and Oliver.

Mom speaks up first. "Honey, it's complicated. We have tried to keep it from you for many reasons. How do you even know? *What* do you know?" She's rambling, caught off guard and uncomfortable.

"I was determined to find out the truth before the ceremony," I explain. "I needed to know what to expect. Granted, it was a little more than I bargained for, but here we are."

"Do you have any questions for us?" Dad asks.

I scoff. "Are you joking?"

My dad shoots me an annoyed look. Okay, no joking.

"Did you know her?" I ask to no one, but everyone.

Zayn's hand reaches for mine, which seems to draw attention. If it wasn't known before that there was something more than friends between us, it is now.

CHAPTER 31

HANDMAIDEN
AURORA DAVIS

My grandma is the one to reply. "Yes. I knew her very well," she says, both in defeat and sorrow.

"How?" I question.

"Aurora, I'm not your grandma. I love you as if you were a daughter to me, but I purposely placed myself in your life so that I could be here one day when you needed me," she admits, her voice thick with emotion. "I was your mother's handmaiden, basically for her entire life. I came with her when she married Gabriel, to the Ariti home. I was loyal to her. When she found out she was pregnant with you, she was so happy. Unfortunately, things didn't exactly go the way she would have imagined.

"Once you were born, I made sure you got to safety. Your dad worked for the Founders when you were born and your biological grandmother and I were best friends before she died. I kept in touch with April and John, so I knew they were looking to have a baby and had been unsuccessful. I contacted April and arranged for John to take you home. I had to act quickly. When you were little, your skin was still so light, you could pass as theirs. So, that's what they did. They claimed that April was pregnant and had given birth to you."

I watch my parents, evaluating their reactions as she tells the story *they* should have told me ages ago. Years of isolation, of questions finally getting answers. I have found out more within the last few months than in my first 18 years of life.

"No one questioned it because they had been trying for a baby for so long. Everyone thought they kept the pregnancy hidden until they knew it was viable," she continues. "I helped them fake your birth certificate so there would be no question on who you were. I gave strict instructions to your parents for you to stay away from the Founding families. You were safest if Gabriel never caught sight of you. So, imagine my surprise when I see Zayn Everett walk in beside you." She shoots my parents a dirty look.

"We had no idea she has been seeing him," Mom snaps. "We would have ended it immediately."

"I don't think that is up to you mom," I bite out, annoyed.

Dad points his finger in my direction. "Watch your mouth, you don't speak to your mother that way."

Zayn's hand grips mine tighter. My anger flares, but I'm not sure if it *is* my anger or his.

"You have all kept everything from me, my entire life. How would you have any idea who I hung out with? How would you protect me from those you want me to avoid, without saying anything to me?"

Oliver tucks his head beside me.

"What?" I whip my gaze to my brother.

"Aurora, I—"

"Fucking what, Oliver?"

"Mouth!" Mom scolds. "This isn't on Oliver, this is on us, he was just doing what we asked. He has kept an eye out on you to make sure you didn't befriend any of the Founders. We had to keep you safe. We can't be with you at school and at home. It was the only thing we knew to do."

"So, you knew who I was this whole time?" I ask Oliver. "You've been watching me? Reporting back? Why did you never tell them about Zayn then?"

"Because I didn't know," he defends himself. "Not until the day you went out with him when he drove you home. I didn't have a chance to say anything before you and I talked. By then, I didn't feel the need *to* say anything. I spoke to Zayn, and it was clear he had no intentions of taking advantage or exposing you. That's what Mom and Dad were worried about. Since it didn't apply, I kept it to myself."

"That didn't answer the question that you knew who I was?" I throw back.

"I didn't, not really," he pleads. "All I knew was that you came from extremely powerful people. So, we needed to keep you off the Founders' radar, so your biological parents could never find you and take you. That was all I knew, I swear. I always wanted to know more, I searched for answers. But all I want is for you to be safe, if I thought keeping you from Zayn was the answer, I would have found a way to make that happen."

I believe him, but I can't help still feeling angry with him, with everyone. Everyone has these small pieces of information about my life and no one was willing to tell me anything. I felt so alone having no clue who I was when in reality, all of it could have been avoided.

Oliver and my parents yell back and forth about him hiding things from them. As my Grandma Louisa sits in silence, watching everything unfold.

None of them stop to think how all of this impacts the trajectory of my future. Everyone would rather argue about who is in the wrong for keeping secrets. When, in reality, none of it matters. None of them were better than the other in trying to control my life by wanting me to live in ignorance. As if one day, I would never find out.

I mean great, I'm not dead, that's definitely a plus. But what if Gabriel found out who I was sooner? What if he saw me on Halloween and immediately knew who I was?

I respect they were trying to keep me safe; I will forever be grateful to them for that. I just would have been so much safer had I even known who I was supposed to be avoiding.

I try to talk to Zayn in my mind, unsure if the thread is

still there. *"Can I stay at your cabin until Academy starts, is it safe? I just need to work through everything and what this means for me."*

There is silence for a few seconds before he sweeps in. *"Depends, are you hiding from me, too?"*

"No, and I'm not hiding from them either. I just need to think."

"I get it. Of course, you can stay at the cabin, I will make sure my dad doesn't have any intentions on going there."

"I need to pack some of my things."

"I will meet you outside and follow you there."

I stand from the couch, effectively silencing their heated discussion.

"I love you, guys, but I need to get out of this house. I am going to pack a bag," I announce.

"You aren't going anywhere, this is your home," Dad says.

"It will still be my home when I get back."

Louisa, steps in. "Let her go."

My parents don't move as I leave the living room, opening the front door for Zayn.

"I will be out soon," I tell him.

He turns to my family. "It was a pleasure to meet you all. I wish it was under better circumstances, but I will always keep her safe."

"That isn't a promise you know you can keep," Dad responds.

"It is," Zayn vows. "And even if it wasn't, your daughter can keep herself safe." He turns and walks out the door, kissing my forehead on his way out.

In my room I pack my bags, taking as much with me as I think I will need until school starts. A soft knock echoes on my door, but before I can tell them to come in, it opens. Louisa shuts it behind her, walking over to my bed. She takes a seat and motions for me to do the same.

She holds an envelope in her shaky hands.

"This is a letter your mother wrote for you the day she died. She didn't know if you would ever receive it or if you were even alive," she murmurs. "She loved you more than this letter could ever put into words. When she lost you, she lost herself. These are your mother's final words to you. But Aurora, please don't go searching for revenge without a plan. You are not ready. You have no idea what they are capable of. When you are, I will be here.

"Your parents and I have stayed on with the Founders for this long to ensure that when the time came, we were in a position to assist you. I know you have her power, we have always known. But to have mind also? Aurora, you have no idea the danger you hold for yourself and against anyone else. You need to do everything you can to focus in on what your mind power consist of. Be careful even with your professors. Only tell them what you need to in order to succeed."

The idea of getting through the next two years lying my way through, trying to hide my powers makes me feel ill. It makes me sick knowing I can't trust anyone besides the few friends that know the truth, and even then, what if they turn on me? If someone reports me to the Founders, I would be dead. It's a shock I'm not already. I can't help rid the Founders from power if I'm dead.

"Unfortunately, most of your education will have to come from practicing on your own," she says. "So it isn't revealed to the Founders how strong you truly are. I need you to remember that we all love you. You will forever be our family. I know right now, it may not seem that way, but one day you will get it. Promise me you will read this letter and then find me when the time is ready?" My grandma hands me the envelope, her eyes rimmed with tears.

I hold it in my hand. It's heavy, more than just a letter. My throat clenches shut, heart racing.

She pats my knees and heads toward the door. "If you need me, I will be right downstairs." With that, she exits my room and closes the door behind her.

I continue to stare at the envelope, wishing Zayn wasn't all the way outside. I know this is something I should do alone, but I don't want to.

This isn't going to get any easier if I wait. I run my finger underneath the flap of the envelope and pull the object into my hand.

It's a locket. I run my fingers over the top of it, opening the lid donning a set of scales. The bottom half has a compass engraved on top of black opal. It's stunning. It looks brand new.

I open the clasp and feed the chain underneath the hair on my neck. I pull it in front of me so I can see it, clasping the locket. Once it's on, it lays just above my chest.

I reach back into the envelope and grab out a letter. A picture falls out in front of me as I unfold it.

A wave of emotion floods through me. I feel a sharp pang in my chest. The picture is of a woman who looks just like me holding a baby. My mother. My eyes begin to sting.

I run my fingers over the picture. She lays in a large bed staring at the baby with such intense emotion.

My heart breaks knowing I will never know her. She killed herself having no idea that I was still here. I will never be able to hug her, talk to her, ask her for advice on how to move forward. I never imagined this would hurt so bad. I always imagined my parents didn't want me.

I set the picture in front of me, so I can look back at it. I begin to read the letter from my mother.

CHAPTER 32
FINAL WORDS

Aurora Penelope,

I did everything I knew how to try to save you. Unfortunately, your story was written long before this. I knew from the very beginning you were a girl. I could feel it in my bones. I paid a fortune to the doctor to alter the documents to say you were a boy. I thought that there was a minuscule chance it would save your life. I couldn't let him take you before I could lay my eyes on you. I thought, just maybe when he saw your face, he would find it in his heart to save you.

I could feel how strong you were from the beginning. I labored for 46 hours before I gave birth. On my final push, I let out an earth-shattering scream. Everyone thought it was because of the pain, but it was my magic ripping from my soul.

As soon as I saw the way your father was devastated to see you weren't a boy, I didn't care. Who cares about powers, I didn't want to be alive without my baby. I knew what was coming next.

His next 4 words shredded every ounce of hope I had. The way his voice dropped an octave, my soul was ripped apart with the words that left his mouth. "Get rid of it," he demanded. You were ripped from my arms. I fought to get out of bed, screaming, thrashing as I was held down. The guards held me so that I wouldn't go after Gabriel on his way out of our room. They put shackles on my wrists that take away the ability to use magic. What they didn't realize was that they were just glorified bracelets to me. I knew I couldn't light a fire, let alone burn him alive. Bloody, basically powerless, and exposed to the world, I was as good as dead.

We never had a loving marriage. We had a marriage of power. I do not come from a Founding family. When I performed the awakening cere-mony, power wrapped around me like I never imagined. I almost burst into flames as soon as the power flooded through me. Fire was my specialization. Something they hadn't seen before.

The Aritis saw an opportunity. An opening to be the most powerful line out of the four. I was a pawn in their game.

Except, not providing a son made me worthless. My handmaiden, Louisa took you away. She didn't return until the next day. When I asked questions, she told me she did what she had to do. I begged and pleaded to be told any little bit of information about you as I could. She wouldn't tell me anything.

A month after your birth, I tried to take my life on the roof of our home. She stopped me. She said, "I was saving this for a day when I knew you would need it to push through. I have carried it with me every single day. I took this picture of you two as soon as you gave birth and had it printed. Gabriel doesn't know I have had it, and he never can. This does not leave your possession."

I looked at the picture she held. It was the moment I gave birth to you. Tears streaming down my face as I held you in my arms. I looked into your eyes; they were as golden as his. Without the menace his carry. No, yours were different, they stunned me, I never told a soul what I saw. As soon as I touched you, the ring around your pupils glowed with fire. My heart broke into pieces at the same time as feeling absolutely in love for the first time in my life.

The picture kept me going. I didn't leave the house much. Gabriel didn't speak to me and moved into another bedroom. I was so thankful he didn't try to bed me for another child. Until today, one day before the anniversary of your birth.

I was in the dining room when he entered and said "Leanne, I've given you an appropriate amount of time to mourn. I'm done. You are to produce an heir. It is your responsibility. I will not be made a fool because you cannot perform your duties. Tomorrow we will begin to try for a male heir." He exited immediately after.

I retired to my room after pushing my food around on my plate. I locked the door. I stare at the picture Louisa gave me as I am writing this letter at my desk.

Praise Lina, I fucking miss you. I would do anything to hold you in my arms. I cannot suffer in a world where you do not exist. I can't risk your life by trying to find you if you are alive. This year has been excruciating. Killing me slowly. I cannot, and will not, bare the pain of going through this again.

I choose to hope that somehow, someway my magic saved you. That all of this pain was for a reason. I hope wherever you are in this world, you know I love you. I hope that one day, the world is different. You are forever my deepest love. I wish I could have done more to save you.

This is the end of my story. I choose to hope is just your beginning. If you are out there in this world with my magic, I don't envy those who cross you. Do not let it burn you alive. Remember to always find balance.

My story will not be yours, if you find a way around the bounds restricting the city, do it. You cannot dismantle the Founders without releasing magic first. Or you will never be able to.

If you do go searching for answers, there are two people I trust who will help you. Angela Everett and Louisa Mae.

I leave my locket, this letter, and picture for you. This locket has been passed down in my family—your family for generations.

Maybe these items will reach you somehow, maybe they won't. If they do, know I am forever with you. Light up this world, baby girl. Make me proud, Aurora.

Love always,
Mom—
Leanne Penelope Ariti

EPILOGUE
AURORA DAVIS

Gabriel Ariti will know my name. He will know that while he was out living his life, my mother was ending hers. When he least expects it, I will be coming for him.

I will make it my life's mission to shred everything they have done to pieces. The time of living under the rule of toxic men who will do *anything* to stay in power will end with me.

I will go to KAE. I will learn how to control and perfect my powers. I will bide my time and sit and wait. Maybe I have help along the way, maybe I don't. Either way, people will really wish I was dead.

I leave my house without looking back, intending to take this summer to learn everything I can about Gabriel before we leave. I will not let my mother's death be for naught.

"I will make you proud, Mom," I murmur as I place a kiss on the locket my mother left me, holding it in a fist against my chest.

See you soon Gabriel.

XO, Aurora Penelope

Also by Kacie Santos

Book 2 in the Fae of Kyrosia Series:

Unveiling Shattered Restraint-Coming Soon

Love Scarred-Coming Soon

ACKNOWLEDGMENTS

Beyond all else, I want to say thank you to my husband. Trying to write a book with a full time job and a one year old is HARD. Thank you for encouraging me. Thank you for telling me to write, even if it was just for me. Listening to all of my ideas, even if you hate to read. You are the love of my life. I don't know where I would be without you, and I really don't want to. You are an amazing role model to our son and an amazing partner.

Thank you to my son, Avery. You made me erase so many characters in the middle of writing sessions. LOL. No seriously, all jokes aside, I was very nervous to start this journey and take time away from you. As I type this, I think of how patient you have been. I hope that one day when you are old enough, I will have books written that are appropriate for you to read. This one is already not it. I love you, son.

Here's to all the women raising boys. May we raise them the best we can. To always be respectful to women/men. To trust their instincts. What they see growing up is the foundation that is set in their minds of how relationships should function. We tell them what is not okay, if you are being treated wrong then you make sure they know that is not how a partner should treat anyone. If you have a loving partner who gives you affection, you make sure they see that. A man is not a pussy because he has feelings. A man is not weak because he shows affection to his wife. A man IS allowed to cry. Love should be shown. Your partner should be your best friend. I'm thankful my husband shows my son what love is. My son showers us, our friends, and family with hugs and kisses. If my husband and I are kissing, he always gets in between us for some love. It makes my heart so warm.

Most importantly, as a parent it is your responsibility to teach your kids this: Regardless of gender, it's just as important. I'm not sure who quoted it first, but it is something that has always stuck with me. "'No' is a complete sentence." If at any point someone is told no, to stop, they STOP. Someone should not have to repeat themselves, not have to justify why.

I'm thankful for my friends who listened to me. Those of you who helped engage in my social media marketing.

Thankful to my dad for offering to take my son while I was writing, or to complete deadlines.

Thank you to Kate Kimbrell, a fellow author, who edited this novel (and hopefully many more). You are beautiful and your writing is incredible and you helped make this story so much better.

Thank you to Katarina Martinez, another wonderful fellow author, who answered my many questions about self publishing and introduced me to Kate. She was one of the very first people I reached out to on TikTok.

Thank you to Brandi, who supported me so very much. You are an amazing friend and I am incredibly thankful you are in my life and my son's life. Thank you for reading my book and telling me over and over that I was going to go far, for listening to me discuss my characters and plot plans, looking at my million covers and most importantly for simply being an open ear.

The beta readers (who actually bothered to read my book) you mean the world to me. Your comments, opinions, feedback; you will never know how much I appreciate you.

To the thousands of creators on TikTok whose videos helped me learn more about the publishing process, fellow authors, readers.

A huge thank you to all of the authors who made me fall in love with reading. Authors such as: Sarah J Maas, Leigh Rivers, Sophie Grace, Shain Rose, Amo Jones, Micalea Smeltzer, Lucy Score, Ana Huang, Shantel Tessier, Sara Cate, Sierra Simone, Kat T. Masen, Monty Jay, Anna Todd, Carley Fortune, Rebecca Yarros and so many more. Your books are incredible, and you should be so proud of the masterpieces you have created. You all have inspired so many people to pick up the proverbial pen and write their own stories, for that you should be honored.

ABOUT THE AUTHOR

Kacie Santos was born in New Hampshire and now resides in South Carolina with her son and husband.

She never enjoyed reading growing up; not until her coworker at the time, Ashlynn, force fed her a book in 2022 (and she's so glad she did)! Kacie couldn't stop after that. She flew through books because she was too exhausted to do anything else.

When her son was born, he would try to rip up all of her

books. She went from a diehard paperback girly, to being in love with her Kindle.

She kept having an itch to write a book and started writing one and then life happened. She got too busy and stopped. A few months later, she had the idea for this book. Only, the ideas would not stop, so she took the leap and started writing it.

Her favorite genres include fantasy, young adult, romance, coming of age, and anything dark and spicy. She loves an enemies-to-lovers trope. Slow burns make her anxious. Forbidden romances are hot as hell. Billionaire romances are forever a great classic, even if they are all mostly the same. She could go on forever.

Her favorite books of all time: Sicko by Amo Jones, Binding 13 by Chloe Walsh, Corrupted Chaos by Shain Rose, A Court of Mist and Fury and Heir of Fire by Sarah J Maas, Little Stranger by Leigh Rivers, Eyes on Me by Sara Cate.

If you have any great book recommendations along those lines, please reach out to Kacie so she can add them to her TBR.

Extra props if you're an Indie Author, she would love to support your journey.

Kacie hopes to write more books in the future. But for now, this is a passion. When it becomes a chore, she'll stop. She really hopes people enjoy this book as her debut novel as an author.

She would love to engage with readers in the future.

Her website is, www.authorkaciesantos.com where you can also join her newsletter.

instagram.com/authorkaciesantos

facebook.com/authorkaciesantos

tiktok.com/@authorkaciesantos